SPECIAL MESSAGE TO

THE ULVERSCROFT F
(registered UK charity number 264873)
was established in 1972 to provide funds for
research, diagnosis and treatment of eye diseases.
Examples of major projects funded by
the Ulverscroft Foundation are:-

- The Children's Eye Unit at Moorfields Eye Hospital, London
- The Ulverscroft Children's Eye Unit at Great Ormond Street Hospital for Sick Children
- Funding research into eye diseases and treatment at the Department of Ophthalmology, University of Leicester
- The Ulverscroft Vision Research Group, Institute of Child Health
- Twin operating theatres at the Western Ophthalmic Hospital, London
- The Chair of Ophthalmology at the Royal Australian College of Ophthalmologists

You can help further the work of the Foundation
by making a donation or leaving a legacy.
Every contribution is gratefully received. If you
would like to help support the Foundation or
require further information, please contact:

THE ULVERSCROFT FOUNDATION
The Green, Bradgate Road, Anstey
Leicester LE7 7FU, England
Tel: (0116) 236 4325

website: www.foundation.ulverscroft.com

Fenella J. Miller was born on the Isle of Man. Her father was a Yorkshireman and her mother the daughter of a Rajah. She has worked as a nanny, cleaner, field worker, hotelier, chef, secondary and primary teacher, and is now a full-time writer. She has had over twenty-five Regency romantic adventures published, among other stories. Fenella lives in a pretty riverside village in Essex with her husband and ancient Border Collie. She has two adult children and two grand-children.

THE DUKE'S REFORM

Devastated by the deaths of his wife and daughters, Alexander, the Duke of Rochester, vows never to love again. Drinking and gambling numb the pain while he searches for a woman to enter a marriage of convenience and produce an heir. The beautiful Lady Isobel Drummond seems ideal for the task, and the union saves her family from financial ruin. But Alexander's high-handed and dissolute ways soon drive Isobel away, just as he acknowledges his growing feelings for her. Can he convince his beloved that he is a changed man? And can Isobel ever regain trust in the man she once loved?

Books by Fenella J. Miller
Published by Ulverscroft:

THE RETURN OF LORD RIVENHALL
A COUNTRY MOUSE
A RELUCTANT BRIDE
A DANGEROUS DECEPTION
MISTAKEN IDENTITY
LORD ATHERTON'S WARD
LADY CHARLOTTE'S SECRET
CHRISTMAS AT HARTFORD HALL
MISS SHAW & THE DOCTOR
TO LOVE AGAIN
MISS BANNERMAN AND THE DUKE
MISS PETERSON & THE COLONEL
WED FOR A WAGER
AN UNEXPECTED ENCOUNTER
HOUSE OF DREAMS
THE DUKE'S PROPOSAL
BARBARA'S WAR
THE DUKE'S RELUCTANT BRIDE
HANNAH'S WAR

FENELLA J. MILLER

THE DUKE'S REFORM

Complete and Unabridged

ULVERSCROFT
Leicester

First published in Great Britain in 2012

First Large Print Edition
published 2015

A catalogue record for this book is available
from the British Library.

ISBN 978–1–4448–2508–4

Published by
F. A. Thorpe (Publishing)
Anstey, Leicestershire

Set by Words & Graphics Ltd.
Anstey, Leicestershire
Printed and bound in Great Britain by
T. J. International Ltd., Padstow, Cornwall

This book is printed on acid-free paper

Prologue

1805

'Your grace, shall I remove the tray?'

Alex glanced over his shoulder at the butler hovering anxiously behind him. 'Take it. I've no appetite.' He turned back to staring morosely over the park. Without Eleanor and the girls Newcomb was an empty shell, no longer a home.

He rubbed his hand over his jaw. He must look like a brigand. His clothes were in little better state than his person. Grief at the death of his wife and daughters had all but overwhelmed him. He was rudderless — like a ship in a storm buffeted this way and that, unable to find a direction to guide him to safety.

What day was it? How long had it been since his life had been torn apart? Weeks perhaps? Visitors no longer called to leave their cards of sympathy. No doubt someone had dealt with them and written suitable replies. He hadn't married Eleanor for love, but had come to love her as the years passed. With her at his side he'd been happy, able to

1

forget his miserable upbringing and make this mausoleum into a happy place.

All that was over. He wouldn't make the same mistake — far better to remain aloof. He vowed never to love again and to remain safe with his emotions hidden. To experience such pain a second time would surely kill him. Sometime in the future he would have to marry; he must provide an heir, but would make sure he selected a suitable girl and not one who would expect him to love her. All he could offer his next bride was affection, respect and his title.

He would abandon this place and travel abroad until his period of mourning was over and then he would live in London and fill his life with mind-numbing activities.

1

Grosvenor Square
1810

Alex glared at his lawyer. How dare he have the temerity to interfere with his life? 'Dewberry, you forget yourself. When I take a wife is my concern.'

'Forgive me, your grace, but I owe it to your father to speak plainly. Your dissolute lifestyle these past five years is a matter of grave concern. If you're determined to destroy your health then find yourself a suitable wife and set up your nursery before matters overtake you.'

'I've no wish to marry again; I've nothing to offer apart from my title and wealth. I cannot expect a young woman to accept me as I am.' Dewberry's look of astonishment almost made him laugh. 'The sort of woman who would be satisfied with just that is *not* someone I'd wish to bear my children.'

'There are dozens of eligible young ladies in the marriage mart this year who would think themselves fortunate to be your bride.'

'It would be a marriage of convenience; my

wife would have to understand it would be a business arrangement: she to provide me with children and I to keep her in luxury for the rest of her life.' He yawned. It had been a late night and he had not yet been to bed. The black crow was staring at him expectantly; he'd get no peace until he agreed. 'I'll do as you suggest.'

The elderly lawyer beamed. 'I'd be happy to arrange for you to meet suitable young ladies. There are several debutantes who would be ideal.'

'I'll do my own selecting, Dewberry.' He raised one eyebrow. 'I don't expect my search to become common gossip.'

The man coloured. 'Of course not, your grace. However, your appearance at Almacks . . . '

'Almacks? I'd rather have my teeth pulled than go there. I'll attend a few functions and see what's on offer.'

He strode from the office, determined to get away from town. Whatever Dewberry said, matchmaking mamas would soon be on the lookout. He would go to Norfolk for some shooting; keep his head down until March.

★ ★ ★

4

Lady Isobel Drummond stormed out of the library. To be ignored by her parents was one thing, but to be told she must marry a wealthy man to save the family from ruin was quite another. Gathering her dogs from the kitchens, she snatched up her cloak and pushed her feet into the wooden clogs she used for gardening.

Othello and Ebony barked and raced around her in circles, as eager as she to be away from Drummond Hall. Today was blustery, a hint of snow on the wind that whipped from the sea. Thank God she didn't have to make a decision about going to London for the season until after Christmas.

Deep in contemplation, she failed to hear the rattle of a carriage approaching at speed. Ebony barked sharply and she looked round. Instinct made her throw herself prone. Her bladder almost emptied as a team of horses, followed by the wheels of the carriage, thundered above her. For a moment she was unable to move. Then, full of righteous indignation, she sat up to see a veritable giant, and not a particularly friendly one at that.

'Good God, woman, what the hell do you think you're doing wandering down the middle of the highway? I could have killed you.'

Spitting mud in his direction, she glared back. 'Are you insane, sir? This isn't a toll road but a country lane. What if there had been a flock of sheep across your path?'

In answer he reached out and hauled her to her feet, then dropping to his knees brushed off the worst of the debris from her person. At every touch she flinched. For some reason her anger dissipated to be replaced by a strange internal heat that followed the path of his fingers. She found herself gazing down at the dark hair which curled intriguingly over the collar of his many-caped coat.

Enough was enough. 'Desist at once, sir. I've no wish to be manhandled. I can remove the dirt myself. Look to your team; your carriage is in imminent danger of tipping into the ditch.'

His head shot up; his eyes were a peculiar shade halfway between blue and black, his nose patrician and his lips mobile. Warmth spread across her breasts and into her face. She couldn't tear her glance away. Then he was towering above her.

'Dammit! Out of the way, madam. Haven't you done enough damage already?'

The spirited team stamped and tossed their heads in impatience and the rear wheel of the vehicle began to slide backwards. She raced to the lead horse and snatched the bit. The gentleman shouted from behind the carriage.

'Good girl. Move them forwards.'

She ignored his instructions. She was well able to handle his horses without his intervention. She urged the chestnut sideways, following her instincts. Going this way would move the wheel away from danger more efficiently. The team threw their weight into the traces and the carriage shot forward. Unfortunately the gentleman fell headlong into the ditch instead.

The air was blue; she'd be wise to leave. She checked the brake was on and the reins securely tied around the pole, then prepared to creep away. Although it wasn't her fault he'd fallen, no doubt he would blame *her* for *his* foolhardiness.

She prepared to make a run for it. Too late! A dripping figure emerged from behind the horses and strode towards her. She couldn't help herself; her scream echoed down the lane. Her dogs hurtled past and for the second time the unfortunate gentleman was tipped into the noxious water.

Not waiting to see him emerge and seek revenge, she raced full pelt down the lane. She scrambled over a five-barred gate and tore across the meadow, scattering cows in all directions in her headlong flight. Her dogs were beside her, tongues lolling out, obviously delighted with the game.

Alexander shook his head, sending foul water everywhere. He scraped the muck from his eyes and watched his quarry vanish down the lane. Who the devil was she? Dressed like a servant but gently born. She was a conundrum. He stepped out of the ditch and propped himself against the carriage wheel to remove his boots and tip out the water.

He tossed his sodden cape on the box and stared gloomily at his ruined topcoat. The blue superfine jacket had cost him a pretty penny and was quite beyond salvage. The young woman was right to castigate him; he *had* been driving too fast. He shrugged; he seldom drove any other way, caring little if *he* came to grief. However, he'd no wish to take others with him, and certainly not the lovely young termagant he'd just encountered.

His horses were unharmed, so he leaped onto his carriage and recovered the reins. His breeches were so wet he slid from side to side as the curricle gathered speed. He had no option; unless he wished to nosedive over the edge, he must return to his hunting box at a walk.

His mouth curved as he recalled the shapely young woman with abundant russet curls and sparkling green eyes. Perhaps that old fool Dewberry *was* right; now was the time to put his house in order and find himself another wife.

For the first time in many years his pulse quickened. He would discover who the young woman was — perhaps she would do? He frowned. What was he thinking of? His wife couldn't be a spirited girl who'd make demands on him. He had his mistress to take care of his bodily needs. What he wanted was a meek, submissive girl of impeccable pedigree who would remain in the country and provide him with the necessary heir.

★　★　★

Isobel slowed her pace as she approached her home. She'd no wish to explain why she'd run like a hoyden across the fields. She slipped inside and returned to her apartment without being waylaid by her parents or a younger sibling.

Mary, her dresser, threw up her hands in horror. 'Lawks-a-mussy! Whatever next! You look like a vagabond, my lady. Did you take a tumble?'

'Something like that. An extremely unpleasant gentleman almost ran me down.' Isobel kicked off her clogs and untied the bow holding her cloak in place. 'But he got his comeuppance. He fell into the ditch twice and ruined his smart clothes.'

Her abigail clucked and tutted as she removed the soiled garments. Who could this gentleman be? She was sure he was a wealthy man, someone used to giving orders. He was handsome, but too autocratic and quicktempered for her taste. He must have a box somewhere and be down to shoot; their gamekeeper might know who he was.

'There, my lady, I'll do what I can with your gown. I've sent for hot water and there's a good fire in your parlour.'

Isobel pushed her arms into her robe and smiled. 'Anything, Mary, as long as it's warm.'

'If you'll forgive me, I think it's high time you appeared in society and found an amenable husband.'

For some inexplicable reason an image of the dark-eyed stranger flashed across her mind. Heavens above! Imagine what her life would be married to him! She turned away, hoping her pink cheeks hadn't been noticed. She wasn't sure what happened in the marital bed, but the idea of him touching her made her pulse race. Her father required an answer. Perhaps spending a few weeks in the capital with her favourite relatives would be enjoyable. At nineteen, she would be one of the older debutantes. Whatever her parents wanted, she'd no intention of being sold to the highest bidder. She'd never marry a man she couldn't at least feel affection for.

2

Grosvenor Square, March 1811

Alex riffled through the pile of invitations on the silver tray. Lord Illingworth was launching his daughter and niece at a ball tonight. He flicked the card and scribbled an acceptance on the back and rang for a footman to take it around. He was certain having a duke at the ball would make up for his bad manners.

He sharpened his quill and wrote down what he was looking for in a bride.

1. *Impeccable pedigree.*
2. *Quiet.*
3. *Not bracket-faced.*
4. *Intelligent.*

He scratched his head with the end of his pen lost in thought. The list seemed rather short. Was there something else he should add to it? His mouth curved. Of course.

5. *Tall.*
6. *Prefers country life.*
7. *Loves children.*

If he found a girl who fitted his criteria he'd offer for her. The sooner he produced the required heir the better; then he could continue his rackety lifestyle without having the family lawyers constantly complaining. He'd no intention of living with his wife once his duty was done. A fleeting image of the lovely russet-haired girl he'd encountered in Norfolk flickered into his head. He'd been obliged to return to town a few days later and had all but forgotten the encounter. He pushed the picture away — she was safely in Norfolk and he must find himself a bride.

★ ★ ★

Isobel stood beside her cousin waiting to greet the crush of people invited to their come-out ball. She must bite her tongue even if seriously provoked. Petunia, a diminutive, fair-haired girl as pretty as a cherub, would have no such difficulty. Isobel felt like an ungainly beanpole at her side. Her hair piled on top of her head added a further few inches. Good grief! Even her evening slippers had heels on them. She'd be staring over the heads of most of the gentlemen present and that must put them off before they'd even spoken to her.

'Isobel, my love, please don't scowl; it's your come-out. You're supposed to be enjoying yourself, not looking as if you're about to have a tooth pulled.'

Her aunt's kindly reminder helped Isobel relax. 'I beg your pardon, Aunt Laura. It's just that I was wishing I were a foot and a half shorter tonight.'

Petunia stretched up to kiss her cheek. 'You're the most beautiful woman here — like a goddess, so tall and elegant. With your lovely red-gold curls and huge green eyes I'm certain you'll be the talk of the town.'

'Thank you, cousin. I can't tell you how unpleasant it is to be staring at the top of a gentleman's head all night.'

Her companions were still laughing when the first guests were announced. Uncle Benjamin hurried to join them, brushing cigar ash from his person. He'd been blowing a cloud in the billiard room and no doubt downing a steadying brandy or two.

He beamed. 'My dears, I'm the proudest man in London. I'll be beating off your suitors with a stick before the evening's finished.' He winked as he took his place beside his wife. He understood what a sacrifice she was making in order to save her family from disaster.

'I think you a trifle premature, Uncle. As there're a prodigious amount of people invited, it would be churlish of me not to find

14

someone when there's so much choice.' His laughter made several heads turn in their direction. 'I'm grateful for the opportunity you've given me, my lord. Tonight I'll make an effort to simper and flutter my eyelids in exactly the way Pet has shown me.'

She loved her relatives; indeed, preferred them to her own family. Whatever the outcome, she was determined to enjoy her stay. She'd attend soirées and at-homes with good grace, but would ride in the park at dawn and visit the sights.

Her smile froze as a tall gentleman dressed entirely in black caught her attention. Her knees almost buckled. He was the one gentleman she didn't want to meet. Her enquiries had assured her the duke didn't attend balls or parties; he was a dissolute aristocrat, more interested in gaming and drinking than finding a wife. There was a sudden flurry of movement and the crowd parted like the Red Sea to let him through. He was staring directly at her.

Had he recognized her as the young lady from Norfolk? Her cheeks coloured and her chest tightened. She couldn't look away; was held by the gaze of his blue-black eyes and the arrogant thrust of his chin. This time he was smiling and she couldn't help responding. The master of ceremonies announced his

15

name with due aplomb.

'His grace, The Duke of Rochester.'

She dipped in a deep curtsy. Presumably his invitation card had stated her name. Her cousin was the image of Aunt Laura so it must be immediately obvious she was Lady Isobel Drummond and not Miss Petunia Illingworth. She straightened, raising her head to discover him watching her. His smile made her toes curl.

'Lady Isobel, I'm enchanted to make your acquaintance. You will honour me with a dance or two.' This wasn't a question but a statement of fact.

'Thank you, your grace; it's I who shall be honoured.' He nodded and was gone. Someone touched her hand; her cousin was staring at her.

'Do you realize who *that* was?'

Isobel smiled. 'He was announced. He's The Duke of Rochester.'

'No, silly, he's the most eligible parti in the world and has singled *you* out. Whatever happens next, your season will be successful.'

Now wasn't the time to say she'd already made his acquaintance. She shivered. Was he planning some sort of revenge? Would he lead her out and then abandon her on the dance floor and make her a laughing stock? 'I think he's an objectionable man, so top-lofty I

16

cannot imagine how he doesn't fall over his own feet. He didn't stay to greet any of you; even a duke should have good manners.'

Aunt Laura looked scandalized and Petunia giggled. Her uncle winked and the moment of excitement was over. Having jumped the queue in his superior fashion, Rochester strolled into the ballroom. An hour later she was free to join the throng. Whoever arrived at her side first, if she liked them, then she'd dance. If she became bored she would sneak away.

Petunia was to lead the first set. No doubt someone would invite her. To her astonishment Rochester appeared, neatly cutting out a small queue of hopefuls.

'I believe this is my dance, Lady Isobel.'

She was tempted to refuse, to say she was promised to another, but something in his eyes made her accept and she curtsied and stepped forward. Just the touch of his hand sent tremors rushing round her body.

'I believe I owe you an apology, my lady.'

Her eyes flew up. His expression was suitably solemn, but his eyes twinkled. 'It's I who must apologize . . . '

His smile made her lose her feet and she stumbled; he steadied her. 'Without your intervention things might have been far worse.'

Her gurgle of laughter attracted the attention of the other couples in the set. 'Shall we agree to forget the incident, your grace?'

He nodded. 'As you wish. May I say that I almost didn't recognize you this evening?'

With wide eyes she replied, 'And I you, your grace. Mud is an excellent disguise, is it not?'

This time his shout of mirth caused an unfortunate young lady to her left to step on her hem and tear the flounce clean off. The dagger look Isobel received almost made her lose her composure. He whirled her away in the promenade and she struggled with her giggles, he not assisting her efforts by smiling wickedly.

The remainder of the ball whirled past and despite her reservations, she wasn't bored; in fact, she had never felt so invigorated in her life. She'd danced every dance but no partner had been as charming or as handsome as the duke.

He claimed her for the supper dance and by the end of the evening she'd quite revised her former opinion and was halfway to liking him. However she didn't expect to hear from him again.

★ ★ ★

The next morning when she returned from her early morning ride she was greeted by a frantic Aunt Laura. 'My dear girl, such an honour. Indeed, it's quite worth the aggravation of rising at the crack of dawn.'

'Aunt Laura, I've no idea what you mean.'

'I told you, my love, the Duke of Rochester has come to call on you. He's been here half an hour already. Poor Illingworth has been obliged to talk to him. I couldn't remain in the same room; he puts me all in a flutter.'

Isobel was dumbfounded. For such an illustrious person to make his appearance but a few hours after the end of the ball was incredible. Had he been as taken with her as she was with him? 'I won't change first.' Her aunt's look of horror made her laugh. 'He cannot expect us to be in our finery if he chooses to call so early. This is a very becoming habit. It exactly matches my eyes, have you not said so?'

Isobel walked across the chequered entrance hall and into the drawing room. Her uncle was patently relieved and the duke showed unmistakable appreciation in his eyes.

She dipped in a deep curtsy; the jaunty ostrich feather on the brim of her cap swept the floor. She gazed at the two men, waiting for one to speak.

'Lady Isobel, forgive me for calling so early, but like you I ride early. I wished to invite you to drive in the park this afternoon.'

He didn't look like a man who relished exercise at any time. Then she recalled his wild appearance last year and reconsidered. He had a slightly jaded air about him as if he spent his days in idle pursuits, not galloping around Hyde Park.

'I should be delighted to accompany you, your grace, if my uncle gives me permission.'

'I'm happy for you to do so, my dear, as long as you're accompanied by your abigail.'

A flash of something passed across the duke's face. Was it annoyance? Had he believed his title allowed him to ride roughshod over her good name?

'Forgive me, gentlemen, but I've to change out of my riding habit . . . ' She stopped, appalled she'd mentioned such a thing. His eyes glittered with something she didn't recognize. Her cheeks blazed. She curtsied and turned to go.

His deep voice followed her. 'I'll arrive at two o'clock, Lady Isobel.'

She was sorely tempted to tell this autocratic gentleman that two o'clock wasn't convenient, but common sense prevented her. A man like him had been born and bred to issue orders. His dark visage had often filled her dreams these past few weeks and driving with the most attractive man in town would be no hardship.

She ran upstairs, smiling at the thought of being seen in his company. If Petunia was to be believed, she would now be the talk of the town. Could one man influence opinion in this way?

★ ★ ★

Mary stood back, her face glowing with pride. 'My lady, I don't believe there's another as beautiful as you. The leaf green of your promenade gown was a perfect choice.'

'It seems a pity to cover the pretty beading on the bodice with my pelisse, but it's chilly this afternoon. It's the end of March, but it doesn't feel like spring.' Isobel lifted the hem of her dress to stare at her new half-kid boots dyed to match her ensemble. 'These are uncomfortable. It's fortunate I shan't have to walk far.'

'They will ease with wear. Your bonnet brim's so deep it's going to stop you speaking to his grace. You'll have to turn your head to see him.'

'That's why I selected it. If I find his company tedious I can stare straight ahead and he'll not know I'm pulling faces.'

'My lady! You mustn't jest about such things; if you offend him your season could be ruined. One word and your invitations will be withdrawn. Remember how you met last November?'

'He's a man like any other; I'll treat him with the respect he deserves.'

She picked up her gloves and reticule and checked in the glass she was looking her best. After all, her appearance was the only thing she had to offer. Being the daughter of an impecunious earl would not impress *this* man. However, unless he engaged her affections she wouldn't marry him. Was it possible he'd been thinking of her since their first encounter?

Good grief! She'd been invited to drive and already was anticipating an offer. On hearing voices in the vestibule she paused at the head of the stairs. She hadn't expected him to leave his carriage and come to collect her. He mustn't keep his team waiting a moment longer.

'Lady Isobel, you are *ravisante*. And equally important, are not tardy.' He bowed and she paused halfway down the stairs to dip in a curtsy.

'Thank you, your grace, for your compliment. I'm famous for my punctuality, am I not, Uncle?'

He nodded solemnly. 'Indeed, my dear, you're an example to us all.'

She hid her smile beneath her bonnet brim, for she was always the last to appear, having had her nose in a book or become lost in her music.

The duke met her at the foot of the staircase. She had no option but to take his arm. Just touching him made her feel odd. She daren't glance sideways; he would see her cheeks were flushed.

'Oh my! A high-perch phaeton — I'd no idea you would drive such a thing.'

'I'm a noted whipster, my lady. Unfortunately, as you can see, I'll be unable to accommodate your maid. However, it's perfectly permissible to drive in an open carriage without risking your reputation.'

Mary was rigid with disapproval. Isobel was tempted to refuse to go, but the resulting fracas would cause distress to her relatives and she wouldn't willingly do that. He was correct — only in a closed carriage must one be chaperoned.

Smiling apologetically at Mary, she continued down the marble steps where the vehicle was waiting. A diminutive tiger was all but swinging from the head of the lead horse as it stamped and pawed the ground.

Without a by-your-leave, she was all but

tossed aboard. The phaeton rocked alarmingly and she clutched the side and did so again as he joined her.

His tiger released his grip and shot to the rear of the vehicle to scramble onto the step at the rear. With a flick of his whip the duke released the team and they moved away. There was no conversation between them. She kept her eyes firmly ahead, fearing the spirited team would spook and deposit her on the road.

Her worries receded as they progressed safely through the traffic. She began to relax and to look about her. This was the first time she'd travelled in such a modern vehicle. Its prodigious height gave one an advantage over other road users. The park gates were visible long before they arrived at them.

There were many like-minded carriages entering the park. Two o'clock was obviously the time to be seen bowling around the paths. She became aware that every head turned in their direction as they trotted past.

'Lady Isobel, delightful as your bonnet is, can I ask you not to wear it on our next excursion?'

She shifted sideways in order to reply. 'I know; it has more the appearance of a coal scuttle than a hat. I cannot imagine what possessed me to buy it.'

His chuckles sent shivers up her spine. He was all but irresistible when he smiled. 'Excellent, my lady. We're already in agreement on one matter.'

'This is an exciting experience. However, being so high from the ground and exposed to the elements isn't something I'd care to do in winter.'

'Shall we ride together tomorrow morning, Lady Isobel? I shall collect you at . . . ' He hesitated as if not sure what would be a suitable time.

'I normally go out at seven o'clock, your grace.' She rarely left the house before half past eight and doubted if he was aware that such an early hour existed.

'Seven o'clock?' He smiled at her and her insides somersaulted. 'I'd no notion you were such a dedicated rider, Lady Isobel. I believe you must have been out for three hours this morning.'

Hoisted by her own petard! Laughing, she nodded. 'I'm discovered; I thought to frighten you by insisting you joined me at dawn. I leave at half past eight and would be honoured to have your company.'

She returned fizzing with excitement. He appeared to find her as appealing as she found him. Had she already met the man she would one day marry?

3

The next two weeks Isobel hardly had time to gather her thoughts. Rochester was constantly at her side and she was whisked to the opera, the theatre and escorted to all the most prestigious social events. Society was anticipating him to offer and so was she.

She was in her sitting room when Aunt Laura came in. 'My dear, I must speak to you, as your mama isn't here to do so.'

'Aunt Laura, there's no need to explain what's required of a bride. I'm aware of what's expected.'

'That's a profound relief, my love. Rochester intends to speak to your uncle this evening. If you've any doubts about marrying him then say so now.'

'I hoped to have longer to decide. I've known him three weeks. I shouldn't hesitate; I'll be a duchess and have everything I could possibly wish for. But I keep remembering his anger. I couldn't marry a man I'm afraid of.'

Her aunt settled comfortably on the chaise longue before replying. 'There are things about his past I must tell you. He was married before. This was, like yours, a marriage of convenience, but from all accounts he came to love his wife.'

'I'd no notion this will be a second marriage. What happened to his wife?'

'Rochester was in London on business, his wife and two small daughters at Newcomb. They were struck down with the sweating fever. All three died before he could be sent for.'

'How dreadful for him to lose his family so suddenly. Small wonder I detect a darkness in him.' Isobel scrambled up and pushed her hair aside. 'I'll make him happy, bear him children and help him forget the sadness.'

'In which case, my love, I'll tell your uncle to accept the offer. We're both delighted. When you came to us I knew you would take, but had no idea it would be Rochester who offered first.'

'Is there anything else you wish to discuss with me, Aunt Laura?'

Her aunt smiled and patted the chintz-covered seat beside her. 'Sit down, Isobel. There are one or two things I don't expect your mama told you. Your husband will be vigorous in his attentions until you are increasing. From that point you will be left in peace until several weeks after the baby is born. With luck you'll become pregnant the

27

first month. It's what all new wives pray for, I'm sure.'

This was a strange conversation to be having. Could intimacy be so unpleasant that a wife preferred to be permanently with child?

'I hope I can give him his heir. After all, it's why he's marrying me. I'm not so naïve, Aunt Laura, to imagine he feels anything for me. But maybe there's a loving man waiting to be discovered.'

That night Mary laid out her newest acquisition. The gown wasn't the white of a debutante, but palest green, silk chiffon, the overskirt in sparkling, silver sarcenet. The neckline was a trifle daring for someone her age, but her emerald necklace filled the expanse of creamy skin. 'Mary, do you think I'm doing the right thing?'

Her abigail shook out an invisible crease in the gown before answering. 'It isn't for me to say, Lady Isobel. If you're happy, then I'm content also.'

With this unsatisfactory reply ringing in her ears, Isobel joined her cousin waiting impatiently in her sitting room.

'Pet, damask rose is perfect for you. I'm so glad you've been allowed to wear colour tonight.' She slipped her arm through her cousin's and twirled her round. 'And when do *you* expect to receive your first offer? Have you decided which of your many admirers to accept?'

'La, Isobel. I've decided to have a second season, as it's so much fun. I'm sure being married couldn't possibly be as exciting. A school friend is already a mother and was only married last summer.'

'Unlike you, my dear cousin, I much prefer to be in the country and not gallivanting all over the place attending balls every night.'

Petunia's tinkling laugh echoed along the corridor. 'Fustian, Isobel, and you know it. You've enjoyed every minute you've spent with the most attractive man in London at your side.'

Giggling, she squeezed her cousin's arm. 'But it will be so much more enjoyable having him to myself in the country.'

Still laughing at their daring conversation, they arrived at the head of the stairs. Isobel all but tumbled headlong in her effort to stop. Halfway up the staircase was the gentleman they'd been discussing. From the amusement in his eyes she was certain he had overheard. She wished the floor would open and swallow her. She was scarlet from her toes to the tip of her ears. Petunia abandoned her and left her to face him alone.

'Lady Isobel, every night you appear in a

different gown and each time you take my breath away. I apologize for eavesdropping. This wasn't my intention, I assure you. Come, sweetheart, I've permission to take you to the library. There's something most particular I wish to ask you.'

The door to the library was standing open, no servants lurking to overhear. He almost bundled her inside and the door clicked shut behind her. Her heart raced. She was about to receive a marriage proposal from the man of her dreams — so why was she apprehensive? Should she find herself a seat or remain trembling in the centre of the carpet? He was obliged to go down on one knee in order to ask for her hand.

'My love, don't look so scared. You know why you're here and my question's a formality.' He walked towards her and she was unable to move. Her feet seemed to be glued to the floor. 'Before I ask you to marry me there's something I must do.'

The distance between them vanished. His arms came around her and she was pulled gently until she could feel his heat burning through the thin stuff of her evening gown. Her knees were shaking. She raised her hands to press them on his chest and tilted her head intending to ask to be released. But his mouth closed over hers in a kiss of such sweetness her fear melted.

His heart pounded beneath her fingertips. He was as disturbed as she and this gave her courage to respond. Her hands crept up until they were around his neck and she buried her fingers in his dark hair. It was smooth and silky; she tugged at the back of his neck to bring him closer.

Then her feet were dangling free, his arms crushing her, and the pressure of his lips increased. His tongue ran along her mouth demanding entry to the moist recesses within. This was too much. She was overwhelmed. Her body was responding to his lovemaking whilst her head was screaming *no*.

Suddenly she was free, but her legs gave way and, without his arms to support her, she would have sunk in a pool of green silk at his feet. 'Sweetheart, I apologize. I didn't mean to frighten you. Here, darling, let me carry you to the sofa.'

'No, I'm quite recovered, thank you, sir.' Her voice was little more than a whisper.

'Lady Isobel, will you do me the honour of becoming my wife?'

Shocked by the abruptness of his proposal, she almost refused. He hadn't bothered to go down on one knee, but remained staring down at her as if impatient for an answer. 'Thank you, your grace, I'm delighted to accept.'

'Excellent. I'll ride down to Norfolk tomorrow to speak to your father and arrange the settlements. We'll be married at New-comb four weeks from today. I'll leave you to organize your bride clothes. Four weeks is sufficient, I hope?'

Isobel wanted to tell him it wasn't nearly enough, that an engagement of a month was too short, but this would be a fruitless exercise. She'd better become accustomed to being dictated to. The man she'd just agreed to marry would brook no contradiction. Had she made a dreadful mistake?

'I'll be ready in time. Are we to have a wedding trip, sir?'

He cupped her face and brushed her lips with his own. 'My love, didn't you say you were eager to spend time in the country with me?'

'I did, and April's the perfect month to spend in Hertfordshire.'

'Come, sweetheart, give me your hand. There's something I must do.'

Obediently she held it out and he pushed a betrothal band with a perfect square-cut emerald onto her ring finger. She gazed down and her eyes pricked. The ring was perfect. It also exactly matched the necklace she was wearing. Her hand strayed to her neck and his eyes followed it. Before she could retreat she was once more within his arms, but this time his lips drifted across her neck, leaving a trail of fire in their wake.

A strange languor made her limbs heavy. She relaxed and tipped her head to give him access to her breasts. She was released abruptly and he moved away to stand with his back to her. Was he unwell? Instinctively, she stepped forward and touched his shoulder.

'Lady Isobel, return to the drawing room and give your family the good news. I'll be with you directly.'

How inconsiderate. It would look strange if she arrived without him. She sighed and did as she was bid. Probably best to start learning to follow his dictums. Once she was his wife he would own her. She would be considered his chattel, of no more value than his horse.

★ ★ ★

The next four weeks flew past. Her parents arrived from Norfolk and her bride clothes were completed. There was no time to repine; everyone told her she was the luckiest girl in the land. Rochester had rarely been alone with her, and then he'd left for Newcomb to oversee matters a week before the wedding.

'Mama, I've scarcely had time to converse

with the duke. How am I going to live with a stranger?'

Her mother shook her head. 'Isobel, child, you've the rest of your lives to become acquainted. There's not a woman in town that doesn't envy you. To be married to a duke who's not in his dotage is good fortune indeed.'

'We're not to have a wedding trip, did I tell you?'

'You have no taste for travelling, my dear. Anyway, as he's marrying you to fill his nursery, it's far better you remain in England.'

No more was said on the matter. Two days before the wedding the baggage carts set off and Isobel and her family followed. There was to be a celebration ball that night for important neighbours, and the next day a garden party for the staff and tenants to allow them to pay their respects. A quiet family dinner would precede her wedding day. Her uncle and aunt and her cousins Petunia and David had joined them.

As the carriage turned into the drive of Newcomb, she lowered the window and craned out like an urchin, ignoring her mother's demands that she sit down immediately.

'Look at that monstrous building — it must

have hundreds of rooms. I've never seen anything so enormous in all my life.'

'Isobel, sit down at once. You should be grateful it's not in the north of England but a mere morning's drive from town.'

'I beg your pardon, Mama, but the thought of spending the rest of my life here's quite daunting. It must require a hundred staff to maintain it. How am I going to manage such a place?'

Her father frowned and cleared his throat noisily. Hastily she sat down, recognizing the danger signals. 'Isobel, I'm shocked at your disrespect. This place won't require your intervention; there will be a housekeeper and butler to take care of things. Your duty is to be a good wife and provide your husband with an heir.'

'Yes, Papa. I know my duty and apologize if I've given offence.'

A small army of liveried footmen waited to greet them. Where was Rochester? Then he appeared in the doorway and strode down the steps and snatched open the carriage door.

'My love, you are here at last. Come, let me show you your new home.' Ignoring her parents and the second carriage that contained the rest of her relatives, he escorted her inside. She was almost running to keep up with him.

'Please, my lord, shouldn't I speak to the staff who were waiting at the door?'

'Absolutely not, darling girl. I've something to show you and it cannot wait. Remember, you'll be my duchess soon. You're answerable to no one here but me.'

She was breathless when he stopped outside handsome double doors. Two flunkies bowed and opened them. 'My word! What a pretty sitting room. Is this to be mine?'

He was delighted by her reaction. 'I've had your apartments refurbished. That's why I've been absent these past weeks. I wished it to be perfect for you.'

Her heart skipped and she threw her arms around his neck and kissed him. Laughing, he swung her round like a child and kicked the door shut in the faces of his staff. 'If there's anything I've forgotten you only have to ask.'

She gazed round the room, her eyes wide as she took in exactly what was there. 'A walnut desk and a harpsichord, and there's an easel and everything I need to paint. I cannot believe it — you've chosen all these novels and they're exactly what I would have picked myself.'

'I spoke to your mother and she told me your interests. I've a stable full of horses you can ride. I don't care for house pets so there are no dogs here for you to fuss over.'

At the mention of her own beloved animals she felt a moment's sadness. She'd miss them, but her siblings had promised to take care of the dogs. 'You're kind and generous. Thank you for doing this for me.'

Her doubts vanished. He might be a reserved man, might not love her as she loved him, but he cared enough to oversee the redecoration of her apartment. This reassured her she hadn't been mistaken in her choice.

4

The ball was a great success and Isobel danced every dance with her future husband. Waltzing for the first time was magical. They twirled to the music in a world of their own. Every time he looked at her his eyes burned with something she wasn't quite sure about. The slightest touch of his hand sent shivers of excitement through her body.

As Mary helped her disrobe she decided to ask how a husband and wife were intimate. She understood somehow they must become as one body in order for the man to transfer his seed, but she was rather unclear exactly how this happened.

'Tell me, Mary, what happens on my wedding night?'

'I'm not sure I should be the one to tell you this. It might be better not to know the details.'

There must be something Mary didn't wish her to know. 'As you're married, and closer to me than anyone else, I'm relying on you to explain.'

By the time all had been revealed she wished she'd remained ignorant. After her abigail left she mulled over what she'd been told. The aperture into which a man's part must go wouldn't even stretch to receive one of her fingers. She would be torn apart — no wonder in the olden days a bloody sheet was held up for all to see.

She slept little that night. She rose early and went to the stable yard. A sleepy groom was only too pleased to saddle up a pretty grey mare and accompany her. The exercise and fresh air cleared her head. She wouldn't think about her wedding night. She would concentrate on the here and now. There was the garden party this afternoon and she mustn't be out of sorts for that.

★ ★ ★

'Where's Lady Isobel, Lady Illingworth? She didn't come into breakfast.' Alexander hoped Isobel wasn't hiding from him.

'I believe she went out on horseback and is now resting so she'll be fresh for this afternoon's event, your grace.'

He relaxed. 'Thank you, madam; I was concerned she might be unwell.'

There was to be a substantial spread set out for his tenants and staff: barrels of ale and jugs of freshly made lemonade, plus pasties and the like. Fortunately the day was fine; it

39

would be a perfect April afternoon, ideal for a celebration. The sooner her tedious relatives departed the better. Isobel would settle once they were gone. He didn't want anyone from her past at Newcomb — this was to be a fresh start for both of them.

The fact she was marrying in order to restore her family's fortune made things easier. She understood their union was a matter of business — she to provide him with an heir and he to settle a vast sum on her impecunious father. His lips curved. It would be no hardship sharing her bed.

There were still two hours until the start of the garden party. As his nuptials drew nearer his mind turned constantly to Eleanor. He would retreat to his study and fortify himself with a much-needed brandy or two. He drank too much — had been doing so for years — but alcohol was the only thing that deadened the pain.

Foster arrived and roused him from his doze. 'Your grace, I beg to inform you the guests are assembled and your tenants arriving in the park.'

Alexander swung his boots to the carpet and eased himself upright. Drinking during the day gave him a damnable headache. He checked his cravat and headed for the drawing room. Isobel curtsied but carefully avoided eye contact. There was something bothering the girl. He must give this some thought. He'd chosen well; she was the perfect chatelaine. She wasn't Eleanor — she was irreplaceable — but Isobel was beautiful, biddable and eminently beddable, and this would have to do. He hardened at the thought of what awaited him the following night.

'My love, you haven't eaten anything. You'll be faint with hunger later.'

'My lord, I daren't risk eating in public. I could be spoken to when I had my mouth full or dribble something on my gown. I'll make up for it at dinner, but I'm touched by your concern.'

By four o'clock his guests were departing and he led Isobel inside and drew her into a small anteroom, closing the door behind them. 'Darling, you've acquitted yourself well. I believe you to be a firm favourite with my tenants already.'

'You've so many in your employ I fear I'll never learn their names.'

'Good God! Don't even attempt it. They know who *you* are and that's all that matters. Leave such things to the estate manager, the butler and housekeeper — that's what I pay them for.'

A slight frown marred the perfection of her

brow. Surely she wasn't going to disagree? Then she smiled and he relaxed. He reached out to gather her close, to enjoy her lips and feel the softness of her breasts against his chest. To his astonishment she skipped sideways and was at the door before he could react.

'Forgive me, my lord, but I've to go to my apartment and change for dinner.'

He was tempted to call her back but refrained. She was right; there was barely an hour before they must all be down in their finery.

He was early and waiting by the open doors of the grand salon. His eyes strayed constantly to the staircase, hoping she wouldn't be long. His guests had stopped trying to engage him in conversation and were grouped further down the room sipping champagne and sherry wine. She was tardy. His lips curved as he recalled their first ride together when she'd assured him she was never late for any appointment.

Then she appeared at the head of the stairs dressed in a confection of silver and gold and floated towards him. His breath stopped in his throat and he gripped the stem of his glass. It snapped, spilling the contents down his pantaloons; he ignored the sharp pain as something embedded itself in his palm.

'Sir, you've cut yourself. Quickly, we must find a cloth to stem the blood.' The concern on her face touched his heart. His butler, Foster, was beside him and offered a clean white square. She smiled her thanks before turning back to him.

'Here, let me do it for you.' She examined his hand, dabbing at the cut with the cloth. 'It isn't as bad as I feared. There, I've removed the glass. We can bind it and then you'll be almost as good as new.'

He wanted to snatch his hand back. Her touch was sending signals to his brain and he would soon be in an embarrassing position. 'Go in and entertain our guests, sweetheart. I can take care of this. I don't wish to mar the perfection of your outfit with my gore.'

'I should not care if you did. However, as I've no idea where your bandages are kept, I'll do as you ask.'

When he returned she was engrossed in conversation with her young cousins. He was apart from them; was of a different generation, almost old enough to be the parent. Was he too old to be her husband? She was little more than a schoolroom miss and he a man of five and thirty — would this disparity of age and experience be a hindrance or a help?

Despite her promise to eat heartily she

scarcely swallowed a mouthful, pushing the food around her plate in order to make it look as though she'd eaten. Something was worrying her; they'd dined together many times and she'd always eaten well. Occasionally she glanced his way and he tried to reassure her with a smile. There was something seriously amiss and he believed he now understood.

★　★　★

Mary handed Isobel a large, flat velvet box. 'There's a note here, my lady. Shall I put it on the desk?'

Isobel had been fidgeting with her easel and looked across. 'No, let me see what he's sent. It's after eleven o'clock. How could Rochester know I was still awake?' Her abigail brought the items over. Isobel broke the seal and the bold black handwriting leapt out at her. The box contained something to be worn at the wedding ceremony.

She opened the lid and gazed at the circlet. 'I've never seen anything so beautiful. This must be an ancient heirloom. See, Mary, how the golden leaves have been constructed and the centres of the flowers are topaz, or perhaps amber.'

'If you're to wear that tomorrow, my lady,

you'll have to have your hair loose, for it won't fit over an elaborate arrangement.'

Isobel shrugged. 'You can braid the front and leave the back hanging free. I wondered why the duke had insisted my gown should be gold. I'll feel like a wood nymph with my floating draperies and this exquisite object on my head.'

She replaced the jewel in the box and returned to her task. Mary sighed. She was being unfair keeping her maid so late. 'I'll retire now. I can't make this wretched thing stand straight. I doubt I'll have time to paint, so it can wait.'

No sooner had her abigail departed than she threw back the covers and got out of bed. She wouldn't be able to sleep. Maybe she'd read a novel in front of the fire until she was too tired to keep her eyes open. Being in the huge bed turned her thoughts to what was going to happen in a few short hours.

She left one candle burning on the mantelshelf and curled up in a comfortable chair, tucking her feet beneath her nightgown and bedrobe. She was almost asleep, the candle burnt out, the only light from the fire, when the communicating door slowly opened.

She shrunk against the seat. He edged into the room carrying an enormous tray from which appetizing aromas floated.

'Stay where you are, little one. I'll put this down and fetch the rest.'

He placed the tray on the carpet in front of the fire and lit two candlesticks. With no more than a friendly smile he vanished. How extraordinary! The sight of the food made her mouth water. She hadn't eaten for twenty-four hours and her stomach gurgled. Surely there couldn't be more coming? There was enough on that one tray to feed a dozen people.

He reappeared with a silver jug and two silver goblets, plus a second jug of lemonade. 'I thought we could share a loving cup, sweetheart, but not until you've eaten. Mulled wine on an empty stomach would make you unwell.'

'I love mulled wine; we always have it at Christmas.' Forgetting she was in her nightwear, not even slippers on her feet, she pushed the poker into the centre of the blaze. 'This will soon heat up. I should like some lemonade to be going on with. Shall I help myself?'

He waved her back to her chair, his expression tender. 'This is my surprise; allow me to be your servant tonight.'

She devoured a substantial portion of the laden tray before she was replete. 'I feel so much better. I'm relieved you joined me in this midnight feast. Can I have some wine now?'

His chuckle made her even more relaxed. He was different, his austerity and coldness gone. In the intimacy of her bedchamber he'd become the man she'd dreamed about. The sweet smell of spices filled the room as he plunged the poker into the jug. He filled both goblets then handed one to her, raising the other in salute.

'To us, my love. May the rest of our lives be spent in happiness and harmony.'

'To us.' She swallowed and the delicious concoction filled her with warmth and a strange excitement. That odd darkness she'd observed before was apparent in his eyes. Hastily she broke the connection and sipped mulled wine, and then the vessel was pried from her fingers.

'Enough, Isobel. You're not used to alcohol. Come and sit with me. There are matters we need to discuss.'

Not waiting for her to move, he scooped her up and, before she could protest, she was resting in his lap. It was pleasant to be held — she hadn't had the protection of another's arms since the nursery. She closed her eyes and didn't flinch when his arms encircled her.

'Would you do something for me?'

Sleepily she gazed up at him; his smile made something most peculiar curl through her nether regions. 'What do you want?'

'Firstly, when we're alone, use my given name — Alexander. I'll call you Isobel.' This didn't seem unreasonable. She nodded and closed her eyes again. 'Secondly, sweetheart, allow me to release your hair. Ever since I saw you waiting in the line at your ball I've dreamt of running my fingers through it. You mustn't ever cut it short whatever the prevailing fashions might dictate.'

She was too fatigued to protest. She raised her head, allowing him access to her braid; if he wished to see it loose then he must release it himself. His fingers were deft. Seconds later she was enveloped in her hair. He gently propelled her forwards and began to draw his fingers through her locks from temples to neck.

Why should such a simple thing be sending shockwaves up and down her spine? An unusual restlessness was building in the very core of her being. Something made her wish to twist in his arms to see his face. Instantly her fear returned and she tried to scramble from his lap.

'Darling girl, you mustn't be scared of me. Whatever you've been told has obviously frightened you. I promise you I'd never hurt you. It's my duty to protect and care for you for the rest of your life.'

His words were soothing, his hands stroking her, easing out the tension and the fear. She couldn't tell him why she was afraid, but he wouldn't lie to her. His fingers buried themselves in her hair and he tilted her head. His lips brushed hers, sending spirals of pleasure around her overheated limbs.

'Trust me, darling; let me show you what it is to be loved. There's nothing to fear. What we're doing is a natural thing; a man and a woman are meant to be conjoined in this way.'

Her arms encircled his neck. She wished to have his lips pressing on hers; for his hands to continue to work their power, stroking and caressing her shoulders and neck. His mouth engulfed hers. His tongue demanded entry and her lips parted to let him in. She was lost in a place she hadn't known existed, her body no longer her own.

When he stood and moved smoothly towards the bed, she made no protest. Gently he slid her down his chest until her bare feet were on the carpet. 'I can't make love to you until you're free of these unnecessary items.'

She was mesmerized; couldn't have moved even if the house had caught fire. The ribbons at the neck of her garments were untied. He pushed the cotton over her shoulders and she was naked before him. Every inch of her was burning. Her breasts tingled and she wanted something from him but wasn't sure what.

Her legs gave way and she fell onto the sheets. With one swift movement he tore off his bed-robe and stood before her as naked as she. Her eyes widened. She hadn't expected this. Before she could prevent it her glance dropped to his stomach — what she saw doused her flames as effectively as a bucket of cold water. Her fears returned and she rolled away, attempting to hide herself in the covers.

She cringed from him but he gathered her close and kissed her softly. His hand moved from her face, and the heat inside her returned. His lips trailed fire from her neck to her stomach. She forgot her fears as his mouth covered hers and she became a woman. She couldn't speak; could scarcely breathe. How could she have been afraid of something so amazing?

'My darling, I hope I didn't hurt you. It's always so the first time.'

'The small pain was worth it, my love. I had never imagined anything so wonderful could take place between us. I can't understand why Mama and Aunt Laura didn't tell me how it would be.'

He laughed and smoothed back her hair.

'They didn't tell you, sweetheart, because not everyone experiences what you did.'

Surprised and intrigued by his answer, she tried to wriggle away from him in order to converse in a more seemly way. His arm around her hips prevented her. 'Surely the process is the same for everyone?'

His answer was to kiss her. She responded willingly and forgot all about her question.

5

When Isobel woke she was alone. The trays had vanished and she could have imagined his visit but for a delicious ache between her legs which told her she was no longer a girl, but a woman. Today was her wedding day, and she'd never been so happy in her whole life. To be marrying the man she loved, who had shown her last night he felt the same way, was something to celebrate.

The sound of water being poured into her bath meant she must rise immediately. Where was Mary? She usually came with her morning chocolate long before this. Isobel leapt out of bed, shocked to see the tell-tale blood stain on the sheets. She had pre-empted her wedding night. Her relatives would be scandalized but she didn't care. Alexander had come to allay her fears. She was the luckiest girl in England; in two short hours would be his wife, and nothing could spoil her happiness.

She rang the bell beside the bed. Mary could remove the sheet and hide it until tomorrow. The dressing-room door opened and a strange young woman came in. She had pinched features and sharp, knowing eyes.

'You rang, my lady? I've your bath ready; his grace said you wouldn't be requiring breakfast this morning.'

'Where's my abigail? I don't wish to be attended by strangers.'

The woman curtsied stiffly; her lips curled but the smile didn't reach her eyes. 'Watkins left here first thing with the luggage. I'm now your maid. His grace appointed me himself.'

Isobel turned away, too upset to remonstrate with this supercilious intruder. Had everything they'd shared last night meant nothing? The man she thought Alexander to be wouldn't have dismissed Mary without speaking to her first. He'd sent away the only familiar face in this barracks of a building. She would be alone with a stranger and was no longer sure of his feelings.

In frosty silence this unwanted woman helped her dress. Her pleasure in the day had gone. This would mean Mary's husband Sam, who was her personal groom, would have gone as well. As soon as the last pin was pushed into her hair, she stalked from the room and along the wide passageway. The church bells were ringing. Newcomb had its own place of worship and she was to be married there.

Her parents were waiting in the vast entrance hall. There was no sign of her other relatives. Their presence would have alleviated the tension and lifted her spirits just a little. 'Mama, Papa, did you know Rochester has dismissed Mary? She's gone without saying goodbye, and after all she's been to me these past years.'

'Isobel, we had no idea she wasn't to remain here. These things aren't under our control; you must abide by your husband's decisions. I'm sure you'll soon come to appreciate the superior woman he has appointed for you.'

'I haven't bothered to ask her name as she's a stiff and unpleasant person. I'll insist she's dismissed, but not today. In a week or two I'll ask my husband to reinstate Mary and Sam.'

Her father scowled at her as if she'd no right to criticize the man who'd given him a fortune in exchange for his daughter. 'I wish to hear no more of your complaints, miss. You're tardy and Rochester has been waiting in the church for five minutes.'

He offered his arm and she took it. Before she had time to think she was being marched down the aisle and standing beside her future husband. A wave of despair engulfed her when he turned to glance at her. This wasn't the man who'd made love to her so passionately — this was the stranger she'd hoped never to see again.

Somehow she mumbled through her vows, smiled bravely during the wedding breakfast, but far too soon she was at his side to wave her parents and relatives away. Without thinking she turned to him imploringly. 'Sir, I'll miss my family sorely. May I invite them to stay later in the year?'

He shook his head. 'No, not this year, my dear. Perhaps they can come when you've produced a child for them to dote on.' His arm was hard around her waist and she was escorted inside. 'Go upstairs and change into your habit. I thought we could ride around the estate. I know you explored the park yesterday, but I'd like to show the rest to you.'

'I should enjoy that above everything. I shan't be long. Do we expect further visitors today?'

His eyes darkened and he lowered his voice so the ever-present butler couldn't overhear. 'I thought you might be tired this afternoon and wish to rest.'

His meaning was unmistakable; there would be little rest involved in his suggestion. Despite her sadness she couldn't help smiling at the thought of what was to come. His lips curved and he dropped a light kiss on her brow.

★ ★ ★

The weeks passed in much the same fashion. During the day he was distant, always aware of his position, never letting down his guard for a second. However, when he came to her room at night he was her darling Alexander, and she lived for these moments. He was assiduous in his attentions and she prayed she wouldn't conceive immediately. If his visits stopped because of her pregnancy there'd be nothing to look forward to.

Maynard, the supercilious housekeeper, appeared at noon each day with the menu but Isobel wasn't required to do more than read it. There was nothing to do apart from playing the pianoforte, painting watercolours of the grounds and reading her novels. Alexander usually rode with her but during these rides she learnt little about the estate as they stayed within the park. Sometimes he was absent and she didn't ask where he went. On the nights he didn't come to her he remained in his study drinking heavily.

When her monthly courses appeared for the third time things changed. His lovemaking became less passionate, as if he considered her incapable of producing the much wished-for child. That this was her fault was indisputable. After all, had he not already fathered two children during his first union?

In October a group of his friends arrived

for the shooting and hunting. They were mostly objectionable gentlemen and she did her best to remain aloof from them. She wrote to her aunt and uncle and heard Petunia had accepted an offer from a young man of impeccable pedigree, deep pockets and unbounded love. She wished she could change places with her cousin, as material possessions were nothing without affection.

Alexander removed to town, returning a few times each month to do his duty. The joy she'd once found in his lovemaking faded. Although he was more relaxed in the privacy of her chambers, he no longer seemed as approachable. It became painfully apparent his sole reason for coming was to conceive a child.

As the festive season approached she asked Alexander what celebrations would take place at Newcomb.

He shook his head. 'Nothing at all, Isobel. We attend church and give Christmas boxes to the staff. Apart from that we have no traditions.'

'May I arrange to decorate the house? Could we perhaps invite our neighbours? It's customary to leave a newly married couple alone initially, but more than six months have passed since we were married and we've received no visitors or invitations.'

'I thought you understood I don't entertain here. The ball and garden party were exceptions. I organized the events in order to mark our wedding day. If you wish to socialize then you must come to London for the season.' He smiled sadly. 'It would appear there's no reason for you to remain here.'

She flushed. There was nothing she could say. She was apparently unable to have children; small wonder he'd little interest in her. To be saddled with a barren wife after he had paid so much to get her must rankle. 'I've no wish to go to London. However, I've no objection if you prefer to be elsewhere at Christmas.'

His eyebrows shot up at her impertinent comment. 'There's nothing to keep me here. I'll do as you suggest, and you must please yourself whilst I'm gone. I'll arrange for your allowance to be paid in coin in future. You have my permission to spend it as you wish.'

When his carriage left the next morning she remained in her bedchamber, unwilling to appear before the staff with blotched eyes and running nose. She would send for Mary and Sam immediately and see if she could find them a cottage nearby, and they could bring her beloved dogs. Being able to visit with them would give her something to fill the empty days.

Sam and Mary were safely installed in a cottage which could be reached by walking through Home Wood. Ebony and Othello were overjoyed to be reunited with her. 'Mary, I'll come as often as I can to walk the dogs. However, I must be vigilant as Foster, Maynard and the unpleasant girl who has replaced you spy on me.'

'I'm surprised Lord Drummond didn't refuse permission. But he seemed happy for the dogs to leave.'

'He obviously doesn't believe I'll return to Bracken Hall to visit. He and my husband must have come to an arrangement about this.'

'Will you be requiring luncheon today?'

Isobel frowned. 'Rochester's bringing a group of his friends for the shooting. The season will be starting next month. Why couldn't they remain where they were?'

'You mustn't be tardy; his grace will want you there when they arrive and you must change.'

'Indeed I must. I shan't be able to visit until they've all gone. Take care of yourselves and my dogs.'

The wind was bitter. Sam predicted there would be snow before the day was out. She prayed it would come soon and prevent the unwanted visitors from setting out. She no longer looked forward to Alexander's return, for there had been no further glimpses of the person she fell in love with. The interludes they spent in bed were still enjoyable, and she responded willingly to his touch, but he was no longer fully engaged in what they did.

She hurried in through the side door, hoping to return to her chambers unseen. But she was waylaid by Maynard with the usual supercilious sneer on her face.

'Your grace, I've been waiting for you to approve the menus for the visitors.'

Isobel stiffened and for once didn't apologize. 'It's of no interest to me what you've been doing, Maynard. It's your duty to be there when I wish to see *you*, not the other way round. Kindly remember that in future.'

The woman recoiled, unused to being reprimanded. She curtsied, her navy bombazine rustling noisily. 'I beg your pardon, your grace. When will it be convenient to see the menus?'

'I've no interest in them, for whatever I say will be ignored. In future don't bother me with such trivia.' Isobel walked off, wishing she'd held her tongue. Her duty was to view these things and Alexander would be displeased when he heard. That he would, was certain. The staff were loyal to him and still treated her as an interloper even after almost a year as their mistress.

She took the little-used back stairs and braced herself for another confrontation. Cranford, the woman he'd appointed, had taken to setting out her gowns. Every morning Isobel felt obliged to insist something else was fetched, although quite often the ensemble chosen by her maid was better than the one she selected.

Her bath was waiting in the small tiled anteroom used for this purpose. She hastily disrobed, glad she'd forbidden Cranford to enter during her ablutions. Today the warm water failed to soothe her and she didn't linger. Quickly donning the necessary underpinnings, she stepped through to her dressing room to see what had been put out today.

'I thought the blue velvet afternoon dress might be suitable, your grace. I don't believe you've worn it more than once.'

Isobel was too dispirited to argue. 'It will do. Please dress my hair plainly; I require no ribbons or feathers.'

In silence she sat whilst her hair was arranged. After collecting her cashmere shawl she left her apartment without a second glance. What did it matter if she looked her best? Alexander no longer noticed and he was the only gentleman she wished to approve of her.

She was standing dutifully in the freezing entrance hall when the party arrived. He strode in first and smiled briefly before removing his caped coat and tossing it to the waiting footman.

'My dear, that's a most becoming gown. The weather has deteriorated. However, we're here now, but I doubt there'll be much shooting.'

'Did any of the wives accompany the gentlemen this time, Rochester?'

'Unfortunately this visit was arranged too quickly to allow the ladies to join us. It might be better if you didn't dine downstairs, but that's entirely up to you.'

Her heart lifted; perhaps this gesture showed he still thought of her a little. 'Thank you. I would prefer to remain apart when there are no ladies present.' The gentlemen drank too much and behaved accordingly; far better to remain in her apartment. There was something she needed to tell him but now wasn't the time as, accompanied by a flurry of snow, the gentlemen poured in.

She retreated halfway up the grand staircase; from there she curtsied and bid them welcome before hurrying to the sanctuary of her own chambers. Her dinner was brought on a tray, as always the meal beautifully cooked but stone-cold. The kitchen was so far from the main part of the house that she rarely ate a hot meal.

The mantel clock struck nine. If she slipped down now maybe she could find Alexander in his study and tell him she was unavailable tonight. Her monthly course had arrived. He usually timed his visits better; she was regular as clockwork so he avoided the days she couldn't welcome him to her bed.

There had seemed no necessity to change, although she was still wearing the blue afternoon gown. The wall sconces were lit along the wide passageway. There was no need to carry a candlestick unless one wished to go downstairs late at night.

The noise coming from the drawing room warned her the occupants were inebriated gentlemen. A footman stepped out and bowed.

'Is the duke in his study?'

'I believe him to be in the billiard room, your grace.'

Botheration! She could hardly speak to him there; she'd write him a note and leave it in his dressing room. Hopefully he wouldn't be so foxed he couldn't read it when he retired. She was about to return when a gentleman holding two glasses of wine staggered out from the drawing room.

'Your grace, have a drink with me. We missed your lovely presence this evening.' He wove his way towards her. She couldn't get past him. Several other guests appeared in the doorway to watch the confrontation.

'Thank you, sir, but I've no wish for a glass. Please allow me to pass; I wish to return to my apartments.'

He leered at her and thrust one of the glasses into her hand; she'd no option but to take it or allow it to smash on the tiles. She waited, her expression icy, for him to move. To her horror he lurched forward and attempted to touch her face. Her reaction was instinctive. She flung the wine into his face. This was enough to stop him. Dodging past the spluttering gentleman, she shot up the stairs before he could do her more harm. The whoops and cheers that followed made her fear they'd decided to give chase.

She tumbled into her sitting room and for the first time since her arrival locked the doors behind her. She rang for her maid; the sooner she was safely in her bed the better. 'I shan't require you again this evening, Cranford.'

She settled back with the latest novel from

Hatchards and became so immersed in this she forgot to unlock the door.

* * *

Alexander heard the shouting and came to investigate. According to his cronies Isobel had thrown a glass of wine over Bartram for no other reason than he'd failed to move aside quickly enough to please her. This was unacceptable behaviour. He'd already had to smooth the ruffled feathers of his house-keeper because of her incivility. Tonight he'd make it clear to her he wouldn't tolerate breaches of etiquette.

His head was thumping; he couldn't recall exactly how many bottles of claret he'd drunk or how much brandy he'd consumed since. Drink numbed the senses, dulled his disappointment and helped him to accept that he'd never have another child to cherish. He paused and leant his burning face against the wall. He closed his eyes, expecting to see an image of his beloved Eleanor; instead a picture of Isobel filled his mind. He rubbed his eyes angrily. No — he wouldn't let her creep into his heart. He'd no room for love in his life. He'd done with this, for it only led to unbearable pain.

He tried her sitting-room door. He rattled,

but it refused to budge. This door was never locked; it must be jammed. He tried to enter her bedchamber through his room, but this door was locked too. Furious, he hammered on the panel. He wouldn't be denied entry to her rooms.

He heard the patter of bare feet cold on the boards. What was the matter with her? Didn't she have a maid? The key turned but the door wasn't opened. He stepped in and glared at the young woman who was staring nervously from beneath the bedcovers.

'Alexander, I came down to tell you that I'm not available this week.'

He felt a flicker of remorse that this lovely young woman was reduced to hiding in her bedchamber in her own home. 'I know that; I'm not a simpleton. I'm quite able to keep note of the date. I came here to discuss the matter of your unbecoming display downstairs.'

'That man was going to touch me. Would you wish me to stand there and let him do so?'

He shook his head, trying to clear his thoughts. She was right. He hadn't given the incident sufficient attention. He didn't doubt her veracity one minute. 'No, of course not. In future you won't respond in that unacceptable way. It'll be the talk of the town, and I dislike being the subject of gossip.'

If he didn't remove himself he'd cast up his accounts on her carpet. This wouldn't enhance his attraction. Momentarily he was ashamed by his lack of control.

'I apologize, Alexander. It won't happen again. You don't look at all well. I wish you didn't drink so much; it's ruining your health.'

Her comment hit a raw nerve. 'Madam, let us get this quite clear. If something similar occurs again don't expect me to be so lenient.' He gulped; he must get to his room before he disgraced himself.

★ ★ ★

Isobel watched him go and her heart twisted. Her husband was no longer the man she'd fallen in love with. He was gambling heavily as well as drinking too much. How long would it be before he was unfaithful? She curled up under the covers and prayed his threat was an idle one, something he'd regret when he was sober. She could forgive his drunkenness, but if ever he mistreated her she would hate him. All hope would be gone. She would let him go to the devil any way he chose.

6

When the unwanted house guests and her husband departed, Isobel thanked God that the snow hadn't been enough to deter them from returning to London. With luck he'd remain in Grosvenor Square all season and leave her in peace. She consoled herself by writing long, untruthful letters to her cousin Petunia and her parents.

Mama no longer enquired if she was increasing and appeared to have accepted the disappointing situation. Her only solace was riding and having her Mary and Sam close by. She visited them more frequently as time passed and spent more time with them than she did in Newcomb.

The summer she spent alone. The younger members of staff, those that hadn't been at Newcomb forever, were now eager to serve her and she was more at ease.

October came around again with the news that two dozen or more guests were expected. There would, this time, be several wives accompanying the gentlemen. It would be pleasant to have someone to talk to other than Mary. Several times she had been tempted to send out cards to the nearby houses but didn't like to go against Alexander.

She waited nervously in the vestibule to greet him. It had been more than six months since he'd been home. Had he changed as much as she? When Foster bowed him in her eyes widened in shock. Who was this man shrugging off his top coat? She scarcely recognized him. His eyes were bloodshot, his face puffy, and his hand had been unsteady when he'd held it out.

She curtsied deeply in order to avoid meeting his eyes. She must school her features and not let him see how dismayed she was. 'Welcome, your grace. It's been too long since you came home.'

She straightened to see him staring as if he couldn't quite place her. He nodded. 'You've lost weight, Isobel. It doesn't suit you.'

With these terse words he strolled off towards the drawing room, leaving her to greet his guests as they appeared. By the time the ladies had been directed to their boudoirs and the gentlemen to the billiard room she was exhausted. She was also bitterly disappointed there wasn't one of the half-dozen ladies she wished to socialize with. They were all as brittle and shallow as their husbands and considerably older than herself.

Unfortunately she must act as a charming hostess for the duration of their visit. How long that would be *he* hadn't told her. At least a married gentleman wouldn't attempt to molest her; she hadn't forgotten the last time and dreaded this happening again. She'd had no opportunity to discuss the matter with Alexander, but she would be blamed if anything similar took place.

Everything went smoothly for the first few days. The men were to shoot and the ladies to join them for an alfresco luncheon. She was almost looking forward to it. To be outside, even in uncongenial company, would be enjoyable. Nothing pleasant had taken place at Newcomb for six months. Unfortunately the heavens opened and the guests were forced to remain indoors. This would mean by dinner the gentlemen would be in their cups and the ladies little better.

At dusk she was on her way to rejoin the guests. The majority of the men had retreated to the billiard room to drink brandy and smoke foul-smelling cigars. The ladies and the remaining gentlemen were in the process of having card tables set out in the grand drawing room.

Isobel was hesitating in the doorway, hidden by a marble column, when a vile creature lurched up to her.

70

'I've been searching for you, your grace. I've noticed your husband ignores you. I'd be happy to take his place. I'm sure you take my meaning.'

Making such a licentious remark was bad enough, but his hand snaked out to clutch her breast. No one touched her breasts but Alexander. Without a second thought she snatched up a large silver candlestick and struck him on the head.

He staggered back, clutching his forehead. Blood poured unchecked down his face. From the screams and cries of distress of the female witnesses one would have thought she'd murdered him. Head wounds bled freely, but she was certain he was not seriously hurt. Then she was surrounded by a ring of accusatory faces and retreated to her apartment.

Alexander was going to be so angry. She huddled under the coverlet, dreading the moment his footsteps approached her bed-chamber. She clenched her fists, her heart pounding, going over the horrible incident which had occurred in full view of many of his cronies.

Should she have brazened it out? Remained in the room and not fled to her apartment in disarray? Maybe she was overreacting — perhaps he would laugh and continue his game of billiards. She might as well be invisible to him nowadays. Was it possible he'd ignore her behaviour?

Her failure to conceive was a bitter disappointment to them. He had selected her to breed in the same way he'd choose a mare to put to his stallion. She had no illusions about her marriage. Her family had been saved from financial ruin by the settlement; Rochester had bought himself a duchess. Her immature fantasies that one day he'd love her had been trampled under his indifference.

How wrong, how naïve she'd been to believe she was anything more than an object, and one that didn't live up to expectations at that. Thank God he spent his time in town, leaving her to her own devices. She should be satisfied with her lot. After all, wasn't she a duchess, dressed in the first stare of fashion, given as much pin money as she wanted? He hadn't repeated his invitation that she join him at Grosvenor Square and she wouldn't have gone if he had.

The mantel clock struck midnight. He rarely retired until the small hours when there were guests. The shooting season was well established and cub-hunting about to start. Her stomach curdled. Why didn't he come and get it over with? She closed her eyes, but the tears spilled anyway. She bit her lip — she would cry no more. She'd done enough these past months. Indeed, she couldn't even recall the name of the obnoxious man who'd waylaid her in the drawing room after dinner.

However justified her actions, she was the Duchess of Rochester. One thing her husband had made abundantly clear was he wouldn't tolerate anything but the most seemly of manners. She shuddered as she remembered what he'd said when she'd thrown a glass of wine over that other gentleman. She was going to cast up her accounts. Her face was drenched with sweat. He'd never raised a hand to her. Tonight would he extract a physical retribution?

★   ★   ★

Alexander downed his brandy before chalking his cue and preparing to take the shot. A hush fell on the billiard room — this was a crucial moment. A thousand guineas had been staked on the outcome of this pot. As he drew back his arm someone cleared his throat loudly and he miscued. The resulting screech of delight from the onlookers fuelled his anger. With clenched fists he turned to find Foster standing rigidly behind him. His butler knew better than to interrupt unless it was a matter of extreme urgency.

73

'What is it, man? It had better be good or you'll be leaving Newcomb tonight.'

Foster's whispered words were barely discernible in the hubbub. 'If I could be permitted to have a word with you, your grace, in private.'

He tossed his cue to one of the gentlemen still celebrating the wager and stepped out of earshot. 'Well?' His head thumped like the very devil. He'd been drinking heavily since early afternoon, which did nothing to improve his digestion or his temper. Even in his befuddled state he saw his servant stiffen as if expecting a blow.

'There has been an incident in the drawing room involving her grace. Your presence is required immediately.'

He'd been angry before; now he was incandescent. The only kind of *incident* he could imagine was that some bastard had made advances to her. He'd put a bullet through the man's heart after he'd beaten him to a pulp. He strode out and the cold air all but flattened him after the fug of the billiard room. The long passageways in this barrack were never heated. The nights were cold and the prodigious amount of glass along this side of the house didn't help. He was obliged to stop for a moment, resting his hand against the wall until his head stopped swimming.

When his stomach settled and his eyes cleared he continued, his fury building at every step. He was about to turn to the grand drawing room when Foster spoke from behind him. The man was slightly out of breath.

'I beg your pardon, your grace, but Sir John is in an anteroom. I thought it best to remove him immediately.'

One thing he could rely on was the loyalty of his staff. Opening the door to a room he couldn't remember entering before, he saw a man slumped in an upright chair: Sir John Farnham. His head was encircled by a clean white bandage and judging by the amount of blood on his garments he had received a serious head wound.

His sharp features were not enhanced by the blood. The man glared at him. 'No one treats me with disrespect. Be very sure every house in town will hear of this.'

Two gentlemen were hovering behind their friend. The shorter one — Alexander misremembered his name — stepped forward. 'It's a disgrace, Rochester. Sir John did no more than exchange pleasantries with your wife and she struck him down with a candlestick. He will demand substantial reparation for this outrage.'

Without hesitation Alexander grabbed the speaker by his cravat, lifting him bodily and shaking him like a rat. 'If my wife was obliged to strike Farnham then it can be for only one reason. He made improper advances.' He tossed the man aside and he fell like an empty coat to the boards.

The second man instantly dodged behind the chair in which the bastard sat. Alexander wanted to throttle Farnham. He loomed over the seated man and Farnham flinched. Isobel would never encourage a gentleman to take liberties; she kept herself apart from his friends and hated every moment he forced her to act as his hostess.

The man shrank against the chair back. Alexander decided he wasn't worth the trouble. 'You and your associates will depart from here immediately. If I discover you when I rise tomorrow I shan't hesitate to kill you.'

As he left the room he heard Farnham call after him. 'You will pay for this, Rochester. I never forget a slight.'

He ignored the comment. The man was of no account. The matter here was dealt with, but there were still his other guests. Before he entered the grand drawing room he needed more brandy to steady his nerves. He detoured to his study, his private sanctum where no one ventured without invitation. He was shocked to find his hands were trembling; another drink should steady him.

This incident would take more than diplomacy to defuse. His anger turned towards Isobel. Hadn't he warned her this kind of behaviour was unacceptable? Whatever the provocation, the family name was sacrosanct; it must never be besmirched. Striking a man with a candlestick in front of his guests was going to send ripples throughout the *ton*. The people he'd gathered around him wouldn't hesitate to gossip about the incident.

He stepped into the drawing room and viewed the assembly through narrowed eyes. There wasn't a person among them he would wish to call a friend; they were sycophants and hangers-on. He shook his head and regretted it as he almost lost his balance. He cared not what this assortment of scroungers thought about his family. They would depart the following morning. The shooting party was over. His icy stare sent shockwaves around the chamber and gradually the chatter stopped and every head turned his way.

'I regret you were obliged to witness the unfortunate incident. Farnham has been dealt with. You'll understand I'm obliged to ask you all to leave at first light tomorrow morning.'

Turning his back on the silent group, he stalked out. He wouldn't demean himself by asking for their discretion, knowing gossip would spread whatever he said. Over the years his real friends had dropped him. He was married to a barren wife. But the one thing he *could* rely on was the family name. Tonight she'd brought it into disrepute and this couldn't be ignored. He returned to the study to allow his guests to retire for the night. Whilst he waited he finished a decanter of brandy.

The house wasn't silent until after midnight. Time for a reckoning. He couldn't blame his wife for being childless, but she could behave with decorum. He paused, heartsick and lonely. Even in his befuddled state he understood the fault was not hers, but his. He was a pitiful specimen and he wasn't surprised he'd failed to father further children.

He punched the wall, the pain sending shockwaves up his arm. He was master here and whatever the provocation, Isobel must pay. His anger grew with each step he took. He'd been too lenient with her; allowed her to run wild when he was absent and to ignore her duties as chatelaine. She'd become impertinent, not at all the submissive wife he thought he'd married.

From tonight everything changed. He'd lavished money and gifts on her, hadn't overburdened her with demands in the bedroom, and what had she done? She'd thrown it back in his face by behaving like a slut. A lady would have fainted, run weeping to fetch him, or possibly slapped the bastard across the face. But no, she must pick up a candlestick and brain the man in full view of a dozen people.

Having left the butler to supervise the departure of those three men, he was free to take the necessary action. His valet was hovering nervously. Alexander smiled grimly. When his evening coat had gone, his cravat, boots and waistcoat also, he held up his hand. 'Leave me, Duncan. I can do the rest myself. I shan't require you until the morning.'

'Your grace, allow me to help you into bed. You're a trifle unsteady.'

'Silence. Know your place or lose it.' What was it about tonight that everyone was defying his orders?

He glared and his valet collected the discarded garments and retreated into the dressing room. The door clicked shut. What was going to take place in the adjoining apartment needed no eavesdroppers.

*   *   *

Isobel tensed at every passing footstep, but so far he hadn't burst in to berate her. The house was quiet, and even the most recalcitrant of the guests had retired to their bedchambers. He wasn't coming. Thank God for that; he'd been drinking steadily for hours. With luck he'd passed out in his study and would wake with a sore head in the morning and no recollection of what had transpired.

She turned, plumping the pillows and finally relaxing. On the verge of sleep, she heard the distinctive click of the communicating door. He entered quietly, pushing it closed behind him. She held her breath. If she feigned sleep would he retreat? Her heart was hammering. A wave of nausea engulfed her.

Through the slit of her eyelids a flickering light showed he was in his shirtsleeves and pantaloons. When he came to her in the usual way he wore only his silk bedrobe and was naked underneath. She couldn't welcome him into her bed when he was angry and in his cups. Here was the only place she was able to cling to the faint hope that one day he'd learn to love her. If he took her in anger, it would be over — with no children to keep them together she would have nothing to hope for. The rest of her life would be lonely and miserable, trapped in a marriage that had failed them both.

Perhaps he wasn't angry but had come to check she was unharmed from the unpleasant experience. She daren't raise her head and reveal she was awake. The sound of further candles being lit could mean only one thing. She could no longer dissemble. He hadn't come to check if she was distressed; he'd come to punish her for besmirching his precious name.

Would it make things easier if she apologized? Pushing herself upright, she forced her lips to curve in a smile of welcome. His face was unrecognizable. His eyes glittered strangely. She tried to find words to mollify him. He wasn't himself; anger and drink had changed him. Her words remained locked behind her teeth. Her mouth was too dry to release her tongue from the roof of her mouth.

With slow deliberation he placed his candlestick on the ormolu table beside the bed. She shivered and feared her bladder would empty. Why didn't he speak?

'Tonight, madam, you brought disgrace to my name. The last time you did this I warned you what to expect. I'm master in this house and it's high time you learnt what happens when you disobey me.' His words were

81

clipped, each one enunciated clearly. This was the voice of a madman. He stepped forward and slung her over his shoulder like a sack of flour and carried her into the anteroom in which she took a bath.

'You disobeyed me. You've only yourself to blame for this.'

The door slammed and he pushed a large piece of furniture against it. She was shut in a freezing room in her nightgown. How dare he treat her like this? There were no other doors in the room and she couldn't escape into the servants' quarters even if she'd wished to.

She pressed her ear to the door. His footsteps faded into the night. Slumping onto the icy tiles, she hugged her knees and tried to stop her teeth chattering. How long would he leave her here to freeze? After an hour she was too dispirited and cold to do more than huddle in a corner praying for release. She shivered for hours until he returned. She scrambled to her feet. His voice reverberated through the door. 'I hope you've learned your lesson, madam.'

She would never forgive him. Rage overwhelmed her. She was blinded by it, her fear and misery burned away by its ferocity. The door swung open and she sprung forward snarling with anger.

Before he had time to react she lashed out,

punching him squarely in the mouth. His teeth ground into her fist, his lip split, and she ignored the hurt that travelled up her arm. He reeled back, blood dripping from his mouth, his eyes wide. Not giving him time to retaliate, she punched him with her left hand. This connected with his eye.

She was incapable of speech. Her cheeks were awash with tears of rage. He stepped away from her shaking his head, wiping blood from his mouth with his shirtsleeve. She turned to see what she could snatch up to hit him with and her fingers closed around a candlestick. As she lifted it his hand grasped her wrist and he took it from her.

'Enough, little firebrand. There are better ways of venting your spleen than that.' He tumbled her full length onto the bed, his weight pinning her down, then held her arms on either side of her head. She bucked frantically to get free.

'Alexander, haven't I been punished enough tonight?'

He disregarded her plea, trapping her. His tongue invaded her mouth — she tasted his blood. Something deep inside her stirred and she tore at his shirt. He took the two sides of her nightgown and ripped them apart. She was consumed by a different heat. His lips closed on hers but they were not hard but soft, persuasive, adding to her passion.

He trailed hot kisses down her neck and her treacherous body responded. Although she hated him, primitive urges took over. It had been too long since she'd made love to him. The all-too-familiar heat spread rapidly until she was unable to control herself. His mouth teased — he sensed she was willing. He was a skilled lover and she was helpless as his fingers worked their magic. Her anger evaporated and she was engulfed by her desire. A wildness flooded through her and her nails raked his shoulders.

Keeping his mouth on hers he stripped off his remaining garments, then hot skin covered her from head to foot. She clawed his back, imploring him, biting his lips in her hunger. Afterwards he gathered her tenderly, believing the passion they'd shared negated all that had gone before. As the pleasure slipped away she became aware of his alcohol-laced breath. She hated herself for becoming a willing participant.

He was dead to the world, exertion and brandy rendering him senseless. She wriggled from beneath him and, blowing out the candles, took the remaining one into her dressing room. She dressed in her plainest clothes, the ones she wore when he was absent. Five minutes later she'd stuffed garments into her portmanteau; then from the depths of her closet she removed two cloth bags filled with golden coins. She'd been hoarding these from her allowance this past year. There was more than enough in her savings to keep her, and her retainers, for a year at least.

She must take her work box, as such items were invaluable. She rummaged inside and found what she wanted. There was something she needed to do before she left. Removing the scissors, she hacked off her braid at the base of her neck. He was always praising her hair, so she would leave it as a memento. She tied the cut end with a fresh ribbon, then threaded on her betrothal ring and wedding band and tied a knot.

There was no need to tiptoe; he was snoring, deep in a drunken slumber. Without haste she gathered up her plait and placed it on the pillow beside him. A bolster pushed beneath the covers made it appear she was still there. She wished she could be in the room when he woke and discovered what she'd done.

With the candlestick in one hand she slipped out through the dressing room door and found her way downstairs without breaking her neck. What she was doing was, in the eyes of the world, a crime. She belonged to him and according to the law of the land he was free to use and abuse her as he pleased. However, *she* would not remain with a man who thought locking her in a small, cold room was acceptable behaviour.

She was thankful everyone had retired, as this made it easy to slip along the dark passageways until she reached the side door used by the junior staff. The sound of the bolt was harsh in the silence, but she didn't hesitate. No time for regrets — her life here was over.

7

Isobel pulled open the side door and closed it quietly behind her. Her bag was heavy but it wasn't far to the cottage where Mary and Sam lived. Her dogs would be overjoyed to see her even in the middle of the night. She doubted her loyal retainers would be so pleased; they would be horrified by her story. There was sufficient money to lease a small house somewhere many miles from here and start a new life. She would defy convention and leave the ruins of her old one behind.

Several times during the walk she set down her bag to lean, panting, against a tree trunk to recover her strength. The hours she'd spent in the cold must have debilitated her. She pushed the memory of their energetic lovemaking aside. She intended to be gone before her husband woke from his drunken stupor and set up a search. His pride would be damaged by her defection. He wouldn't let her go willingly. He would rather die than do so.

It took longer than usual to reach the cottage. The path ran like a white ribbon in the moonlight and she'd never been so grateful to see the small front door. She hammered with the remainder of her strength and woke her pets. Minutes passed and then Sam was calling to the dogs telling them to hush. The clatter of his boots on the wooden staircase meant he was on his way. The door swung open and the animals threw themselves at her; too tired to push them away, she tumbled backwards.

'Your grace, let me help you. Get away, stupid dogs; haven't you caused enough harm?'

'No, Sam, don't blame them. Mary must get up at once. We depart from here immediately. I've left him; nothing on this earth will make me return. My life at Newcomb is over and I shall make a new one elsewhere.'

'Come along, let's get you inside and Mary can see to you. I'll get out back and harness up the gig.'

With his support she stumbled inside. Mary rushed to her side, guiding her to a wooden rocking chair that stood to the left of the fireplace in the main room.

'He shut me in the bathing room for hours; I'm still frozen to the marrow.'

'The monster! You should never have married him. I always thought him a cold fish, not good enough for you, my pet.' Mary gestured angrily to her husband. 'Didn't I say, Sam, how much weight the mistress has lost these past few months? See, she's shaking; hasn't the strength of a kitten because of what he did to her.'

'Don't worry, your grace, I'll get you away from Newcomb. We'll keep you safe.'

As she rested against Sam's broad shoulder she told him of her other decision. 'Please, don't use that title again. I'm done with it. From now on I am plain Mrs . . . ' She was unable to think of a single name to replace her own. All her life she'd been known by a title: first Lady Isobel, eldest daughter of the Earl of Drummond, and since her marriage she was a duchess. Would life be simpler if she was a commoner?

'Don't fret, madam. We'll come up with something soon enough. Here, sit yourself down. Mary shall make you a hot drink whilst I get the horse out.'

Isobel settled on the cushions. She closed her eyes, leaving Mary and Sam to do what was necessary to ready themselves for their flight. Sounds became distant; she wasn't quite asleep, but far enough from reality to gain respite from the pain in her heart which was far worse than any physical injury.

'Come along, my dear. Everything's done. It will be light in an hour or two. Do you have any idea where you wish to go?' Mary offered her arm and pulled her gently from the chair.

She closed her eyes and an image of the

huge skies, white sand and the flat green fens of her birthplace filled her head. 'I'd like to leave Hertfordshire and return to Norfolk. It can't be anywhere near Bracken Hall, for that's the first place *he* will look for me. But if we go to the north of Norwich we should be safe enough.'

'That's what we thought; it's going to take us several days to get there. With only one horse, we'll have to take it in stages.'

'And it's imperative we don't use the toll road, and we must travel at night if possible. *He* will send out search parties. I can't go back and he mustn't find me.'

A cold nose pressed into her hand. She rubbed the silky head, knowing it to be Othello, as Ebony was already at the door waiting. The one light in this darkness was that she would be with her beloved animals.

Sam assisted her into the vehicle; he'd prepared a snug nest in one corner and she curled up. Mary scrambled in beside her. The two dogs flopped down in the well and they were ready. The first faint glimmer of dawn coloured the sky. There was no need to light the lanterns that hung on poles on either side of the carriage. The gentle rocking of the vehicle helped to soothe her misery; with luck she would sleep through most of the journey.

Alexander forced his eyes open. Where the hell was he? He'd no recollection of the previous night; this wasn't uncommon after consuming so much brandy. Moving his head made his stomach lurch; he took a deep breath through his nose. This was Isobel's bed and he was naked. He reached out a hand and his fingers brushed her long braid. Odd — when they made love he always released it.

His fingers closed around it. The ribbon refused to give way beneath his fumbling. He tugged and the plait slithered across his chest. What the hell? His stomach clenched and he rolled to one side to cast up his accounts. When he'd finished he wiped his mouth on the sheet. He gazed at the bolster where Isobel should be. His eyes misted, he slumped as he recalled what had happened the night before.

Holding her hair against his chest, he moved into the space she'd occupied, breathing in her scent, his face wet with tears of shame and loss. Something clinked against his shoulder. He slid his fingers down the severed braid and found her betrothal and wedding bands tied to the ribbon.

Isobel couldn't have made things clearer.

She'd gone; his lovely young wife had gone and he didn't blame her. He buried his face in her pillow and his shoulders heaved. For the second time in his life he'd lost the woman he loved, and this time the fault was his. His brutality had driven her away.

The stench in the bedchamber made his stomach roil. Unsteadily he swung his legs to the floor and attempted to stand. The pain thumping between his eyes was worse than he could ever remember. He deserved to suffer, deserved to be horsewhipped for what he'd done. How had he come to this?

He tottered through the communicating door and back into his own rooms. The long braid bounced behind, jingling as it hit the boards, the sound a reminder of what he'd destroyed. His misery deepened. She was cutting him out of her life in the same way she'd cut her lovely hair.

How was he going to live without her? The death of his wife and two daughters had all but killed him; made him frightened to love again. He'd been given a second chance to find happiness and had ruined it by his base behaviour. Last night had been the culmination of his callousness. She'd offered him nothing but love and support over the past year and he'd spurned it, treating her as if she were of no importance. He'd remained aloof because he'd fallen in love with her and was terrified of being hurt again.

There was no need to send out a search party. She would be with the Watkins couple. Isobel believed this to be a secret, but nothing happened at Newcomb undetected. Initially he'd intended to confront her, but after consideration he'd decided to leave her servants where they were. She needed a bolt hole.

As he splashed his face with cold water he felt less anguished. Maybe matters weren't as bad as he feared. After all, Isobel was his wife and had promised herself to him. If given time to reconsider, she would come back. He'd allow her a day or two to recover and then visit. He wouldn't demand she return immediately but suggest she visit one of his estates in the north. There she could live in seclusion, untrammelled by responsibility, for a few weeks.

His spirits lifted. He'd behaved unforgivably but he'd change; become the man she deserved. She might hate him now, but she would love him again. Isobel would return for the seasonal festivities, and what a time of celebration that would be. However much she loathed and despised him she was his wife and, and unlike himself, wouldn't shirk her duties.

He rang the small brass bell which stood

beside his bed, then ramming his arms into his bedrobe he waited for Duncan to appear. The click of the dressing room door heralded his arrival. 'Duncan, I require a bath and a jug of coffee.'

'At once, your grace. Mr Foster has asked me to inform you all your guests have departed.'

Alexander raised his hand in acknowledgement and wandered to the window to stare morosely across the park. Usually the magnificent stand of oak trees in their autumn glory and the ornamental lake filled him with satisfaction. Today it meant nothing. What was the use of having so much when he'd no one with whom to share it? Until she returned he'd gain no pleasure from this view.

★   ★   ★

'What do you mean, the place is uninhabited?' Alexander glared at his man of business, William Hill, whom he'd sent to check on the cottage.

'The place is deserted, your grace. The shutters up and the stable empty. I reckon it's been like that for a day or two.'

'Thank you. You may go.' The man bowed and retreated.

Alexander wanted to hurl the nearest

object through the window. This was an unmitigated disaster. Why hadn't he had the place checked immediately? He gripped the edge of his desk, forcing his anger back. Never again would he let his temper rule him. He had driven Isobel away. He sank into the nearest chair, dropping his head in his hands in despair.

He wouldn't relinquish the search until he was certain she was well and had sufficient funds to live comfortably. He prayed the scandal never reached the outside world. With luck no one, apart from the staff would know she had gone. She rarely joined him in London and there were no close acquaintances to make enquiries.

Perhaps her disappearance could be kept secret? He was certain the unfortunate chambermaids who'd been obliged to clear his mess wouldn't risk their position by gossiping. He'd let it be known Isobel had gone to Norfolk to be with her ailing mother; no one would dare question this. His fingers clenched. What was he thinking of? Let the scandal mongers say what they wanted; he'd willingly sacrifice his good name if it brought her back.

Where would she go? He wouldn't mount a full-scale pursuit but send out a few discreet enquiries. They shouldn't be too difficult to find despite having had two days' start. A gig containing two large black dogs, along with a beautiful young woman and her maid, was bound to be noticed when they trotted through a village or town.

The thought of Isobel being tossed about in that ancient vehicle filled him with remorse. He'd never drink to excess again and would immediately root out the bad influences in his life. From this moment forward he'd be a better man. He intended to spend the rest of his life making amends. He wouldn't take her for granted again if she consented to return.

He'd never considered the notion of bringing her back by force. If she wished to remain estranged then so be it. He would retire from society. Now the wretched war was over he could travel abroad and leave his heartbreak behind. Ten years ago he'd been a different man. This mausoleum had been a happy place filled with the laughter of his little daughters and his beloved Eleanor. He'd taken due interest in his tenants, paid attention to his friends and wasn't the arrogant, hedonistic bastard he'd become.

Small wonder those that used to be his intimates had begun to refuse his invitations. To fill his loneliness he'd surrounded himself with toadies, sycophants and people not worthy of his attention. Into this hellhole he'd brought his innocent bride and tainted her by association. Look what this degeneracy had led to.

He strode to the door and roared down the corridor, 'Foster, have Hill return immediately. I'll wait for him in my study.'

His butler must have been lurking in the shadows, for he stepped forward bowing obsequiously. 'You haven't taken breakfast again this morning, your grace. Shall I have something sent to you?'

Alexander was about to refuse but he needed his strength; he couldn't afford to become unwell. 'As you wish. I want coffee served with it.'

His study was the one place he was comfortable. Eleanor and the children had never entered so it held no sad memories. He'd no idea if Isobel had investigated this room in his absence; he hoped she had, for then he could feel closer to her.

The thought of what she'd endured since their marriage almost unmanned him. He'd kept her cloistered like an inmate of an asylum. Her wardens had been his too-attentive staff. He'd been so immersed in his own selfish affairs he'd never considered how unhappy she was without friends or family around.

Hill arrived at the same time as his breakfast and on impulse Alexander invited him to join him. They sat and munched and Alexander was surprised how hungry he was. 'I want you to select three discreet and reliable men. Have them ride out and make enquiries. They mustn't make themselves known, merely follow. When she's settled, they can send word to me.'

'My lord, might I suggest we send the men in pairs? That way one can come back with news whilst the other continues his surveillance.'

'Good man. Arrange that. I intend to wait two weeks and then close Newcomb. I'll take the staff and move permanently to town. Make sure these men are aware of this.'

'Do you wish me to remain in your absence, your grace? Or shall I accompany you to London?'

'Come with me; set yourself up somewhere. God knows there are enough rooms in Grosvenor Square.' He reached into his desk and withdrew a wallet filled with paper notes. He added a substantial bag of coins and the matter was settled.

When the chambermaid had removed the empty tray he stretched out on the daybed in front of the fire. He hadn't slept since Isobel ran away; every time he closed his eyes he relived his actions and woke sweating and ashamed. He no longer slept in his room, but took cat-naps in his study.

As he was drifting off to sleep he reviewed what he knew about her flight. He was certain she'd at least one hundred pounds in her possession. Each quarter she had the full amount of her allowance and, as far as he was aware, had spent none of it on frills and furbelows. The cost of maintaining her two servants was negligible. Had she somehow anticipated one day this moment would come and she would need funds to escape?

When Foster informed him Isobel was hoarding money he'd been horrified his staff believed he wished them to spy on her. He'd told Foster in no uncertain terms to mind his own business and make sure the staff did the same. No further reports were given to him, but with hindsight he realized this surveillance had probably continued. Should he ask his butler if he knew where Isobel intended to go? What was he thinking? He would never discuss his wife with that dried-up stick of a man.

He jack-knifed, all desire for sleep vanishing. There was one thing he *could* do which would prove how much he'd changed. He would get his lawyers to ferret out his heir. There must be one somewhere, as his grandfather had had several younger brothers. One of them would have managed to produce a male between them. He'd groom this gentleman; teach him everything necessary to become the next Duke of Rochester. Surely this would prove to Isobel he was happy to live his life without setting up his nursery?

The two weeks passed with no news of Isobel. She appeared to have vanished without trace. He could procrastinate no longer. He'd had word from his lawyers that one Richard Bentley, Esq had been located and was on his way to meet him in town.

Newcomb was under holland covers; several diligences had departed with items of furniture that he couldn't live without, plus the majority of his wardrobe. The exodus was like a military operation. Transferring over a hundred staff and their belongings, as well as his own, to Grosvenor Square required careful planning. He would be glad to turn his back on this place. The building held nothing but unhappy memories. His first wife and daughters had died here and then Isobel had left him.

He was resigned to the fact she might never come back; that he would have to spend the rest of his life alone. He would never divorce her. He had no wish for another wife. Isobel was everything a man could want.

Lady Fulbright, his ex-mistress, had cornered him at a card party the last time he'd been in town and made it blatantly obvious she was more than willing to resume their relationship. He shook his head. He would never be so self-indulgent; stopping his drinking and gambling was only half the task. To give in to the demands of the flesh would make him a lesser man. Indeed, he was in every way a much reduced specimen. His years of overindulgence showed in the flab on his once lean frame. If he attempted a round at Jackson's he would be floored in seconds. That was something else he would pay attention to. He would get himself back in shape; be someone Isobel could respect, even if she could never forgive.

One day his men would discover her whereabouts. He would ride to her and she'd see the difference in him and know he was a changed man. He closed his eyes and her image filled his head. The way she used to smile at him; the way her eyes lit up when he entered the room; her delight when he returned to her; and the refreshing innocence with which she welcomed him into her bed. How could he have been so stupid? She had offered him something precious, and like a fool he'd crushed her gift beneath his feet.

8

Isobel sat back, her forehead clammy, her head spinning, and thanked God the retching was over. Mary removed the basin and replaced it with a clean vessel. Isobel accepted a cool drink, rinsed her mouth and spat the last of the noxious matter into the bowl. There was no doubt; she had to accept the impossible. She was increasing.

'I must return to Newcomb, Mary. I don't wish to, but I'm with child. I've suspected so for some time but could scarcely believe it. I haven't had my courses since we arrived and that must be more than eight weeks ago. Whatever my feelings for the duke, I can't deny this child its birthright.'

Mary nodded. 'I've known for weeks, madam, but didn't like to say considering the circumstances. I've been waiting for you to draw the same conclusion. You needed time to recover from what happened without further anxiety. But Sam and I have things organized. We can be ready to leave immediately.'

Sally Harris, who'd been turned off by her previous employers, had joined them a few days after their arrival at Home Farm. The young woman now acted as her abigail. Isobel turned to her. 'Sally, I'll be returning to Hertfordshire, to Newcomb. Are you willing to accompany me?'

'I'd be delighted, madam, if you're sure the likes of me will be allowed to serve you at such a grand place.'

Isobel stood up, smiling at the young woman she'd become quite fond of these past weeks. 'It will be very different from living here. I intend to have my own people around me. You'll be answerable to me and no one else.'

Sally curtsied. 'I'll start packing your clothes, madam, if you don't require my services.'

'No, I wish to speak to Mrs Watkins. I'll ring if I need you.'

The two basins were removed to the dressing room, leaving Mary alone with Isobel. 'I'll not be browbeaten by the staff this time; I intend my return to be on *my* terms.'

'You have our full support, and I'm certain the others you've taken on will be more than happy to come with us.'

'Bill has made an excellent footman, so he'll be my butler. His experience serving as a valet has given him all the skills he needs for this post. His leg injury has been no impediment to his efficiency.' She considered the other staff. The cook and kitchen maid were a mother and daughter who'd been made homeless when the man of the house died. These two would be pleased to accompany her. However, the two women who came in to do the heavy work had families of their own. They would wish to remain in Norfolk. She would leave the maintenance of the house in their capable hands.

'Will you please inform everyone, Mary? Betty and Ada will require sufficient funds to tide them over until I return.'

'Yes, madam.' Mary fiddled with an apron before continuing. 'Shall we call you by your title? Being plain Mrs Baverstock is all very well in the country, but at Newcomb things are different.'

Isobel was relieved her friend made no comment about her intention to return. 'I've no choice so I suppose it's better to resume my title now and become used to hearing it. I wish to leave the day after tomorrow; I'm sure the roads will have dried by then.'

They would need the gig and the ancient travelling carriage Sam had purchased in order to transport everyone to Newcomb. The two outside men were competent with horses, so could act as coachmen, leaving

Sam to ride the gelding she'd acquired from a local farmer.

She'd been thinking about her return for the past few weeks. She'd guessed she was pregnant but refused to accept it. When the baby was born, whether boy or girl, she intended to leave the infant with her husband and return to Home Farm. Alexander would never let her take the baby with her. Unless she was prepared to live with him again, she must abandon her child. She swallowed the lump in her throat at this hideous thought. She blinked back tears — time enough to consider this when the baby arrived.

The farm was almost self-sufficient and with good management it might even produce a surplus to be sold on. The day workers must continue to take care of the livestock in her absence.

'Mary, I don't mean to move into Newcomb; I'll occupy the east wing. The old part of the house hasn't been used for many years. It will require cleaning and refurbishment but will be ideal for my purposes.'

Mary ignored this unusual suggestion. 'Sam's sending a man ahead to reserve accommodation, your grace. In your delicate condition it would be best if we completed the journey slowly.'

'Thank you, Mary. I'm not looking forward

to being jounced around when I feel so sick, and will be happy to travel in stages.'

Being left in idleness gave her too much time to think. She wasn't the same girl who'd married Alexander a year ago. Today she would stand her ground and insist he did as she requested. The horror of a public scandal should work in her favour. She would agree to act as his hostess if there were guests, but the remainder of the time would remain in the east wing surrounded by those she trusted.

She prayed the baby would be a boy. Although she no longer had any feelings for Alexander, she'd spoken her vows in the house of God. By refusing to share his bed she was breaking them. Therefore, if she produced an heir, at least she could leave knowing he had the son he so desperately wanted.

The Marquis of Newcomb, as their son would be called, would have everything he needed without his mother being in residence. No doubt the baby would be removed from her as soon as he was born and be given over to an army of retainers. A nanny brought out of retirement would hand him to a wet nurse. Isobel would have no control over his well-being and only see him when the nanny chose to bring him down. Someone of her status wasn't expected to be involved in childcare, merely to produce the necessary children.

This was a highly unsatisfactory system but accepted in wealthy and aristocratic households. However she'd recently read in a pamphlet about such matters and this had stated quite categorically that all mothers, not just the poor folk, should feed their babies themselves. The author was calling for women at every level to do what nature intended. She shrugged. This was another decision she could put off for a few months.

They travelled at a leisurely pace, taking three days to complete the distance. The gig, which contained staff and baggage, had gone ahead in order to ensure the overnight accommodation was suitable. When the carriage arrived at Newcomb, Isobel's confidence slipped. Making rash decisions was one thing, but carrying them through in the face of her formidable husband might prove a different proposition.

Mary fussed with her bonnet, shook out the folds of the travelling cloak and smiled a trifle nervously as the vehicle rocked to a halt outside the enormous building. Isobel expected the usual army of liveried footmen to pour from the front door. Foster and Maynard would no doubt be waiting to greet her with sneering faces.

To her astonishment the door remained closed. She stepped down and stared at the building, only now seeing the shutters were closed. The house was unoccupied. Alexander had removed to Grosvenor Square. He'd shut the house and given up on her.

She felt a moment's regret but forced it away. So much the better; she would have free rein to set herself up before he heard she'd returned. There must be a skeleton staff. Fires had to be lit regularly or the place would become damp and uninhabitable.

'Mary, ask Sam to hammer on the door. There must be someone in.'

Mary relayed the message through the window and Sam dismounted and went to speak to those in the gig. Othello and Ebony whined to be released. She pushed open the carriage door and let them out to explore their new home. They'd never been here but it would soon become familiar territory. Animals didn't worry about etiquette and preserving their good name; if they wished to relieve themselves a hovel was as good as a palace.

Sam's thunderous knocking eventually produced the required result. The door was unbolted and a flustered middle-aged woman, with her cap askew and her apron strings flapping, gawped at him. This wasn't someone she recognized.

'His grace has moved to London. The house is under covers and I haven't been told to expect any visitors.'

'My good woman, her grace, the Duchess of Rochester, has returned. You'll do well to mind your tongue.'

The servant glanced at the travelling carriage. The woman paled and threw her apron over her face as if by so doing would become invisible.

Isobel laughed. 'This is quite ridiculous.' She walked forward and gently pulled the apron down. 'My arrival's totally unexpected. I don't intend to live in the main part of the house. As soon as it can be cleaned I'll remove to the east wing.'

The woman was too distressed to do more than curtsy clumsily and step to one side to allow her to enter. About a dozen servants were arriving, hurriedly buttoning livery and straightening their caps. They more or less curtsied and bowed together.

Sam and Mary took charge, leaving Isobel to head for the small parlour at the rear of the house which would be far easier to heat than any of the enormous rooms.

The maid curtsied nervously. 'I'm acting housekeeper here; Smith's the name, your grace. His grace has taken the rest to Grosvenor Square. There's no one left inside, apart from us few. And all the grooms and such have gone with him, and all the horses too.'

This was exactly the news Isobel wanted. Without the objectionable Maynard and Foster to interfere she might well be installed in the east wing before Alexander became aware of her presence at Newcomb.

'I'm delighted to hear you say so. I've need of loyal staff of my own. From now on you're in my employ and shall become *my* retainers. Mrs Watkins is my housekeeper, Mr Watkins my man of business, and Mr Brown my butler. I'll leave them to organize matters as they see fit.' She turned to Mary. 'Send someone along to light fires in the small parlour and also in the yellow guest suite. I'll sleep there until the east wing is ready.'

A tall young man bowed to her. 'If I may be permitted to speak, your grace? There's nothing we'd like more than to serve you. We've not had an easy time working here. We're all recently taken on, that's why Mrs Maynard and Mr Foster left us here on half-pay.'

'Good — I require my staff to be loyal to *me*. I wish no mention of my arrival to reach

110

London. Do I have your assurances on this matter?'

A chorus of assent ran round the circle. Satisfied she'd made her position clear, she left her staff to get on with what they did best. In less than an hour she was warm and cosy and drinking tea served on the best china.

The next few days were a bustle of activity as her minions cleaned and prepared the east wing. Mary insisted she remained with her feet up, reading and sewing.

'The east wing is in good shape, your grace, considering how long it's been left unoccupied.'

'How long before I can move in?'

'I've fires burning in every chamber. I reckon the place will be warm and dry in no time. The furniture and curtains you've selected are being transferred this afternoon. Sam says you can come and see for yourself later on.'

At three o'clock, just as night was drawing in, Sam escorted her from Newcomb and into her new home. This section was accessed by its own front door and there were no communicating entrances. The east wing was beginning to look like a place where she could be comfortable. The ceilings here were considerably lower, the rooms less vast, and although it didn't have the modern appointments of Newcomb, it made up for it in other ways. The building was of ancient construction and had been the original Newcomb before the current monstrosity had been added by Alexander's grandfather.

For the first time she was in control, not beholden to her parents or her husband. By the end of March the entire staff had transferred to join her. Extra servants had been taken on from the village and so far no one had seen fit to send news to Grosvenor Square. Mary had the house running like clockwork. Bill was a magnificent butler, firm but fair and, more importantly, he was almost as tall as her husband and much younger and fitter. She was praying he wouldn't allow the duke to barge his way in when he eventually arrived to confront her.

She hadn't been in residence long when the estate manager, Mr Reynolds, approached her. 'Your grace, forgive me for bothering you, but your tenants and their cottages are in dire straits. There have been no repairs or improvements here for years. Two children died from lack of warmth last week.'

'That's appalling, Mr Reynolds. I give you permission to instigate any repairs necessary. Get the men to do the work themselves and pay them for it. Make sure there's enough fuel for everyone and give food where it's in short supply.'

How could the duke have been so lax with his duties? He prided himself on his birth and yet had neglected the most crucial part of his inheritance — taking care of his dependents.

Reynolds beamed, his cheeks glowing from the cold. 'Thank you, your grace. I've access to funds for day-to-day matters. If we get started right away by the time the depredations are noticed the work will be completed.' He grinned, and looked almost boyish in his excitement.

'Do whatever you have to, spend what you need, but I suggest everything's done as rapidly as possible. I'm sure you understand the necessity for speed.'

'I do. What's done can't be undone. I reckon we've got a month before . . . well a month to get things finished.' The estate manager departed, leaving her to contemplate the scale of what she'd set in motion. This was tantamount to stealing; as the duchess she'd no legal right to her husband's money. He would come hurtling down from Grosvenor Square when he noticed the discrepancies in his accounts. Was that why she'd given her permission without a second thought? Was it time for him to know she was pregnant?

Word had spread around the neighbour-hood that she'd returned and had authorised much-needed improvements. Everyone knew she'd no right to do so, but the artisans had done the work anyway. When the duke eventually came he'd be faced with a *fait accompli*. His tenants would be well-housed and all he would be able to do was rant and rave. She'd take the blame; no one else would suffer.

Isobel was sitting quietly in front of the fire reading a new novel recently arrived from London, entitled *Pride and Prejudice*. She'd never read anything so enjoyable and was so engrossed she ignored the faint fluttering in her stomach. When it happened a second time her book fell from her fingers. She placed both hands on her distended belly. Yes, there it was again. The baby was kicking, telling her she was going to be a mother in a few months. Her heart contracted. The idea of handing over her baby appalled her. But could she learn to live with a man she feared and didn't trust?

9

Alexander ran his fingers through his hair and frowned at the column of figures. There was something amiss here; the amount of money leaving this account was astronomical. His estate manager was either corrupt or had run mad. The man had had no authorization to draw so much from the bank. He pushed the papers to one side. He'd visit Newcomb and see what was going on. This was a damn nuisance, as the season was about to begin and he was determined to complete the process of re-establishing himself.

He had easily resisted the voluptuous temptations of his erstwhile mistress and doused his physical needs by vigorous exercise. To the astonishment of his staff he'd taken to running round the park at dawn and hurtling up and down the staircase at regular intervals during the day. He'd also resumed his sparring at Jackson's and during the last bout he'd only been floored once.

Being fit and clear-headed for the first time in many years had sharpened his intellect. Unfortunately it had also made him more aware of the sins of the flesh. One thing was very certain: however much he might lust after a woman, he'd never be unfaithful to Isobel. She was constantly in his thoughts. He prayed every day for the Almighty to give him a second chance.

A sharp tap on the door reminded him to gather up the papers and drop them into the desk. For some reason he didn't trust Richard Bentley, the young man his lawyers had tracked down as being next in line. Bentley was altogether too unctuous and already showing an inclination towards fast play and fast women.

'Come in, if you must.'

The door swung open and Bentley stepped in. Alexander struggled to remain expressionless. Good God! The idiot could scarcely turn his head because his shirt points were so high.

'Your grace, I beg your pardon for disturbing you, but I've a matter of the utmost urgency to bring to your attention.'

Even his voice irritated. It was slightly high-pitched, and he ended sentences as if asking a question. 'As you see, I'm busy. Can't it wait?'

The young man smiled and nodded as if in understanding, but looked as if he intended to stay all morning.

'Well, get on with it. What do you wish to tell me?'

Undeterred by the brusque response, Bentley leaned forward, placing his hands on the desktop. 'I beg your pardon but I've heard the most disturbing rumour, your grace. It's being said in more than one drawing room that the Duchess of Rochester is missing.'

His gripped the edge of the table. How dare this jackanapes ask him such a question? The man had been in residence three weeks and was already behaving as if he were a member the family. 'My wife's at Newcomb. She doesn't come to town. In fact, I'm going to visit her today.'

He was damned if he was going to sit here and be interrogated by someone who was only a relative in the most tenuous of fashions. According to his lawyers Bentley was his heir, a clear line of descent from an ancient uncle, but he was a cousin so many times removed Alexander felt him not to be kin at all.

The wretched man sprung to his feet, all eagerness and conciliation. 'How delightful! Then if you'll permit me I'll accompany you. I can't tell you how much I am anticipating the pleasure of meeting your wife.'

This was too much. With one swift stride Alexander was beside him. He was a head taller and twice his weight. Bentley took a step backward and, tripping over his feet, landed heavily on his backside. He couldn't prevent his bark of laughter at the man's expense.

'Get up, man. And get rid of those high-heeled boots; you'll break your neck falling off them.' He offered his hand and pulled him to his feet.

'Thank you, sir. I do beg your pardon for being so clumsy. I take it you've no wish for me to accompany you. I quite understand. Perhaps I may join you in the country next week?'

The young man was a buffoon. Bentley had been brought up in different circumstances, but maybe he would improve. 'Very well. If I don't return before then you're welcome to follow me to Newcomb.'

Bentley bowed and retreated, leaving him to consider his options. He wouldn't disturb his staff; they could remain *in situ* as his visit would be brief. He would deal with Reynolds and then depart immediately. Newcomb would be cold and unwelcoming, with only a handful of servants to receive him.

He frowned and rubbed his chin. The season was about to start — why did Bentley have this sudden urge to visit Newcomb? That he wanted to meet Isobel was fustian.

Surely he wasn't already running from his debts? He shrugged and dismissed this unpleasant notion. It could be dealt with on his return.

Today was clear and crisp, the storms and poor weather of the previous months gone. March weather was notoriously fickle, but spring appeared to have arrived early this year. He decided to ride. The distance was no more than twenty miles and his restlessness demanded the extra exercise.

There had been no word on Isobel's whereabouts but he was determined to find her. When he did, she would see he was a different man, not the one who'd mistreated her last year. Somehow he would persuade her to return and then spend the rest of his life demonstrating how much he loved her, and how their lack of children made no difference to him.

He was resigned to passing on his title and estate to a virtual stranger. He shuddered at the thought of what damage Bentley could do when *he* became the Duke of Rochester. God willing, that wouldn't be for another thirty years. Hopefully the man would have grown out of this sartorial extravagance and profligate tendencies and learnt what it meant to be in a position of power. He scowled. Small wonder Bentley was going astray — the young man would know all about his lifestyle and believe he was expected to sow his own wild oats.

His valet was following behind in a closed carriage with the luggage. Alexander didn't require much for an overnight stay and there was still a closet with garments at Newcomb. He was aware the majority of his older staff treated young Bentley with barely concealed contempt. They weren't quite disrespectful — that would have been easier to deal with — but they'd closed ranks at his appearance. Were they refusing to accept the inevitable — that he would never produce a son of his own?

The ride from London to Hertfordshire was invigorating. He'd purchased a magnificent chestnut stallion with a fiery temper to match his own. The horses in his stable were more than adequate but he'd been taken by this beast the moment he'd seen him.

He had two grooms in attendance mounted on equally impressive horses, but they were hard-pressed to keep up. Rufus could gallop across country all day, taking huge hedges and ditches in his stride. He halted at midday to rest him and take refreshments. He'd made good time and would be at his destination long before dark.

As he cantered down the drive he was

aware there was something odd about Newcomb, but he couldn't quite place it. He reined back and studied the huge edifice with interest. The main building was, as expected, shuttered and dark. But there was quite definitely smoke spiralling into the sky and it could only come from the east wing. Had the remaining staff moved in there for some reason?

He kicked Rufus and the stallion responded. He arrived outside the stable yard, sending dirt in all directions. He vaulted from the saddle and pulled the reins over his mount's ears in order to lead him through the archway.

To his astonishment, several equine heads turned to view his arrival. The stables should be empty. Someone had taken up residence in his absence.

★   ★   ★

Isobel was sitting contentedly in front of a roaring fire, completing a small garment. She wasn't a skilled needlewoman but was determined to make something for the baby. This was the least she could do if she actually stuck to her plan of abandoning it.

She looked up as the door burst open and Ellen, the senior parlourmaid, came in. They stood on no ceremony here; this was a happy establishment. 'Good heavens, Ellen, why are you in such a fuss?'

'He's come. He's just ridden into the stable yard. What shall we do, your grace?'

Isobel was on her feet, her sewing slipping unnoticed to the carpet. 'Who's come? Are you telling me the Duke of Rochester is here?'

The girl nodded, her complexion pale. 'He is, your grace. What shall we do? There's nothing ready for him and Newcomb's abandoned and we work for you here.'

Isobel was confident she could face Alexander and not be bullied into making a permanent return. Her hands were damp and her stomach churned at the thought of seeing him. He was terrifying when he was angry.

'Inform Mrs Watkins to prepare a guest chamber for the duke. No doubt his man will be travelling separately and he can fetch whatever his grace requires from next door.' He was stronger than her; if he wished to abuse her there would be little she could do to stop him. The idea she could use Sam and Bill to protect her was nonsensical; Alexander would see them on the gallows if they raised a hand to him.

She must make sure he didn't vent his spleen on the staff that had deserted their posts in order to join her employ. His appearance wasn't unexpected. Mr Reynolds would require protecting from Alexander's wrath, for the agent had withdrawn the money for the repairs and refurbishment.

She glanced around her cosy parlour. She wouldn't receive him here as this was *her* domain, the way the study had been his. She would greet him in the salon. The fires were lit throughout the ancient edifice so it would be perfectly comfortable.

Mary met her in the corridor, her face anxious. 'Your grace, Ellen says we're to let him in. Are you sure this is wise?'

'I've no option, Mary. I've my people around me and he's by himself. He owns Newcomb so we can hardly leave him standing outside.'

'I'll prepare the blue room and Cook has instructions to make a more substantial dinner. Unfortunately it will be delayed an hour, but his grace never liked to eat early anyway.'

'It's no matter to me, Mary, when I eat. It's my authority that matters; here *I* make the decisions and you answer to me. Please make sure the staff remain aware of that.'

Her words were mere bravado. Alexander could do as he wished and there was nothing she could do about it. She checked in the overmantel mirror that her cap wasn't askew, her velvet gown hung straight and that the bulge of her pregnancy was not immediately apparent. The high-waisted gown dropped in tiny pleats from under her bosom, the rich russet colour matching what little of her hair could be seen. The emerald-green sash and matching slippers completed her ensemble perfectly.

Her shorn locks were so much easier to manage than long hair. She'd never let it grow again. Now it curled into her neck, framing her face and emphasizing her eyes. The baby fluttered and she placed a protective hand on her stomach. Five months had passed since that dreadful night; she'd moved on. She no longer hated Alexander but she neither loved nor respected him.

He strode in without knocking. If she hadn't been braced against the back of a chair she might have swooned. She scarcely recognized this smiling man as the husband who'd mistreated her. The love she saw in his eyes was genuine. Why did he finally love her now? However much he'd changed, she'd never trust him again.

'Isobel, I can't tell you how delighted I am to see you, and looking so radiant. I'm bewildered to find you living in the east wing. Why didn't you send for me?'

Even his voice was different. The edge had gone, his tone was soft and charming, and there was no hint of the chilly aristocrat. His appearance was changed also; somehow looked years younger. What could have happened to bring about this transformation?

'I had no need to bother you, sir. As you can see I'm happily established here. I've no intention of returning to live as your wife next door.' She stared at him, daring him to disagree. His eyes flashed but he held his tongue. Emboldened by his restraint, she continued. 'You also look remarkably well. I believe you've lost weight. Would you care to be seated? Coffee's being fetched for you.'

She pointed to a chair on the other side of the hearth. Then, not waiting to see if he complied, she arranged herself in an upright chair, making sure the folds of her gown concealed her pregnancy. She was certain her nervousness hadn't been apparent even to someone as sharp-eyed as he.

He moved to the chair she indicated, allowing her time to compose herself. There was no doubt he was a different man. Her eyes filled as she thought of how things could have been, but he was five months too late. He'd killed her love and nothing could rekindle it.

'What brings you down here at the start of

the season, Alexander? I didn't expect to see you until May.'

He smiled lazily. 'You know why I'm here, my dear. As soon as I saw you I realized it was you who must be behind the withdrawals from my account. Tell me, Isobel, how did you persuade a man of such probity as Mr Reynolds to steal from me?'

★　★　★

Her eyes narrowed. 'Mr Reynolds hasn't been stealing from you. He has been doing what *you* should have done. On my instructions he has repaired the cottages, farms and outbuildings you've neglected these past years.'

Alexander swallowed a brief surge of anger. She was right to castigate him. He stared at her and his spirits sunk to his boots. She'd become someone else entirely. There was a rigidity about her person, a darkness in her eyes that hadn't been there before.

His brief flash of ill humour vanished, to be replaced by the all-too-familiar shame. His self-indulgence these past years had caused her and his unfortunate tenants to suffer. His neckcloth became unaccountably tight and he ran a finger around it. He cleared his throat, for the first time in his life unsure what to say.

Should he apologize and clear the air between them?

'Isobel, I can't tell you how ashamed I am of my past behaviour. No, please let me finish. I don't expect your forgiveness; I can't forgive myself for what I did. But I give you my word it'll never happen again. You're looking at a changed man; I no longer drink to excess, I've cut free from the toadies, and have re-established contact with my former intimates.'

He waited for her response but there was none forthcoming. Her expression remained friendly but distinctly unimpressed. He ploughed on, hoping she'd receive this next piece of news with more enthusiasm. 'I've also had my lawyers discover my heir, one Richard Bentley, a young man of nine-and-twenty years. The matter of your childlessness is no longer an issue between us. I'll attempt to turn Bentley into someone deserving of this title before I kick the bucket.'

'How interesting, Rochester. Do I have your permission to speak?' Her eyes bored into him. This wasn't going well. He nodded and waited. 'I've something important to tell you.'

She glanced down at her hands and a slight smile played about her lips. She raised her head and met his eyes with a strength equal to his own.

'I returned for one reason only. I'm carrying your child. The baby will be born in July. I intend to remain here until delivered. However, when I'm certain the child's well established, I'll depart. At no time will I reside next door.'

His glance followed her fingers as she smoothed the material over the quite distinctive mound of a pregnancy. He felt a rush of such happiness, such joy, he didn't take in the full import of what she'd said. He wasn't going to die childless; he'd been given another chance. Whatever she thought, somehow he'd convince her he could be a good husband.

★　★　★

Alexander's eyes blazed. 'My love, I can't believe it; we're going to have a baby together.'

Isobel almost capitulated under the weight of his happiness. The door opened and Ellen appeared with the coffee. She waved her hand and the girl hastily placed it on the table to her right and vanished in a rustle of petticoats. She must disabuse him immediately. She couldn't allow him to continue in this vein, but he forestalled her.

'I'm stunned, but overjoyed at your

announcement. I'm sad to think our first child was conceived in such a way, but I'm sure . . . '

'Enough. You didn't listen. I don't intend to remain once the baby's born. I'll leave the child in your care and return to my home elsewhere.' She paused, too upset to continue. 'Of course, I'd much prefer to take my baby with me, but I assume that would be out of the question.'

His expression darkened. 'I can't believe you intend to abandon our baby. I didn't take you for a heartless woman. I grew up without a mother's love and look what happened to me. Do you wish to deprive your own child of his most important parent?'

Her determination faltered as the baby kicked beneath her fingers. She would be firm. Her treacherous body would betray her if she allowed it to. However much she wished to resist him, he would persuade her into his bed if she remained within reach. 'You'll make an excellent father. I'm certain you'll provide a retinue of loyal retainers for the infant's nursery. I should scarcely see the child anyway. You know how things are for people like us.'

In this great household a son would be sent away to school at an early age, and a girl would have a governess. Parents were expected to have little involvement in the upbringing of their children. No, she had made the right decision; she'd not remain here any longer then she had to.

'Things can be however you wish them to be. If you want to break tradition then you'll have my support. Please, Isobel, think about this. Not for me, but for the baby.'

'You must understand that night's forever between us. I'm as much changed as you. I know you were in your cups but I can never forgive you. I married you because I loved you and not because you offered to save my family from financial ruin.'

He leant forward but she stopped him. 'No, it's far too late. Maybe your feelings have changed, but mine have also. You'll always be the man who mistreated me. I want your word as a gentleman that you'll respect my wishes and leave me in peace here, and allow me to go when I wish.'

He lowered his head; she wasn't sure if he was hiding grief or anger. Then he looked up and the wretchedness in his eyes almost broke her heart.

'I agree, my love. It's not what I want but I'm in no position to argue. Everything you say about me is true. If I could take back what happened, even though it could mean there would be no baby, I'd do so. I've learned my lesson. I know it's far too late for a reconciliation and promise I shan't pester you.' His smile was tender and she couldn't help responding. 'However, can I ask you to slightly alter your plans?'

When he was at his most charming he was impossible to resist. 'Go on, sir. What do you wish me to do?'

'Promise me you won't leave until the child's at least six months old. If you still want to go, you can do so then with my blessing. I'll give you an annual income of £10,000; you can live anywhere you please and return whenever you want to see your child.'

'There's no need for so much. I know you're a wealthy man, but such a large amount will strain even your deep purse.'

'This isn't negotiable. I'll never divorce you, never remarry. You'll be my duchess until you die and as such it's only right you live in the luxury and comfort your status deserves. I'll sell my Scottish estates, manage my others more prudently and invest more wisely. I've also stopped gambling.' His lopsided grin made her toes curl. 'That will restore a deal of buoyancy to my finances. Have I your promise, Isobel? A few extra months in return for a life of luxury? What harm can there be in that decision?'

She nodded scarcely able to believe he was offering her so much. 'I agree; I'll remain until the infant's six months old. This will give you time to draw up my settlement. I'll get my man of affairs, Watkins, to start looking for somewhere suitable. I enjoy being involved in the management of an estate; it will be a pleasure to have one of my own.'

Bill appeared in the doorway. 'Your grace, I wish to inform you that his grace's apartment is now ready for occupation.'

Isobel stood. Alexander had no choice but to do likewise. 'Dinner will be served in an hour. Do you wish to send a footman to collect a change of raiment from next door?'

For a second his expression hardened at her dismissal. The formidable duke was in there somewhere; however much he tried, he couldn't eliminate all his pride and arrogance. This was bred into him.

He bowed his head, hiding his face from her. 'My trappings will arrive later. I came across country and my man's bringing my luggage. I'll go with your footman. I'll see you at dinner, my dear.'

He strode off and she breathed again. She wished he wasn't under her roof, but as she'd stolen his staff she could hardly send him packing. He must remain for the moment. No doubt he'd return to town after speaking to Mr Reynolds. She must endeavour to keep up her guard for the short time he'd be here.

The encounter had gone more smoothly than she'd expected. She'd remained in command and he'd acquiesced to her demands. Indeed, he'd volunteered to pay her a fortune when she departed. But for all his sweet talk and generosity he'd no intention of letting her go. She must have her escape well-planned for when the time came.

10

Isobel dined in her room. All things considered, it might be wiser not to spend time with Alexander alone. He was very persuasive when he wished to be and she'd no intention of falling under his spell again.

'Sally, you may take my tray down. I've had sufficient, thank you. Please return to assist me to retire.'

For the first time since her return she slept without nightmares and woke early feeling happier than she had in months. She would get up. There was no need to summon her abigail. The gowns she'd had altered to accommodate her increasing girth were high-necked and long-sleeved. No doubt she'd be obliged to have some lighter gowns adjusted for the final months.

The sun was barely up and there'd been a sharp frost, but it wasn't too early to go outside with the dogs. There was nothing they liked better than to race across the silvered grass searching for unwary rabbits. Lacing up her boots was going to become more difficult but at the moment she managed perfectly well.

She put on her thickest cloak and found her muffler and mittens and was ready. Her early appearance caused two of the maids, on their knees scrubbing the floor, to look up in surprise. With sacks tied around their waists they were barely recognizable as the smart girls one saw about the house during the day.

'Good morning, Eliza, Annie. Pray don't disturb yourselves; I'll walk around your pails.'

As there were only two dozen staff employed in her domain she knew all of them, which was how it should be. Her dogs slept in front of the fire in the drawing room and bounded out to greet her.

'Get down, you silly things. Yes, you're quite correct, we're going for a walk.'

It had been her intention to exit through the boot-room door, but the sound of the bolts being drawn back behind her meant one of her footmen must have heard her voice and come to open the front door.

'Good morning, Isobel. I didn't expect to see you abroad so early. I wake at dawn nowadays and take a brisk walk before I break my fast.' Alexander bent to stroke Ebony's ears. 'I should like to join you but fully understand if you'd prefer to walk alone.'

It would be churlish not to let him accompany her when he'd spoken so charmingly and given her the option to refuse. 'You may come with us, if you wish, but I'm afraid the excursion will be far from brisk. More a stroll, as I can't dash about as I used to.'

He offered his arm and she took it, relieved she didn't feel the slightest bit flustered by the contact. The dogs circled around them, barking, and he took the hint and found a suitable stick to throw. Thus the walk progressed. When one or other of the dogs returned with a piece of wood, she released her grip on his arm so he could throw it again.

'There's really no necessity. They're perfectly content just to sniff and chase anything that moves.'

Laughing, he wiped his hand on his breeches. 'I enjoyed it; I'd forgotten the pleasure of playing with dogs. Do you wish to walk as far as the lake? It will be spectacular when the sun rises in the next few minutes.'

She nodded, finding his behaviour disconcerting. The old duke would never have ruined his pristine appearance; neither would he have risked tearing his jacket by throwing sticks. Was this a genuine change, or was he trying to ingratiate himself?

They were returning to the house when a figure on horseback cantered into view. She recognized the rider; this was Reynolds, the estate manager. He was unconscionably early. Did he really expect the duke to be so eager to see him?

'Reynolds is upon us, my dear. I sent a message for him to come first thing. I wish to spend a day examining the improvements and arranging for anything further that needs to be done. I've been delinquent in my duties; I shan't be so in future.'

'So you're not going to ring a peal over both of us? That's a great relief. I feared that you might . . . ' Her voice trailed away and she swallowed the bile in her throat. Just thinking about that awful night made her unwell.

'Isobel, what I did to you was unforgivable. I know that, but I've given you my word whatever the provocation, I'll never be unkind to you again.'

She glared at him. 'Provocation? It is *I* who is more likely to be provoked.'

He grinned and raised his hand as if he thought to touch her, then thought better of it as she frowned. 'I know; you're perfect in every way. How could I think there was even the remotest possibility you would do anything to irritate me?' He released her arm, nodded, and strolled across the turning circle to greet his visitor.

Mollified by his good humour she went in, her optimism renewed that somehow they'd get through the next few hours without upset. However, the quicker his business was completed the better. She wasn't entirely comfortable in his company. He wouldn't manhandle her; whatever he'd been in the past he wasn't given to making false promises. The danger lay in his ability to soften her resolve.

He was out all day and returned only as darkness fell. To hear him chatting companionably to the footmen he met in the vestibule was a revelation. If he continued to improve she would no longer recognize him as the man she'd married. Perhaps she could make more effort to be civil; after all, only Mary and Sam knew why she'd left him. She'd no wish for her staff to believe she was being curmudgeonly.

She reached the door as he prepared to ascend the staircase. 'Rochester, I'll join you for dinner tonight. I'd dearly like to know what you thought of the improvements.'

'I'll look forward to it, my dear. Do you wish me to put on my evening rig?'

She was surprised he should ask, for she could not remember an evening when he hadn't appeared in formal attire and she in an evening gown. 'I should much prefer to eat in the small dining room and not have to change at all.' She smiled wryly. 'In fact I don't have anything suitable to wear at the moment. I haven't bothered to alter my grand ensembles.'

'Excellent.' He pointed at his mud-spattered clothes and laughed. 'However, I can assure you I shan't reappear in disarray.'

He took the remainder of the stairs two at a time. How could she not be aware his physical appearance had improved over these past months? His eyes were clear and no longer bloodshot. His toast-brown hair was shining with health and he moved with a vigour he'd never previously displayed. She giggled at the thought that he was becoming thinner, as she was doing the exact opposite.

Mary appeared in answer to her ring. 'I wish to have dinner served in the small dining room. Make sure Cook doesn't serve an elaborate meal; we're not dressing for dinner.'

'Do you wish to eat at the usual time, your grace?'

'No, we'll dine at half past five; that will allow the duke plenty of time to bathe.'

Bill, now referred to as Mr Brown by the staff, rang the gong at the appointed hour.

Isobel walked towards the door. She was hungry and didn't wish to waste further time dawdling in the drawing room. The duke hurtled down the stairs, as eager as she to dine. He was dressed as before, but this time in a dark blue superfine jacket, blue waistcoat and skin-tight unmentionables. Her eyes were held by the muscles in his thighs. She couldn't drag her gaze away.

Aware of her scrutiny, he paused and his eyes blazed with that all-too-familiar fire. This wouldn't do. She wasn't going to be bamboozled into acquiescence. She was made of sterner stuff; was her own woman and had no intention of allowing him to breach the walls she'd erected.

'I'm famished, my dear. You might remember I didn't come in for breakfast and had no time to stop for midday refreshments.'

'Good heavens! I'm surprised you didn't come to grief galloping all over the countryside with nothing inside you.'

He laughed. 'As I keep telling you, Isobel, I'm not the man you married. That degenerate is no longer me. I'm returned to the fellow I once was. I'm hoping you'll come to see me as my true self.'

She stiffened. Did he really believe his reformation could possibly remove the scars of that night? 'Dinner is waiting, sir. I don't as a rule serve wine, but I've asked Brown to fetch claret from your wine cellar next door.'

She waited for him to tell her he no longer drank. Instead his eyes twinkled.

'I'm reformed, but not become a Puritan, my dear. I drink in moderation as any gentleman should.'

'I didn't know imbibing alcohol was a prerequisite for being a gentleman. However, I'm always ready to learn from an expert.'

Content in his company, she led the way to the small dining room she used in preference to the larger chamber which seated more than twenty around the oak table. The evening passed without discord and she returned to her chambers pleased she'd been able to enjoy his friendship without being beguiled by his charm.

He had assured her he was leaving the day after tomorrow and would remain in town for the season. Whilst there he would speak to his lawyers and have them arrange the settlement. Her family would think this a disgraceful arrangement; even her aunt and uncle would be shocked to the core by her desertion. In May, two months before she was due, he'd reopen Newcomb and take up residence next door. Everything was working out as she'd hoped and when the baby was six months old she'd be able to take her leave and move to whatever small estate Sam had found for her. She must also arrange for Sam to dispose of Home Farm; she'd never return there.

Her digestion rebelled the following day and she was unable to leave her bedchamber. Rochester sent his commiserations and hoped she'd be well enough to speak to him before he left the next morning. Sam asked to see her that afternoon and, as she was now sitting in her parlour, she agreed.

'Madam, his grace has just called me in to speak to him; he told me I'm to start looking for a suitable estate for you. Have I mistaken the matter? Are we not to stay here permanently?'

'No, my life is no longer here. Once Newcomb is occupied by the duke it will be untenable to remain here. It's far better I make a new start somewhere else.'

He looked away and his cheeks coloured. 'I beg your pardon for questioning your decisions, your grace. I believe there are more than a dozen estates held by his grace. Do you wish me to visit all of them?' His tone was formal, his expression sad.

Should she tell him he was mistaken, that the estates he was to look at were not those owned by her husband? It might be better to leave him in ignorance. 'I haven't thought about it. You can be sure I shall inform you in good time. Do you know if Rochester has approved all the changes made on the estate?'

'His grace didn't see fit to discuss the matter with me.'

'Thank you for coming to see me, Sam. If there's nothing further, you may go.'

She must get accustomed to disapproval. If even her dear Sam thought her wrong, she might find it difficult to re-establish herself elsewhere. She would be obliged to be known by her title and not revert to Mrs Baverstock. Abandoning her husband was beyond the pale; to do the same to her child wouldn't be forgiven by society. It would break her heart to do so, but he wouldn't allow her to take the baby with her. No doubt he was relying on her maternal instincts to make her change her mind.

Feeling more the thing the next morning, she was up early to take her walk. She half expected him to join her and was disconcerted to find herself disappointed he did not. At a little after eight o'clock she returned. Breakfast would be waiting and, after her enforced fast yesterday, she was more than ready to eat.

'Good morning, Isobel. I'm glad to see you're fully recovered. Why don't you sit down and let me serve you?' Rochester put down his cutlery and stood at her entrance.

'Thank you, I'm famished. Tell me, what's

under the covers this morning?'

The meal was accompanied by light-hearted banter. How pleasant to have someone to talk to, especially when her companion was so amusing. 'What time are you leaving?'

'My horse is being saddled. Duncan will follow with my baggage in the carriage. Promise me, my dear, that you'll send for me if you've a problem of any sort.'

'Of course I will. Perhaps you'll come down and tell me when matters have been arranged by your lawyers?'

'I'll write to you.'

She was tempted to ask him to leave things to her but he was smiling at her openly; was making a kind gesture, nothing more. 'That would be most helpful, thank you, sir.'

* * *

Alexander forced himself to eat heartily. He was damned if he would let her see how much her formality was hurting. He pushed his plate aside and stood up. 'Pray don't disturb yourself, my dear. Finish your meal. Remember to send a message to Grosvenor Square if you need me.'

He bowed and strode from the room without a backward glance. He nodded to the butler and walked out into the crisp, cold morning. It had been purgatory to be so close and not able to touch her, to show her how much he loved her. One thing was certain: Gloria would never get her claws into him. If he couldn't make love to his wife, he would remain celibate. Seeing her again had served to reinforce his decision and confirm his love for her.

He swung into the saddle, his two grooms did likewise, and he urged Rufus into a canter. As he rounded the curve in the drive a carriage turned in. God's teeth! What was Bentley doing here? Had he not told the young man to remain where he was? The last thing he wanted was for Isobel to meet him. Time enough for Bentley to know if the infant turned out to be a boy.

The coach rattled to a halt and he leant down to speak to Bentley through the window. 'Turn round. I warned you I wouldn't be here above a day or two. I'll wait for your vehicle. We can stop for refreshments in an hour or two.'

'I say, my lord, I do beg your pardon. I set off at first light determined to arrive before you left. It would be a shame if I didn't meet your duchess now I *am* here.'

There was almost desperation in his words. Had something occurred in town that he was fleeing from? Even if that were so, he couldn't risk a premature meeting between Isobel and his putative heir.

'The duchess isn't receiving.' He glared and Bentley hastily withdrew his head. The coachman looked down expectantly. 'Mr Bentley will be returning forthwith. Will your cattle take a double journey?'

'I doubt it, your grace, not without a couple of hours' rest. Mr Bentley insisted we travelled at a spanking pace. The beasts are all but done.'

Alexander frowned. Yes, there was a solution to this. The unwanted guest could return with Duncan and this carriage could remain here until the animals were rested. 'Bentley, you travel back with my valet. His carriage is about to leave.'

The dark head emerged nervously. 'I'll do that, of course, your grace. At what hostelry are we to meet? You mustn't keep your stallion waiting whilst I transfer my belongings to the other vehicle.'

This was reasonable. 'The Green Man. You follow the toll road and I'll cut across country.'

The other carriage appeared behind him. Excellent — it shouldn't take long for the exchange. He could leave knowing he'd avoided a potentially difficult situation.

Isobel was in the entrance hall when there were carriage wheels outside. Goodness, who could this be? Duncan had departed and he wasn't likely to have forgotten anything. He was the most frighteningly efficient gentleman's gentleman. She hurried to the window and looked out making sure she couldn't be seen. A young man descended. He looked vaguely familiar but she was certain no one of her acquaintance would appear on her doorstep with a sky-blue jacket and a pink-and-gold waistcoat.

'Bill, we're about to receive a visitor. I'll retire to my sitting room. I don't wish to speak to him. He's a stranger to me; no doubt he's lost his way and called in for directions.'

Whoever this was, he must have seen Duncan and Rochester and could have got directions from them. She was decidedly uneasy about this. Something wasn't quite right about her unexpected guest.

11

Ten minutes went by and then there was a rapid knock on the door. Bill appeared looking somewhat bemused. 'I beg your pardon, your grace, but the young gentleman insists I give you his card. He won't depart until you've seen it.'

Isobel examined the writing. 'Good heavens! Mr Bentley — he's next in line to the title. The duke told me about him but I'd no idea he intended to visit. Show him into the drawing room; I suppose I must speak to him.' She called the butler back. 'I doubt if he's eaten. Ask the kitchen to put something out in the small dining room.'

Small wonder he'd seemed familiar. Rochester must have suggested he call in and introduce himself before returning to the city. It would be better if her pregnancy remained unnoticed. If she fetched her cloak this would disguise her bump and he'd assume she was going out with the dogs.

'Sally, quickly, we need our bonnets and cloaks. Mr Bentley, a distant relative, has called in unexpectedly and I don't wish him to remain here long. I shouldn't be entertaining in the duke's absence.'

Soon she was on her way to the drawing room, Sally following behind and both dogs gambolling at her feet. Pausing in the shadows, she viewed the young man who was lounging on the chaise longue with his booted feet resting on the upholstery. This wasn't a good start. How impertinent of him. She stepped in and stared frostily.

Instantly he was on his feet smiling and bowing. 'Your grace, I do beg your pardon for intruding. I can see that you're about to go out, so I shan't delay you long. Richard Bentley, your husband's heir, at your service.'

She inclined her head a fraction but didn't suggest he sat. 'Mr Bentley, I've arranged for you to eat before you leave. It isn't seemly for you to be here in the duke's absence.'

His cheeks turned puce and he clutched at his ridiculously elaborate neckcloth. 'I beg your pardon. Cousin Alexander doesn't know I called in. He believes me to be travelling with his manservant. Forgive me, your grace, but I couldn't leave without meeting you.' He stared at her, his watery blue eyes innocent. 'I didn't believe the rumours in town that you had disappeared. Now I can assure society you're at Newcomb.' He glanced round rather pointedly and raised an eyebrow.

'I've spent the past few months in Norfolk

with my family, as my mother was ailing. Fortunately she has recovered. As I don't enjoy the season and much prefer to be in the country, I move into the east wing whilst my husband's away.'

'Ideal arrangement. It leaves you both free to . . . ' He paused, looking self-conscious. 'I beg your pardon. I was about to say something inappropriate.'

To what had he been referring? She couldn't help herself. 'Free to do what exactly, sir?'

He looked at his feet; he was wearing the most ridiculous pair of high-heeled boots. 'It's not my place to discuss gossip, your grace. But as you *insist*, I'm obliged to tell you what's being said in the drawing rooms of the *ton*.'

She tapped her foot and waited. He appeared to shrink under her disdainful stare.

'They're saying Cousin Alexander has renewed his friendship with Lady Fulbright. I'm sure they're wrong and I beg your pardon for mentioning it.'

If the wretched man begged her pardon once more she'd scream. 'And so you should. I'm appalled at your indelicacy.'

Slowly she let her gaze travel from his heavily pomaded brown hair down his gaudy waistcoat to the gold tassels that ornamented his boots. He shifted uncomfortably. There was a slight sound behind her and Bill stepped forward.

'Your grace, breakfast is served for the gentleman. Shall I escort him?'

'Do that, Mr Brown. Mr Bentley will be leaving directly he's eaten.'

The young man edged forward. 'I fear the horses won't be sufficiently rested for another hour or two.'

This was the outside of enough; she was beginning to heartily dislike this mushroom. 'In which case, sir, you can occupy your time exploring the grounds. I bid you good day.'

Bentley stepped forward and swept her an extravagant bow. Ignoring his silliness, she stalked out. Bill and the three footmen would ensure the irritating gentleman was ejected when he'd finished his meal. She'd make sure she was inside before he came out. She patted her stomach. God willing this would be a boy.

★ ★ ★

Alexander had been kicking his heels at the Green Man for almost an hour when he spotted the carriage trundling into the yard. Striding across to greet Bentley, he was shocked to discover only Duncan inside.

151

'Devil take it, Duncan, what have you done with Bentley?'

His valet shook his head. 'Should he be travelling with me, your grace? He said nothing about that when he stopped to speak to me; merely told me to meet you at this hostelry.'

'We have to go back, damn him! If I didn't know him for a fool, I'd think he was leading me this dance deliberately. I'll cut across country again; rest the horses and then follow me.'

Rufus needed no further time in the stable but his grooms' mounts weren't fit to return immediately so he didn't bother to have them fetched. He tacked up the huge beast himself as there were no ostlers available. His return ride was far swifter: not only did he know the route, but was also concerned about the behaviour of the nincompoop.

He thundered across the park, his horse kicking up huge clods of earth which would take his groundsmen days to replace. There was no sign of the carriage waiting on the turning circle — was it in the coach house whilst the horses recovered? By his reckoning more than four hours had passed since his departure and it would be dark soon. He wouldn't allow Bentley to remain at Newcomb; the buffoon must put up at the nearest coaching inn.

There was no sign of the team that had pulled the coach. He swore volubly. Isobel had sent her unwanted guest on his way. No doubt Duncan and Bentley would pass on the lane somewhere. This was a ridiculous situation. What was the matter with him? His wife was perfectly capable of dealing with the situation without his assistance.

A stableboy, startled at his sudden appearance, jumped off the pail he was sitting on and tugged his forelock. No doubt the entire staff would think him fit for Bedlam after today. He vaulted from the saddle and tossed the reins to the boy. Then his irritation vanished to be replaced by amusement. His sudden laughter sent Rufus skittering across the cobbles and the unfortunate stable lad lost his footing, falling headfirst into a pile of freshly swept manure.

'Stand, Rufus. Enough of that nonsense.' His horse quietened and he tied the reins to a metal ring before hoisting the boy from the dung. 'Up you come, lad. Are you hurt?'

The urchin grinned as he spat out a mouthful of straw. 'Right as rain, your grace. A bit of muck don't hurt nobody.'

Still chuckling, he tossed the boy a coin and strolled from the stable yard to the east wing. God knew what Isobel would make of all this. He hoped she'd see a comical side to his reappearance when she had all but told him he was unwelcome.

* * *

Mary bustled into the room, her homely face split by a huge smile. 'Well I never! His grace is back, and poor Johnny got tipped headfirst into the muck by that big horse.'

Isobel tossed aside her sewing with a smile. 'I'm not surprised. He would have realized Bentley had intruded and would wish to make sure I was managing.'

'The chamber he used previously is ready for occupation. His man will still be on the road, so I'll send George to help him. He's the most able of the footmen.'

'Make sure a bath is drawn, and send someone next door to find him clean clothes. Oh, Cook will need to be informed as well.'

The dogs barked furiously. He was here and she wished she'd had the forethought to change her gown. Too late to repine — he was on his way to speak to her. She had recovered from the shock of hearing he was once more involved with his mistress but the infidelity still hurt.

He hadn't wasted much time before re-establishing Lady Fulbright as his *chère amie*. It was inevitable he'd look elsewhere for his physical needs. Her stomach lurched. How naïve she was. He must have been seeing that woman for more than a year, since the time he'd stopped making love to her.

The marriage was definitely over. She could never be intimate with him knowing he was sharing his body with another woman. She would remain seated. He'd understand she wasn't overjoyed to see him.

Alexander strode in. She gasped. She'd never seen him in such disorder. His many-caped riding coat was slung around his shoulders and his usually pristine Hessians were barely recognizable beneath thick mud. As for his breeches, they were not only dirty, but ripped and bloodstained. This drew her attention to a nasty gash running across his thigh. If the injury wasn't attended to immediately he might well succumb to a putrid wound.

Forgetting her vow to treat him coldly, she scrambled to her feet. 'Alexander, did you take a fall? Look at your leg; it needs the attentions of a physician.'

He glanced down as if noticing it for the first time. He frowned and looked almost embarrassed. 'My dear, I beg your pardon . . . '

Laughing, she interrupted him. 'Please, don't do so. Bentley was forever begging my

155

pardon, and if I hadn't sent him packing I believe I should have thrown a book at him.'

'I was going to apologize for appearing in my filth but obviously that's unnecessary. I take it the idiot has gone?'

'Indeed he has. I'm afraid I didn't take to him. He was served breakfast and then evicted. I made myself scarce until he departed.' She tugged the bell-strap before continuing. 'Give me your outer garments. Good grief! Where's your hat?'

He grinned ruefully. 'I believe that went when I had my altercation with a tree branch. I didn't take a tumble. In fact, until you mentioned it, I hadn't realized the damage I'd sustained.'

The butler appeared, followed by two footmen. 'Brown, his grace has injured his leg. He will need it attending to.'

'Right away, your grace.' He bowed to Alexander and stepped in to remove his coat. 'If you'd care to come with me, your grace, I've considerable experience with wounds.'

Alexander was given no chance to refuse. Isobel watched with amusement as he was bundled from the room. He smiled at her over his shoulder. 'When I'm repaired, my dear, do I have your permission to join you down here?'

She was on her feet watching anxiously.

'Don't you think you should remain in your bedchamber and have your dinner brought up to you?'

'Certainly not. And anyway, my love, the amount I intend to consume would require three chambermaids to fetch it.'

His chuckles filled the room. Should she send for Dr Jamieson? Perhaps it would be better to see what Bill said after he had dressed the cut. One thing she knew, he couldn't ride back to London tomorrow. Of course he could travel in the carriage with Duncan, but the horses would need twenty-four hours to rest.

He must take no risks with his health. What if he were to die? The very thought of Bentley inheriting was enough to make her hair stand on end. Although she no longer loved him (he would never be Alexander to her again), she didn't want him to perish. He was the father of her baby and despite everything she still cared enough to wish him well.

The dinner gong sounded before he reappeared. She'd resisted the urge to change and remained in her gold velvet. He, however, was resplendent in a fresh jacket. This one was green, his shirt crisp, his neckcloth tied intricately and his waistcoat of gold silk. His inexpressibles had been exchanged for panta-loons and he'd slippers on his feet instead of

157

his boots. He was leaning heavily on the banister as he descended the staircase.

'I know, Isobel, I should have remained where I was. It's a damn nuisance. I've no more wish to be here than you do to accommodate me.'

Shocked by his abruptness, she was unable to answer. There were lines of pain etched either side of his mouth. His injury must be worse than she'd thought. She hurried to his side and offered her arm.

'Lean on me, Alexander. I do wish you hadn't come down. I'll send for the physician straight away.'

'You'll do no such thing. Your butler has put sutures in; he did a neat job too. I doubt Jamieson could do any better. I'm fatigued; I haven't slept for days and have spent more time in the saddle than I have on my feet. I fear I shan't be able to leave tomorrow.'

'Of course not. You must remain until you're fully recovered. Has your man arrived yet?'

'No, he will be benighted. The weather's deteriorated but I'm sure he had the good sense to find himself a bed. He'll appear when the storm's abated. The man acting as my valet is perfectly competent and I've enough garments to not appear unkempt.'

With some difficulty she guided him down the passageway to the dining room. When a footman approached he scowled and the young man backed away. They were both relieved when they arrived without mishap.

'Alexander, you take the seat nearest the fire. You don't look too well; I'm most concerned.'

'Don't fuss, Isobel. I should be looking after you. God willing, you're carrying the next Duke of Rochester. Heaven forefend that numbskull takes the title after my demise.'

There was little she could add to that heartfelt comment. There was something she didn't quite like about Bentley and it wasn't just his ridiculous appearance and flowery manners. She shook her head at her fancies. Mary had told her to be wary of false emotions. Wild imaginings were quite common when a woman was increasing.

The meal was eaten in silence, she too concerned to make chit-chat and he too busy eating enough for three men. When he finally pushed away his plate she laughed. 'I'll stop worrying about you, Alexander. If you were truly ill you couldn't have eaten so much.'

He smiled that special smile and her insides melted. 'I'll be perfectly fine after a good night's sleep. However, I fear I shan't be able to depart until it's more clement.'

'If you've finally finished there are several things we must discuss. Can you manage or shall I send for someone for you to lean on?'

'I'm quite well, but my leg hurts like the very devil and I can barely keep my eyes open. Could our conversation keep until tomorrow, my dear?'

Carefully he pushed himself upright. His knuckles were white where he gripped the table. He wasn't as well as he pretended. 'Remain where you are, Alexander. I'll send for assistance. No, don't scowl at me. You'll never ascend the stairs under your own volition. Do you wish to add a cracked head to your injuries?' She spoke to him as if he were a child. How things had changed — he'd addressed her like this last year.

Bill and two hefty footmen appeared so rapidly she guessed they'd been expecting to be called. 'His grace will require your help to return to his bedchamber.'

This time he didn't argue but slung his arms around the shoulders of the two young men and hobbled out. She was concerned to see he put no weight on his injured leg. As soon as he was comfortable she would attend to him. There could be no disagreement about her being in his bedchamber; after all she was his wife, and who else had more right to be there than she?

12

Isobel left Alexander in the capable hands of George, his temporary valet. There was nothing further she could do for him as he was sleeping peacefully. In her bedchamber Sally was waiting to help her disrobe.

She was woken later by someone beside her. 'Mary, is he worse?'

'Yes, your grace, he is. George came to fetch me; Sam said as I was to get you. The duke's burning up and there's no way we can fetch a doctor. A foot of snow has fallen this past hour and no one can get in or out of Newcomb.'

'You did right to rouse me. Fetch Bill; he'll know what to do.'

She pulled on her bedrobe and rammed her feet into slippers. Then with candlestick held aloft she hurried through the icy passageway to the guest chamber at the rear of the house. She entered through the private sitting room. She pushed open the door and reeled back.

'Good grief! This room's like a furnace. Small wonder his grace is overheated.'

George looked mystified. 'I made the fire

up a treat, your grace. I thought that was right.'

'Not in my experience. It tends to make the fever worsen. Quickly, open the windows and I'll do something about the flames.' There was a half-filled jug of water on the wash and expense stand in the dressing room and she threw it over the fire. Immediately the room was full of hissing coals and choking steam, but the fire was out.

Mary rushed in with Bill, who coughed and looked round in astonishment but nodded at Isobel. 'Exactly what I would have done, your grace. Bring down the fever as quick as possible. I've seen men dropped in icy water, but that's kill or cure.'

'I hope my drastic measures won't prove fatal. Mary, we'll need water to wash him down and a jug of barley water or lemonade.'

The room had cleared and a howling gale whistled through. The curtains were almost horizontal and flurries of snow spiralled across the boards. 'George, I think you can close the windows; the temperature's dropped sufficiently.'

She was chilly in her night apparel. The fire was a sullen glow in the grate; they could do with slightly more heat but it refused to burn any brighter. The water she'd thrown on it earlier still puddled on the hearth.

'His grace will do very well now, madam. He's sleeping peacefully, the flush on his cheeks all but gone. I can take care of him if you'd like me to.'

'I intend to stay. You all return to your beds; I'll ring if I require any assistance.'

Mary was the only one who seemed pleased by this suggestion. When Isobel was alone she looked around for somewhere warm to curl up. Alexander was cool, so perhaps it would be safe to leave him. She shivered and glared at the fire, which refused to burn.

The bed was the only place in which she could be warm. If she crept in the far side, remaining on top of the sheets and not inside them, he shouldn't know she was there. Kicking off her slippers, she slipped under the covers and drifted to sleep.

A short while later she woke. Botheration! She must use the chamber pot behind the screen. Comfortable again, she scrambled into bed this time, removing her bedrobe, for she'd all but suffocated with it on. She settled into a deep sleep and her dreams were filled with images of the man she'd once loved.

His arms were round her, his heat burning through the thin cloth of her nightdress. Then his lips found hers and she drowned in the sweet sensation. The dream was so vivid that desire curled through her, sending wave after wave of delicious pleasure from her toes to the top of her head.

She moved restlessly and his kiss deepened. She forgot everything as she was swept away until her world exploded into ecstasy. She lay exhausted in his arms, too shocked by what had taken place to move or speak. The discomfort of her nightgown bundled up around her waist eventually roused her. For a second time he'd taken advantage of her; made love to her when he knew she didn't wish him to.

'Darling, I can't tell you how happy I am you came to me tonight. I never thought to be able to love you again. I . . . '

'Let me go. I did not *come* to you for this. I came because you were delirious earlier.'

His arms tightened and he pulled her closer, ignoring her words. She struggled and screamed to be released. Immediately his grip slackened and she scrambled out of bed. She couldn't see his face in the near blackness but he'd be certain he'd re-established his ascendancy.

'I hate you, Alexander. You're despicable; you know how I feel about you and yet you took shameful advantage.'

'You were in bed beside me and responded to my kisses. This was hardly the action of a woman who doesn't wish to make love.' His words were clipped as if he was angry.

'I was asleep, I thought I was dreaming and when I woke it was too late to stop you. The only reason I was beside you was to keep warm. The fire's out in case you haven't noticed.'

'But my dear, the fact you were dreaming about making love tells me everything. There's no point denying it, Isobel: you want me as much as I want you.'

This was too much. 'I've lived more happily these past few months away from you than at any time when you were here. Unlike you, I had no recourse to slake my physical needs with a lover. You promised me you would never be unfaithful; that you would take care of me and make me happy. You have broken every one of those vows.'

Too distressed to remain, she fled to her own apartment and sobbed herself to sleep.

⋆   ⋆   ⋆

Alexander cursed his stupidity. He'd been half-asleep when his bare thigh had touched hers. Unable to believe what his senses were telling him, he'd reached out and found his darling girl curled up beside him. He hadn't stopped to think — had just reacted. When she was in his arms rational thought was impossible. His hand came away from his leg bright red. Making love had reopened the wound. This was a job for the physician now; he would need fresh sutures to staunch the blood.

Keeping one hand firmly pressed on the gash, he stretched out and rang the brass bell, praying someone was within earshot. He couldn't remove his hand in order to get out of bed and pull the bell-strap. He was beginning to despair when the butler rushed into the room.

'My leg — it's bleeding profusely. You need to send for the doctor to stitch it again.'

'That's not possible, your grace. The snow's too deep. Here, let me bandage the injury. It should hold until I can fetch what I need.'

In the feeble light of a single candlestick his leg was dressed efficiently. The bed was ruined; it looked as if someone had been murdered within the sheets. He felt light-headed and not at all well. From a distance he heard voices, then someone propped him up in the bed and tipped cool lemonade into his mouth, which immediately revived him.

'I'm putting extra stitches in the wound, your grace. It might hurt, but I reckon to give you brandy or laudanum would do more harm than good after the bout of fever you had.'

'Get on with it, man. Then I can remove myself from this bloodbath.' Several extremely painful minutes later the job was done. 'Can I get up now? I'll sit in the chair whilst the bed's changed.'

'Allow me to assist you, your grace. Then Mrs Watkins can set things straight.'

Only then did he remember what had taken place between those sheets. Would the evidence of their lovemaking be visible? Too late to worry. He was married to Isobel after all, and making love was perfectly natural between a man and wife.

His cheeks stained. The housekeeper was Isobel's confidante and knew how things stood. Would she believe Isobel had been unwilling for a second time? He slumped into the chair, despair overwhelming him. How was he going to convince her he'd believed her to be there from choice? It might be a week or more before the roads were clear enough for him to leave. Would this be sufficient to repair the damage?

★   ★   ★

The rattle of the curtains being drawn back woke Isobel. Her head ached, her throat was dry and she had no wish for breakfast. Sally placed the tray with tea and buttered toast on the bedside table.

'It's fair freezing outside, your grace, and more snow is falling. I doubt anyone will get in or out of here for a week.'

'I think I'll stay in my apartments today, Sally, as I didn't have much sleep last night.'

'Very well, your grace. There was a right to-do last night, I can tell you. His grace needed Mr Brown to stitch up his leg again, for he lost a deal of blood, but George says as he's fine now.'

'I'm glad to hear it. Ask Mrs Watkins to come and see me, please, Sally.'

The girl left the tray and vanished through the dressing room. Isobel toyed with the toast but drank the tea. A polite tap on the door heralded Mary's arrival.

'Good morning, your grace. I think it wise to remain here today; it's warmer upstairs than down.'

'Mary, tell me what happened? I left the duke because he was sleeping peacefully and his fever gone. There seemed little point in me shivering in a chair when he was well.'

'It would seem the injury was worse than we thought. Bill said he had to probe into the wound in order to remove a large sliver of wood. His grace must have nicked a vein, and

168

what with all that tossing and turning with his fever he reopened the wound.'

'But the duke's in no danger?'

Mary beamed. 'Bless you, no; he's sleeping like a baby. I doubt we'll keep him in bed.'

'You'd better find him a cane if he insists on getting up. Has someone taken the dogs out?' Her erstwhile abigail looked uncomfortable. This was the first time since they'd returned Mary had forgotten to address her correctly. 'I regret we don't spend much time together, Mary. You're my dearest friend and I insist in future you come and take tea with me every afternoon.'

The smile returned. 'Thank you, your grace. Perhaps I could come later and show you what I've made for the little one?'

Isobel's spirits rose and her appetite revived. When there was a second rap on the door she looked up with a smile, but this faltered when she saw Alexander standing there.

'You shouldn't be out of bed; you were at death's door yesterday.' She could hardly tell him to go away, even though that was what she wished to do. Sally was in the dressing room sorting out the mending and could hear everything.

'Isobel, we have to talk. No, don't frown at me, my love; there are things that must be said to clear the air.'

She gestured towards the dressing room and he nodded. Before she could prevent him he limped across and told Sally to go and not return until called for. His high-handed behaviour steadied her nerves. Her annoyance made her ready to face him.

She pushed herself straight, ran her fingers through her hair and pursed her lips, waiting for him to return. 'You may sit on the chair by the fire, Alexander. I would prefer it if you did not come any closer.'

With an amiable smile, he nodded and was soon comfortably seated. 'There's no point in my apologizing again, for whatever I say you'll think the worst of me. Therefore I don't intend to do so. I'm marooned here for several days. Do you intend to skulk until I go?'

'Don't be ridiculous. In case you haven't noticed, I'm increasing. What took place last night has debilitated me.' She glared at him and something prompted her to continue in the same vein. 'If I lose this child it will be your doing, and you can be very sure there will never be another legitimate heir whilst I'm alive.'

His face drained of colour and his eyes widened. 'My God! Is there a likelihood you'll miscarry? I don't care what the weather's like; I'll fetch the physician myself even if I've to dig my way out.'

She wished the words unsaid. She'd wanted to hurt him; to make sure he didn't attempt to make love to her again, but not send him out to meet his death. 'I'll remain in bed; there was no more than a twinge. I'm sure with rest all will be well.'

His expression stabbed her heart. He looked so relieved, so abjectly miserable, that she was driven to broach the subject she'd intended to talk to him about last night. 'Alexander, your Mr Bentley believes that *my* home is intended for him when he comes to live with you. As I always meant to move back into Newcomb for the birth, I think it might be prudent if I return in May, before you get back. However . . . '

Something flashed across his face. Could it have been triumph? 'I'll be eternally grateful, my dear, if you do. The thought of being obliged to share my home this summer with that ninny quite appalls me. At least in here we shan't be seeing him every time we turn the corner.'

'Alexander, you didn't allow me to finish. I'll only return if I can have my own staff. I've no wish to be waited on by those presently in London.'

He nodded thoughtfully. 'I can dismiss anyone who has offended you.'

'Good grief, there's no need to do that. Most have been with you this age; they believe they're doing their duty by keeping me from damaging your reputation. Do I have your word on this matter?'

'You have it, Isobel. Tell me who you don't want at Newcomb and they can serve Bentley.'

'Thank you, that's an excellent notion. I suppose we must set up the nursery in readiness for the arrival.'

'Leave that to me. As you don't intend to be here, I believe it's my prerogative to select who will do the job for you.'

She quailed under his frosty stare. 'Of course, Alexander. No doubt you've an old retainer lurking in a cottage somewhere who can be recalled.'

Talking about the baby was distressing. She wanted him to go, but unexpectedly he was beside her. 'Don't cry, sweetheart. Things will work out for the best one way or the other. I'm sorry I was so brusque, but the thought of you not being here is as upsetting to me as it is to you.'

His thumb caught the tear trickling down her cheek and rubbed it away. She turned her head. When he was being like this she could feel her anger melting; could almost believe they might have a life together after all.

13

The snow showed no sign of melting and Isobel was resigned to Alexander remaining. She became accustomed to sharing her meals and her home with him once more. He was so pleasant, so charming and such lively company, that being with him was no hardship.

The fourth night of his visit they'd been playing an entertaining game of Piquet, which he'd won, when he tossed his cards on the table and walked over to the window. 'I believe it's raining. The snow will be gone by tomorrow.' He peered behind the heavy curtains and nodded.

'Listen to the flames spitting. It must be heavy to come down the chimney. The roads will be a quagmire; I think you'd best wait until the carriage arrives. Your leg isn't sufficiently recovered for you to ride back to Grosvenor Square,' Isobel said.

He grinned and stared ruefully at his injury. 'As always, my dear, you're quite correct. In which case, you must endure my presence for a further day or two.'

Resuming his seat, he stared into the flames while she picked up her novel.

Unexpectedly, Sam appeared at the door, his face creased with concern. He looked from one to the other and then addressed his mistress. 'Excuse me for interrupting, your grace, but I've to tell you the ceiling has just collapsed in your bedchamber.'

'Good grief! How can that be? The roof was sound when I moved in, and we have had several heavy downpours since with no leaks at all.'

'I reckon the weight of the snow cracked the tiles and then with this downpour it came right through.'

Alexander got to his feet. 'Is it just this one room or are others affected?'

'There's leaks springing up all down that side of the building, your grace.'

'The tiles are ancient. There's been nothing done to this place for generations; small wonder they've given up. Move her grace's belongings into my bedchamber.'

Isobel shot up, sending her novel flying into the grate. Alexander grabbed the poker and flicked it from the flames before it burnt. Picking up the book, he extinguished the remaining sparks with his fingers. 'Not seriously damaged. A trifle pungent, but definitely still readable.'

Her protest about his high-handed suggestion that she move into his bedchamber remained unspoken. 'But what about your hand? Have you hurt it?'

He waggled his fingers in front of her face. 'See, no damage to them either. I must go and see — '

'Alexander, I'm quite sure my staff are capable of placing buckets under the drips. There's something I wish to say that's more important than you overseeing the positioning of receptacles.'

Shrugging, he returned to his chair and raised an inquisitive eyebrow. 'Well, my dear, what do you wish to say?'

'If you think that I . . . '

'There's no need to fly into the boughs, Isobel. I've no intention of remaining in my bedchamber once you're safely installed there. You can be quite certain Watkins will be moving my belongings as we speak — after all, he knows how things are between us.'

Isobel ignored his comment. 'There's something I've been meaning to say to you about the settlement.' His eyes were watchful but he made no comment. Emboldened by his silence, she continued. 'Sam was under the erroneous impression you were sending him details of the estates you own and I didn't disabuse him. On reflection I think it might be better if I moved somewhere within your demesne. I've no wish to cause unnecessary scandal for you or the child.'

He thumped the table, scattering the cards on the floor. 'Devil take it! Why didn't I think of that myself? There's already an estate you have undisputed claim to. Highfield House in Epping is held for each duchess in her lifetime. The revenue from the farms, which is substantial, will have been banked in your name since our marriage.'

'Why doesn't this estate pass down to the eldest daughter? It seems strange it should move from one duchess to the next like this.'

He stared at his boots. 'This estate comes through my maternal great-great grand-mother. You're not the first duchess to wish to live apart from her husband.'

'Are you telling me unhappy marriages are expected in this family?'

'I believe the Dukes of Rochester are infamous for their infidelities. My grand-mother died at Highfield House, as did my own mama.'

Her stomach curdled. She stared at him as if seeing him clearly for the first time all week. Was he incapable of being the kind of man she wanted because he was genetically disposed to philander and abuse? Tears pricked her eyes as she recalled what Bentley had said about Lady Fulbright.

Carefully placing her singed book on the

table, she stood up and walked across to pull the bell-strap. When the footman appeared she gave her instructions. 'Go upstairs and see if the bedchamber being prepared for me is ready. I wish to retire.'

She couldn't resume her place; needed to be as far away as possible from him. Music would soothe her and the pianoforte was at the far end of the drawing room. She needed no extra candlelight; she could play her favourite sonata from memory. Settling onto the piano stool, she raised the lid and ran her fingers over the keys. Soon she was lost in the melody, her distress slipping away as the beauty of the music enveloped her.

★　★　★

Alexander slumped back into his chair. He'd seen the accusation in her eyes. That little bastard Bentley had told her about his ex-mistress, Gloria. Lady Fulbright had invited him back to her home and he'd accompanied her, gone inside and dismissed his carriage. However, that was as far as it went. He'd changed his mind and told her the liaison was over, irrevocably so.

He'd not even removed his beaver or topcoat, had left the house no more than three minutes after entering it and walked home regretting the impulse that had made him accept the offer in the first place. Someone had seen him go in and drawn incorrect conclusions. He didn't blame Isobel for believing the worst. Had he not just told her he came from a long line of unfaithful dukes?

He closed his eyes, letting the beautiful sound wash over him. Then he was on his feet, limping softly towards the far end of the room from which the glorious music was coming. Why hadn't she played for him? He'd no idea she was so talented; in fact, he barely knew the woman he'd married so precipitously. This was another serious omission on his part.

He positioned himself against the wall where he could see her face and watch her hands moving confidently up and down the keys. Her eyes were closed; she was lost in a world of her own — somewhere he couldn't reach her. Her glorious hair had grown and now curled around her face in a russet cap emphasizing the beauty of her magnificent green eyes. Her face was thinner than he remembered. Despite the growing mound of her pregnancy, she was obviously losing weight.

This was his fault, as was everything else that had befallen her. Whatever she wanted from now on he wouldn't quibble — would make no demands on her of any sort — and let her find happiness where she could. She'd loved him once and maybe in a year or two, when she saw he was completely reformed, she might love him again.

★ ★ ★

Isobel finished the sonata and slowly returned to her surroundings. A slight sound beside her made her turn her head but there was no one there — she must have been mistaken. With a sigh she closed the piano.

Alexander was standing by the fire, his eyes alight with admiration. 'I'd no idea you could play so brilliantly, my dear. You're a virtuoso; I don't believe I've heard that piece played so well.'

'Thank you. It's a great favourite of mine. Music has always been a solace; I can lose myself when I'm playing.'

Mary appeared at the door looking somewhat flustered. 'Your chamber's ready, your grace. Shall I send up a supper tray?'

'No, thank you. I need nothing else tonight. Have you found somewhere for his grace to sleep?'

Her housekeeper glanced nervously at Alexander. 'I'm afraid the only chamber available isn't really suitable, but it's the only one that isn't leaking apart from the room you're occupying, your grace.'

He nodded. 'It matters not where I sleep, Watkins. I'll be leaving at first light.' He stared at Isobel, daring her to contradict; to tell him he wasn't fit enough to ride.

This was his decision; she wouldn't gainsay him. 'In which case, Mary, make sure breakfast's available at dawn.' She smiled briefly at her husband. 'As you'll be leaving before I rise, I bid you a safe journey, Alexander.' She didn't add she hoped he would return soon.

When, heavy-eyed, she came down the next morning, he'd already departed. The snow had all but gone, and a watery sun lit up the soggy park. Alexander was mad to leave on horseback, but he was a man grown and made his own decisions. It might be several more days before the roads were passable and his valet arrived with the carriage. Therefore, with so much tension between them, she was relieved he'd chosen to go.

Even the dogs were subdued. They moped about the place as if their best friend had departed, not someone they'd only known a few days. The fine weather meant repairs could be done to the roof and the other bedrooms with damaged ceilings. Sam liaised with the estate manager and soon the place was filled with the sound of hammering and banging.

She'd insisted the employment was given to those who most needed it. Work was scarce everywhere at the moment. Resigning herself to spending the next few days with the house shrouded under holland covers, Isobel retreated to the small sitting room at the rear of the house.

Into the middle of this chaos Duncan arrived with Alexander's missing luggage. Closely behind him was Bentley, who'd been obliged to spend the past few nights at a disreputable roadside inn where he'd met with the most unfortunate accident.

'Mr Bentley, how distressing for you.' The young man was no longer dressed immaculately, nor was his hair oiled or his shirt points freshly starched. Now he was a bedraggled sight, looking as if he had been sleeping in his clothes for the past week, which wasn't far short of the truth.

'I do beg your pardon for returning here like this, your grace, but I'd no option. The robbers left me with no money to pay my shot. They took my trunk, and everything I own was in it. I was obliged to leave my fob watch behind as surety. I can't return to London as I am.'

181

'Of course you can't. You must remain here until you've fully recovered. Unfortunately I don't believe the duke's garments will fit you, but no doubt we can find something.'

He looked pathetically grateful. He was no longer the bombastic young man who'd arrived on her doorstep the previous week. Her heart went out to him. He must stay with her until something could be done about his wardrobe, but where he would sleep was a conundrum she'd leave to Mary.

'Your grace, I do beg your pardon for intruding a second time. I see the house is under covers. Has there been some sort of disaster?'

'The roof collapsed under the weight of the snow and it's being repaired at this very moment. This means you'll be obliged to sleep in the nursery, but Rochester did so without complaint.'

'I thought his grace returned to London.'

She could hardly tell him why Alexander had galloped back. The poor man had suffered enough indignities these past days. 'His horse cast a shoe and he was obliged to return, and then the weather closed in and he stayed until the beginning of the week. We must send word to Grosvenor Square that you're with me. His grace will be worried when he finds you absent.'

Hiding her smile behind her hand, she turned away. Alexander was more likely to be enraged than worried Bentley wasn't in town. The man was harmless now the starch had left his person as well as his apparel, and might be amusing company for a short while.

'I've no wish to cause you any aggravation, your grace, especially as matters stand. I'll endeavour to bother you as little as possible whilst I'm here.'

Whatever could he mean? Then she saw his eyes resting on her bump. She'd forgotten to disguise her pregnancy. Too late to repine, she'd make him feel wanted despite the fact his position as the duke's heir was possibly to be of short duration.

'My husband, when he set about the search for you, didn't know I was in an interesting condition. We both believed we wouldn't be blessed with children. By the time we realized, the lawyers had contacted you.'

This feeble exclamation was the best she could do. He would no doubt draw the correct conclusion — that they'd been estranged at the time. He accepted the information with equanimity. 'I'm more than delighted for you both. To tell you the truth, I never expected to inherit the title. However, his grace has seen fit to set up a generous annuity for me and for that I'm extremely grateful. This means I can live comfortably and mix in the highest circles, something that wouldn't have been possible if the lawyers hadn't discovered me.'

'I'm glad you're not disappointed. Whatever happens, you are now a member of the family.' What had prompted her to say such a foolish thing? The very last thing she needed at the moment was someone else watching the disintegration of her marriage. It would be impossible to hide her intention to depart after the baby was born. If the child turned out to be a girl, how would things be then?

He bowed, looking decidedly silly in his dishevelled state. 'I thank you, your grace. I've no close family of my own. In future I'll consider Cousin Alexander and yourself as my dearest relatives.'

This embarrassing conversation was brought to a halt by the appearance of Duncan. 'Your grace, I've found some garments for Mr Bentley. Shall I act as his man for the present?'

'Yes, that would seem a sensible solution. Mr Bentley, if you would care to go with Duncan, he'll take care of you.'

No doubt Bentley was anticipating with some dismay what he'd be obliged to wear for the foreseeable future. Duncan must have discovered items Alexander had worn in his youth. Nothing he possessed at the moment would do; he was a head taller and almost double the width of his heir.

*　*　*

The ride back to London was decidedly unpleasant and Alexander and his two grooms were more than grateful to dismount in the stable yard behind his palatial home. The head stable lad appeared to take the reins of his mount.

'He'll need walking to cool down. Also check his tendons carefully; the going was sticky.' He limped to the side entrance, surprised word of his arrival hadn't reached the house. He stepped in to come face to face with Foster.

'Your grace, I must apologize for not being here to welcome you. We didn't expect you back today.'

The butler made it sound as if he was remiss by not sending word of his arrival. He stared frostily and Foster recoiled, unused to such treatment. 'I'll need someone to act as my valet, as Duncan is elsewhere.'

'I'll see to it, your grace. We have several suitable footmen. Shall you be requiring luncheon?'

'Soup and fresh bread and cheese will be sufficient. Have it sent to my chambers; I'll eat there whilst I wait for my bath to be drawn.'

He was halfway up the staircase when he recalled Bentley must be in residence somewhere. 'I wish to speak to Bentley. Have him come to my study one hour from now.'

'I'm sorry, your grace, but Mr Bentley isn't here. We thought he was with you at Newcomb.'

God dammit! Surely he should have made his way to Grosvenor Square by now? He was no doubt waiting for the roads to clear and would be along later today to annoy him. 'He must have stayed en route. Make sure his apartment's prepared. He'll be here shortly.' The butler hovered as if he had something on his mind. 'Well, what's wrong?'

'Your grace, there have been three letters delivered for Mr Bentley; I've put them in his rooms.' Foster shifted from one foot to the other. 'I must also report that two unsavoury characters called, demanding to speak to him. They were sent about their business but I fear Mr Bentley might have fallen in with some rogues.'

Alexander frowned. He'd been correct in his first assessment of the situation. Bentley had got himself in financial difficulties. 'Thank you for bringing the matter to my attention, Foster. I'll speak to him when he returns.'

If the wretched man wasn't in Grosvenor Square by tomorrow he'd send someone to look for him. The young man might be irritating, and from the looks of it was going to be a serious drain on his purse, but he was his responsibility. He was damned if he was going to make the journey again himself. He'd done enough gallivanting these past few days after that particular person.

There was no sign of either his valet or Bentley the next day. What could be keeping them? The toll roads were fit to travel on and the weather was good. By the next morning he was concerned, so when Foster arrived with a letter sent express, he hoped it contained news of the missing pair. He didn't recognize the writing. Impatiently he broke the seal and read the contents.

Dear Alexander,

I do hope that you returned safely and have suffered no ill effects from your travel. I am writing to ask for your assistance. Mr Bentley was robbed of all his possessions whilst benighted at a disreputable roadhouse. He made his way back here and I've no idea what to do with him.

187

I've discovered a local tailor, who is endeavouring to make him something fresh to wear, but Mr Bentley's requirements are too stringent and I fear the outcome won't be successful for either party.

Mr Bentley has taken the news of our happy event with good grace. I am in a quandary as to how to proceed for the best. I shall eagerly await your advice.

With kindest regards
Your wife,
Isobel.

He slammed the letter down on the desk. What a disaster! He'd no option but to rout out Bentley's tailor and drag the unfortunate man down to Newcomb along with samples and pattern books. He could hardly blame his cousin for being robbed, but it was a damned nuisance nevertheless. He'd no wish to return to his country estate. He was unwelcome there and his presence would only exacerbate the rift between himself and Isobel. Only time and separation might mend the damage his appalling behaviour had caused to the marriage.

Thoughtfully he picked up the letter and examined it more closely. This was the first missive he'd received from her. The note was hardly a *billet doux*, but on the other hand she'd addressed him by his given name and was asking for help. He ran his fingertip around the loops and whorls — her writing was a revelation to him. It showed a flamboyance he'd not suspected in his wife. How many more things would he learn before he truly knew her?

Duncan returned the following morning and Alexander was relieved to hand over the search for a suitable tailor to his capable manservant. Alexander realized he'd no recourse but to return to Newcomb.

14

Two days after Isobel had sent her plea for help to London, she was returning from a brisk walk around the park with the dogs when a travelling carriage bowled around the curve of the drive. There was no doubting to whom this belonged, for emblazoned on the handsome black paintwork was the Rochester crest.

She sincerely hoped Alexander had come to remove her guest, who'd taken to sulking in the drawing room, his gloom pervading the whole house. Without his sartorial elegance to bolster his self-confidence he was a pitiful creature. No doubt the smaller coach contained the tailor. With a sigh she returned to the east wing, glad all the rooms were now usable and she was safely installed in her own apartments.

Ebony and Othello shot off ahead, somehow sensing who was in the carriage. By the time she made her way to the turning circle Alexander was playing with her dogs. How could this youthful gentleman with a ready smile for everyone be the austere man she'd married what seemed like years ago?

'Good afternoon, my dear. You look enchanting. I expected to see you over-wrought.'

'I'm very well, thank you, sir. Bentley is far less intrusive this visit.'

'Where is he? I can't wait to see him dressed in my cast-offs. I'm sorry you've been bothered a second time. I'm here to organize his new wardrobe and take him away.'

Isobel laughed. 'He'll be moping about in the drawing room bewailing the fact that his clothes were stolen and he can't return to town until properly dressed. He'll also be complaining the local tailor is useless and stating he'll refuse to wear anything he makes.'

'He'll wear what he's damn well given and be grateful. I've brought his tailor with me in the second carriage. He has a selection of articles for Bentley to choose from. He also has his pattern books and samples so can start making up what's needed.'

They strolled companionably around to the east wing where the front door was open and Mary and Bill were waiting to greet Alexander. Two footmen rushed by to collect the baggage. Inside, Alexander stared up at the ceiling enquiringly.

'Have you managed to repair the roof? Am I in the nursery with Bentley?'

'You may relax, Alexander. Everything's as it should be. If Bentley is to live here it must be re-roofed before next winter. However, it's sound enough now, thank goodness.'

They agreed to meet at dinner and she vanished to her own domain at the rear of the house, leaving him to take care of matters with her less welcome guest. Hopefully both men would depart the following morning and her life could return to normal.

She paid particular attention to her appearance that night as there were two gentlemen to entertain. 'Sally, I think you've done a splendid job altering my evening gown. It's fortunate the high waistline is ideally suited to someone in my condition.'

'Emerald silk is a perfect match for your eyes, your grace, and there will be more than enough room to accommodate the baby over the next few months.'

Isobel's hair was long enough to dress in a more elaborate style. She preferred to have it loose, but tonight she made the effort to appear as the Duchess of Rochester and not a country squire's wife. 'No, Sally, I won't wear emeralds. This is an informal occasion not a grand event.'

Disappointed, her maid returned the necklace to its velvet box. 'I could wear the pearls, and you could thread the smaller strand through my hair.'

This was the first opportunity her abigail had had to show she was capable of dressing a duchess. Up till now Isobel had worn the simple gowns best suited to her condition.

Despite the extra preparations she was on her way downstairs in good time. There were already voices in the drawing room. Bentley had asked if he might call her Cousin Isobel. Her lips twitched as she recalled Alexander's terse reply to this impertinent suggestion, so things remained as they were. Formality would be observed until her husband decreed otherwise. She paused in the open door and he strolled in her direction, his toe-curling smile still having the same effect even after all this time.

'Good evening, my dear. Permit me to say you look enchanting tonight. That's my favourite gown and it suits you to perfection.'

She smiled and dipped in a shallow curtsy. He bowed and taking her hand raised it to his lips. She was uncomfortably aware Bentley was avidly observing this play between them. Gently removing her fingers, she turned and nodded to the young man.

'Mr Bentley, I see your tailor has found something that meets with your approval. You look exactly as you did before.'

She heard a strange choking sound behind

her; Alexander was doing his best not to laugh. Bentley preened and smoothed down his lurid cherry-pink and gold waistcoat.

'Mr Smith knows exactly what I like; I do beg your pardon for my previous appearance.'

Fortunately dinner was announced and she was saved from having to dissemble. Alexander offered his arm and she took it, leaving Bentley to follow behind.

The dinner was served as she'd instructed. The removes were plain and as the last cover was cleared she rose gracefully and nodded to both men. 'I'll leave you to your port, gentlemen. No doubt you'll join me in the drawing room later.'

Alexander pulled a face as she walked past. He wouldn't dally. Not wishing to be trapped in further tedious banalities, she removed to the pianoforte. Alexander had brought her several sheets of music from London and she was eager to try them out.

As always, once she started playing she was unaware she had company until the final notes died away. The silence was shattered by raucous cheering and loud applause from Bentley.

'I say, your grace, that was excellent playing. I've never heard better.'

'Thank you, Mr Bentley, and thank *you*, Alexander, for bringing this new piece. I don't have it perfectly, but practice will improve my performance.'

Once they were comfortably settled in front of the roaring fire Alexander leant back in his chair. 'Bentley, you've yet to tell me exactly what took place at this inn. I need the name of the place so I can send your reckoning to them and recover your pocket watch.'

The man looked worried and fiddled with his exaggerated shirt points. 'To tell you the truth, your grace, I misremember the name of the establishment. There was a blizzard blowing and the driver stopped at the first hostelry we came upon.' He paused and then his face lit up. 'I have it. The coachman will be able to tell you. After all, he could see where we were going.'

Alexander nodded. 'I'll speak to him tomorrow. Never fear, your watch will be returned. Do you wish me to pursue the matter of the robbery?'

'No, sir. I expect it's far too late to apprehend the varmints. They'll be long gone and the landlord won't inform on them. Those sort of people tend to stick together, do they not?'

'In which case there's no more I can do. I'll pay for your wardrobe; you shan't be out of pocket. Another thing, Bentley. The east wing will be yours if you wish to reside here.

However, when we reopen Newcomb this place will need extensive repairs to the roof. Therefore I suggest you remain in Grosvenor Square until your accommodation is ready.'

'Of course, I don't wish to intrude. I can assure you, your grace, I appreciate your generosity and I beg your pardon for being a trial. I understand I'm unlikely to remain your heir, but now I can live the life of a gentleman, something I'd never aspired to before.'

Isobel had heard quite enough. Time she retired to the blessed peace of her own apartment to read her novel without interruption. 'If you'll excuse me, I shan't remain for the supper tray.'

Alexander was up before her and offered his hand to assist her from her chair. With a smile she accepted. The young man bowed politely.

'Your grace, forgive me, but as I've no wish to intrude, would it be possible for me to know at what time you take your dogs out? I also enjoy an early-morning stroll and will ensure I don't come down at the same time as you.'

She looked at him in surprise. He'd not risen before noon so far. However, his question was perfectly civil and demanded a similar reply. 'I no longer come down at first light but around eight o'clock. Please, Mr Bentley, feel free to get up whenever you wish. We stand on no ceremony here. If you require breakfast earlier you only have to ask.'

'No, your grace, I do beg your pardon; I've no intention of asking your household to change arrangements on my account. I'll take my constitutional first thing.'

What an odd conversation. Alexander raised his eyebrows. The evening hadn't turned out as wearisome as she'd feared, but she'd had enough for tonight.

Bentley had talked only of fashion and gossip, and there was nothing more tedious than hearing *on dits* about people one had never met. Alexander was the exact opposite; with his every word she'd found herself being drawn to him again. She wouldn't be taken in a second time, for he could turn the charm on and off at will.

★   ★   ★

The following morning Isobel was woken by voices beneath her window. How curious — who could possibly be outside so early? Then she recalled Bentley had told her he was taking an early morning walk. He must be speaking to an outside man.

Something about the conversation bothered her. She rolled out of bed and went to the window, peeping around the heavy curtain and pressing her nose against the shutter.

Good heavens! Bentley was talking to two unpleasant individuals who were certainly not employed at Newcomb. The taller man, his face obscured by a muffler and pulled down cap, was angry.

'You ran away from us. Don't think your belongings are enough to settle what you owe my master. He has your vowels and he wants payment.'

'I told you, I've nothing of my own. I'm dependent on Rochester. You have my word I'll pay you as soon as I'm solvent.' Bentley sounded desperate. He grasped the tall man's sleeve. 'You shouldn't be here. The duchess is increasing and the duke will toss me aside if I anger him. If your master is patient, then he'll get his money eventually.'

Bentley glanced up — had he detected her presence at the window? She retreated, deeply disturbed by what she'd heard. The young man had gambling debts and the person he owed was prepared to use violence to recover the debt.

She must speak to Alexander. He'd know what to do. She rang the bell and paced the room until Sally appeared.

'Please send word to the duke; I wish to see him urgently.'

Sally curtsied. 'Yes, your grace. I'll go myself.'

Scarcely ten minutes later her bedchamber door flew open and Alexander appeared with his cravat poorly tied and his hair on end. 'What's wrong, sweetheart? Are you unwell?'

'No, nothing like that.' She explained what she'd overheard.

'Devil take the man! He's an infernal nuisance. Don't worry, my love; I'll have the intruders apprehended and settle Bentley's debts this time. However, I'll not do so again.'

His face was hard, his eyes slate grey. 'Thank you, Alexander. I'm afraid I can't like your cousin, but I feel a trifle sorry for him. He seems to attract disaster.'

'Return to bed, my dear. Leave matters to me.'

★   ★   ★

By the time Isobel eventually went downstairs there was no sign of her husband or Bentley. Bill followed her to the breakfast room.

'Your grace, I'm to inform you Mr Bentley has returned to London. His grace accompanied him but will be back before dark.'

'Thank you, Bill. Do you know if the intruders were discovered?'

'No, your grace. The outside men scoured the grounds and outbuildings but found no one. I reckon they said their piece and then took off.'

Alexander returned at dusk and she was obliged to contain her curiosity until he'd changed and joined her downstairs.

'I've sent for coffee. Do you wish for anything more substantial or are you happy to wait until we dine?'

He flopped into an armchair and stretched his booted legs towards the fire. 'Coffee will be fine, my dear. I'm relieved to be back. Rufus is a magnificent animal but even he is shattered after making a double journey to town.'

'I've no wish to hear about your horse, Alexander. Tell me what you've been doing all day.'

A footman came in to place the tray on a side table. Alexander nodded and waved him away. Not waiting for her to scramble up and serve him, he leant forward and picked up the silver jug and poured himself a steaming cup.

'That's better. Now, I'll tell you everything. Three hundred guineas is a substantial sum but it could have been worse.' He swallowed another mouthful of coffee and she watched the strong column of his throat convulse.

'I can't believe you've ridden almost forty miles today and are still upright. You couldn't have done so a year ago.' Her cheeks flamed and she wished her incautious remark unspoken. 'I beg your pardon . . . '

He grinned at her inadvertent use of Bentley's irritating expression. 'Don't apologize to me, sweetheart. You've every right to comment.'

His eyes gleamed above the rim of his cup and she smiled. 'I'm still waiting — stop procrastinating and tell me who the money was owed to.'

'Bentley wouldn't reveal that information however much I tried to persuade him.' He frowned. 'There's something a bit havey-cavey about it. One would have thought he'd be relieved to have me speak for him. But no, he was adamant. He said he'd deal with the matter himself and that we wouldn't be troubled again and I must take his word for it.'

'So Bentley wasn't waylaid by footpads but by the two ruffians who came here?'

'Apparently so. It hardly seems credible he could have got himself in such a mess so quickly; I'm beginning to suspect he brought the villains with him from his past.'

'Oh dear! From your expression, Alexander, I take it you don't intend to let the matter go?'

'Hill's investigating for me. I intend to discover who sent those men here. You may be very sure, my dear, that they'll regret their actions by the time I've finished with them.'

She was woken in the night by her dogs barking. What had disturbed them? She sat up to listen — were those footsteps outside her door? She was about to scramble out of bed when the dogs settled. She must have been mistaken.

15

Next morning she was woken by a shrill scream, the noise of smashing crockery and a series of thumps. This was followed by a ghastly silence. The disturbance had come from somewhere in the main passageway. It sounded as if someone had fallen down the main staircase.

She tumbled from bed and paused to adjust the belt of her robe. Satisfied she was decent, she ran into the corridor but Alexander was there before her. He vanished down the staircase.

She reached the top. Her early morning chocolate was spilt over the boards. Her hands flew to her mouth and she reeled against the balustrade. He was crouching over what could only be her own, dear Sally.

'Isobel, stay where you are. There's nothing to do here.' He glanced over his shoulder. His eyes glittered and his face was pale. Sally was dead — she'd been killed by the fall.

'I don't understand, Alexander. She brings up my tray every morning. I insist she uses the main staircase and not the back stairs in order to keep her safe.' Her voice sounded strange — reed-thin, as if someone else had spoken through her lips. This was her fault. If Sally had used the servants' staircase she wouldn't have fallen to her death.

Then the entrance hall was full of people. Mary arrived and close behind were Bill and Sam. Alexander shielded the body with his own. Only when someone else could take his place did he turn and bound up the stairs to her.

'My love, your abigail tripped and toppled backwards. She broke her neck; she'll have felt no pain and died instantly.'

She heard his words but couldn't take them in. Her head felt light and she fell forward into darkness.

★ ★ ★

Alexander caught her. He was shocked; she weighed little more than a child in spite of her advancing pregnancy. The stress and the shocks she'd endured might prove too much for her delicate health. Whatever her objections, from now on he would remain at her side and take care of her. He strode back to her apartment, his precious burden held close to his heart. He must do whatever was necessary himself.

He placed her tenderly on the bed, then sat

chaffing her hands and calling her name. With considerable relief he watched her colour return and her eyes flicker open. Withdrawing her hands, she turned her head away, trying to repress her sobs.

'My darling, let me hold you. This has been a terrible shock. It's a tragedy a young girl has died. Let go of your grief — it doesn't do to bottle it in.'

She stiffened, rolling further from him. He must ignore this; she needed his comfort. 'Sweetheart, let me hold you. You'll feel better if you cry.'

Gathering her up, he returned to the daybed with her cradled in his arms. For a further moment she was rigid, resisting, but then she relaxed and rested her head on his shoulder. He stroked her hair, her back, her face, as she sobbed. Eventually she was quiet, her breathing even. Thank God; she'd fallen into a deep, restorative slumber. He became aware the housekeeper was in the room.

'Your grace, if you would place her grace in bed, I'll take care of her. You're needed downstairs.'

The woman's tone was terse; she hadn't forgiven him for what he'd done to her beloved mistress. 'Thank you, Watkins. I know she's in capable hands. This is a wretched business; I don't understand how this happened.'

Downstairs was quiet; a reverent hush had descended over the building. The poor girl's mortal remains had been removed and both the butler and Sam Watkins were waiting to speak with him.

'Your grace, there's something you need to see. This is a strange business and no mistake.' Watkins led him to the top of the stairs and pointed to the boards. 'See here, Sally's slippers have made marks where she lost her footing.'

Alexander dropped to one knee to examine the place. There was a smear of something on the top step. He dipped his finger in the mark and touched his tongue to it. As he'd thought — somehow the unfortunate girl had trodden in lard and this had caused her feet to slip on the polished surface. How this had happened, he'd no idea, but servants were in and out of the kitchen all the time. All it took was a careless scullery maid and the deed was done.

'Do you see this? You were right to draw my attention to this grease mark; at least it explains how it occurred.'

The butler, who'd accompanied them to the top of the staircase, shook his head. 'It's right peculiar, my lord. If Sally had walked in fat, then why didn't she slip when she left the kitchen?'

Alexander frowned. 'The girl must have

walked on the central carpet, and then when she stepped on the boards at the top, her foot slid from under her. She would have had no chance of saving herself as she was carrying a tray.' This was not a satisfactory explanation. Walking on carpet would have rubbed off most of the grease. However, they appeared to accept his explanation.

'It's a very sad day, your grace. If I discover who was the cause of this death they'll be dismissed on the spot and no references to take with them neither.'

Alexander straightened and patted the butler's shoulder. 'It would do no good to take such action. Accidents happen. Put it behind you, Brown.' He turned and addressed Watkins. 'Can I rely on you to take care of funeral arrangements? Has the family to be informed?'

'No, your grace, Sally was an orphan, that's why she was pleased to be taken on as a lady's maid. Her grace will be devastated. My Mary must take care of her now; this is no time to employ a stranger to look after her.'

'An excellent suggestion, Watkins. I assume there's someone who can take over the role of housekeeper?'

He nodded. 'Yes, your grace. You may have no fear on that score.'

These matters were not Alexander's concern. He must go and see how Isobel was faring. He was sure a shock of this sort might cause a miscarriage.

★ ★ ★

'Sally? What time is it?' Then Isobel remembered: her maid was dead and the accident was her fault. Her throat clogged and she couldn't stop fresh tears from soaking her pillow.

'There, there, my dear. All this crying will do no good to your baby. Sally wouldn't want you to make yourself ill on her account.'

She sniffed and dried her eyes on the sheet. 'Mary, what are you doing here? You have the house to run. Ellie will do very well.'

'Bless you, your grace, I'd not let anyone else take care of you. It's only a small establishment. Young Bill can manage everything as well as I can.'

'It will be a comfort having you close, but only until I've recovered from the shock. Then you must return to your duties.' She was heavy-eyed, her throat raw from crying, and she'd no idea what time it was. Pushing herself upright, she stared at the mantel clock.

'Good grief! It's almost noon. I must get up at once.'

'His grace insists you remain here, your grace. He's taking care of everything — the funeral is tomorrow and staff can attend.'

'I've no wish to cause distress, Mary, but I'm not remaining in bed. I feel perfectly well. I'm deeply grieved but won't break down again. I'm the mistress here; I should be on my feet, not malingering here like an invalid.'

Mary had no chance to remonstrate as Isobel threw back the covers and hurried into the dressing room. She had a pressing need to use the chamber pot. Twenty minutes later she was in her sitting room waiting for a tray. Once clothed, her desire to go downstairs became less urgent. She kept seeing the limp body spread-eagled at the bottom.

The door opened and her mouth rounded. 'Good heavens. Alexander, you're the last person I expected to arrive with my luncheon.'

He smiled but his eyes were sad. 'I wished to speak to you, my love, and thought I would share your repast.'

His gesture reminded her of the night before her marriage and her gaze softened. 'There's certainly more than enough for both of us. Mary has cleared the table, so put it there.'

He did as suggested then smiled at Mary. 'If you would care to return to your duties,

Watkins, I'll be here for the remainder of the afternoon.'

Mary curtsied; she didn't smile but looked slightly less disapproving than usual. 'Thank you, your grace, but I'll be back before it's dark.'

When they were alone he approached her, his expression reflecting his concern. 'Sweetheart, how are you now? Your eyes are red — have you been crying again?'

'I'm recovered, thank you. It's my condition; according to Mary, it makes me more tearful. I haven't eaten since dinner last night. Tell me, what has Cook sent?'

After removing the white cloth he examined the plates. 'There's a tureen of soup — from the aroma I'd say it's leek and potato — and there's fresh bread and butter. Then game pie and chutney, a decent wedge of cheese and a generous slice of plum cake.'

Her mouth watered as he listed the food, then her stomach gurgled loudly much to his amusement. 'It sounds delicious. Please may I have soup and some bread; no butter? Did Cook send up lemonade?'

He removed the small beaded cloth from the jug and sniffed the contents. 'Yes, it appears we're both to drink this for there isn't anything else.'

He sounded so offended she giggled.

'Honestly, Alexander, it will be to your taste. Far better than wine or beer, I can assure you.'

The meal did much to restore her and his kindness and attention warmed her heart. 'I'm replete; I couldn't eat another morsel. Between us we've almost cleared the tray.'

'Excellent — your cook's an asset; I'd forgotten what good plain food tasted like. My *chef de cuisine* smothers everything with a rich cream sauce so most of it's unrecognizable.'

'And I don't remember ever having a meal served hot.'

'You're quite correct; it's ridiculous for food to arrive cold.' He brushed off the crumbs and carried the tray into the corridor. She thought he might leave but he returned and folded himself back on the chair with a sigh of what could have been contentment.

A stab of guilt jolted her. How could they be sitting here enjoying each other's company when poor Sally was in her coffin? 'Where's the service being held tomorrow?'

'In the family church, where else? She'll be buried in the churchyard alongside other staff who died in our service. That's something I wish to discuss with you, my love. Have you any suggestions for her headstone?'

'Let Mary decide. She'd know better than I

211

what Sally would like.'

He stretched out his legs towards the fire and she noticed his breeches were no longer stretched taut across this thighs. She wasn't the only one to have lost weight recently.

'I've decided to reopen Newcomb. Watkins and George have gone to select sufficient staff to run the place. Maynard and Foster are to remain in Grosvenor Square with the rest of my people; they can take care of Bentley. I've told him to accept invitations on my behalf and enjoy himself. This will be his first experience of the *ton*; he can benefit from my absence.'

She shook her head in disbelief. 'I've no wish to live next door. You may move there but *I* am remaining here.'

'Isobel, I thought you'd prefer to be away from where your abigail died. Every time you ascend the stairs you'll be thinking of her. If you prefer to stay, then that's entirely your prerogative.'

Her eyes filled. She couldn't keep pace with his new persona. 'I beg your pardon . . . ' She half-smiled. 'I must try not to use that phrase; it reminds me of Bentley. You're quite right; that thought has kept me here all day. But I still don't understand why George should need to accompany Sam.'

His cheeks flushed. 'George will know

exactly which members of staff to bring back; he won't select anyone likely to make you uncomfortable.' He leant forward, his expression earnest. 'I should have been aware how unpleasant things were for you. In future only people with *your* best interests at heart will work here.'

She was nonplussed by his consideration. 'I don't know what to say. Newcomb is your home. My wishes should come second.'

His grin made him look almost boyish. 'I intend to remain here, in the east wing. I'll oversee the repairs. I've no wish to cause you any further distress. I can assure you Newcomb will no longer be an unfriendly place.'

'I'll still be obliged to eat cold food,' she said, laughing, 'and if my cook is to remain with you, then *you* shall have the best of the arrangement.' There was something about his suggestion that didn't sit well. What was it that bothered her? Her good humour vanished as she realized she'd been bamboozled into accepting the fact he didn't intend to return to Grosvenor Square.

'Why aren't you going back to town?'

His expression was wary. 'You're not looking after yourself; you're too thin. This tragedy has made me decide my place is here, taking care of you and my unborn child.'

Jumping from the chair, she glared at him. 'I'm quite capable of taking care of myself, Alexander. It's very strange that now I'm carrying a possible successor to your title, you're all attention. Where were you a year ago when I was miserable and lonely and you were gallivanting all over London with your unpleasant acquaintances and *chère amie*?'

He loomed over her, his bonhomie replaced by a fearsome scowl. 'Madam, you're impertinent.' He stared down his aristocratic nose and her bravado shrivelled. 'I've never been unfaithful. I've my faults, but I don't intend to follow . . . ' Biting back whatever he'd been intending to say, he nodded coldly and strode from the room.

This didn't bode well if they were to spend the next few months under the same roof. No — he was intending to live apart from her. She wished her intemperate words unspoken. He was sacrificing his comfort in order to remain close by and she'd rejected his kindness by accusing him of infidelity. She must apologize to him. If Bentley hadn't drawn her attention to the existence of a mistress she wouldn't have considered the possibility.

Miserably she returned to her bedchamber. The sound of someone moving in the dressing room startled her. Her eyes filled. It couldn't be Sally; she was dead. She sank onto her bed in despair — everything was in disarray. The thought of having Alexander watching her every move wasn't a happy one.

'Your grace, Mrs Watkins said as I was to come up and see if I could do anything. I've been sorting out the mending.'

'Ellie, I'm pleased to see you. I believe you can look after me quite adequately if Mrs Watkins shows you what's required.'

The girl curtsied and managed a wobbly smile; her eyes were red and puffy, no doubt very like her own.

'I'll be ever so grateful for the opportunity, your grace.' She hurried across the room. 'Shall I help you disrobe?'

Isobel had been going to lie down as she was but Ellie was correct, she'd ruin her morning gown if she did so. 'Thank you. I shan't be going downstairs today. I'll require a supper tray.'

★　★　★

She found it difficult to descend the staircase next morning but, unless she intended to remain trapped in her apartment, she had to face her fears. The funeral was in an hour or so. The house was quiet, all the staff given leave to attend. This was unusual as females

215

rarely attended such an occasion. In the absence of any close family, Mary and Sam decided Sally would like everyone to be there. No one even knew her real name or how old she was — she'd just been Sally to them.

Isobel drifted around the place unable to settle, and eventually decided to take the dogs to the ornamental lake. This was a considerable distance, but the weather was fair and she needed time to clear her head. There was still the matter of the apology. With luck, his anger would have been forgotten by the time she met him.

Ebony stayed at her side. However, Othello saw something in the woods and raced away, ignoring her calls to return. This was unlike him. He was usually an obedient animal. He must have unearthed something particularly interesting to remain in the trees barking and growling.

Fortunately Home Wood was closer than the lake, so taking a detour wouldn't add to her perambulations. She was breathless when she arrived and leant for a moment against a nearby trunk to regain her breath.

Ebony's hackles rose and a deep rumbling growl echoed through the naked branches. The interior was too gloomy to see what was upsetting both dogs. A shiver flickered down her spine. It could be a poacher. Although they weren't normally violent, being caught red-handed might promote an unpleasant retaliation.

She must collect her dogs and return to the house. The gamekeeper could investigate when he returned from church. She shouted for Othello but he continued to bark and snarl as if he had someone, or something, cornered. Should she leave him to rely on his instincts to find his own way home?

Then the matter was decided for her. Ebony dashed from her side, barking ferociously. A gun shot ripped past her. Forgetting she was almost six months pregnant, she rushed into the trees intent on coming between her dogs and whoever had fired the gun. A shadowy shape was sitting halfway up an oak tree whilst both dogs leapt and growled below him. If she could attract the poacher's attention, and tell him he could leave freely, then all might yet be well.

⋆ ⋆ ⋆

Alexander returned from the funeral eager to make his peace. The dogs were nowhere to be seen; she must have taken them for a walk. He would find them. Far better to smooth things over away from the disapproving stares of her retainers.

He stared across the rolling green and saw a movement at the edge of the trees. Why the hell would she want to go in there in her condition? As he walked briskly towards the wood he heard both dogs barking and growling. Something wasn't right; he broke into a run, cursing his damaged thigh which still impeded his movement.

He was a hundred yards away when a shot was fired. He covered the remaining distance flat out and burst into the wood to see her scrambling through the undergrowth in the direction of the tree in which he could clearly see a man with a rifle.

God's teeth! This was no poacher — this was far more sinister. She paused and called out to the figure.

'Please don't shoot my dogs. Let me collect them and you can go.'

She didn't realize what she was dealing with — how much danger she was in. Should he call out and warn her, or approach stealthily and try and apprehend whoever was skulking above them? Then his heart all but stopped. The rifle was being raised. It was pointing directly at Isobel. He was too far away to dislodge the gunman. How could he save his beloved?

16

Desperate to reach her dogs before the poacher lost patience and shot one of them, Isobel forgot to gather up her skirts. Her boot snagged in the hem and she stumbled forward. As she fell a second gunshot exploded and a missile thudded into the trunk of the tree above her.

'Isobel, for God's sake stay down! Someone's trying to kill you!'

Alexander was shouting a warning. She curled into a ball and covered her head with her hands. Crashing feet, shouts and curses were added to the noise her dogs were making. She cowered on the ground, too terrified to get up in case she was struck by a third bullet.

Then she was snatched into his arms. 'My darling, he could have murdered you. What were you thinking of, coming in here on your own?'

She clung to him, needing his warmth and his strength to stop her teeth chattering. Her pets were pressing against her legs and gave her the courage to look round. She expected to see bloody carnage. 'Where is the man who fired?'

'He's abandoned his rifle and taken off through the trees. I'll organize a search after I've taken you home. Can you walk, my dear?'

Experimentally, she straightened. Her legs no longer trembled. 'I'm perfectly well, Alexander. However, my promenade gown hasn't been so fortunate.'

Chuckling at her attempt to break the tension, he kneed the dogs aside and brushed off the worst of the leaf mould from her skirts. 'That will have to do. We must get back. The sooner I get after that bastard the better.'

With his support she began the long trek to the house. They hadn't been travelling far when she realized he was carrying the rifle. 'Why did you bring that?'

'Someone might have come for it. Being able to handle such a weapon isn't common — whoever was in that tree was probably an ex-serviceman. There's a remote possibility this rifle might lead us to him.'

She was finding it increasingly difficult to keep up with his long strides; he must slow down. Then he tossed the gun aside and swept her up and continued to walk as fast as he had done before. With a sigh of resignation she relaxed and let him do what he did best — take command.

His arrival was greeted with cries of distress and much muttering from the footmen.

'Put me down, Alexander. I'm quite capable of walking now I'm not obliged to keep up with you.'

Reluctantly he placed his precious bundle on the parquet floor. 'I do beg your pardon . . . '

'Oh, please don't — I'd much prefer you to say you're sorry.' Her eyes were alight with laughter and his heart skipped a beat. This was how it should be — sharing intimate moments and not constantly at odds.

'I *was* intending to ask your forgiveness for dragging you along but now I'll refrain. You're a baggage, madam, and show me no respect at all.'

The housekeeper bustled up her homely face anxious. 'Your grace, are you unwell?'

'No, Mary, but there's a poacher in the wood and he shot at my dogs.'

Her announcement caused further consternation. 'Isobel, wait for me in your sitting room. I'll return as soon as I can.'

He watched her walk away, her back straight, her wonderful russet curls tumbling onto her neck. No other woman had ever affected him in this way. He would desire her however advanced her pregnancy or her years. However, this wasn't the time to be thinking of carnal pleasures; there was a murderer to apprehend.

He returned to the wood with four men. His pistols were primed and ready in his pocket but he doubted there'd be anyone to shoot. Their quarry would be long gone but they might be able to follow the trail.

He picked up the rifle he'd cast aside earlier and examined it as he jogged. The gun was in poor condition and in need of a good clean. 'That oak tree's the one where the poacher sat. One of you climb up and tell me what you can see when you're sitting on the large branch.'

The youngest and most agile of the group shinned up the trunk to sit astride it. 'I can see clear to the lake, your grace. The break in the trees is right opposite. You'd not know anyone could get a clear view from so deep in the wood.'

This was no random event. Whoever had been in that tree had been waiting for the opportunity to shoot Isobel. She walked her dogs in this part of the park every day. All he had to do was remain hidden; the range of the rifle meant he could have killed her from where he sat.

His eyes misted with rage. There could be

only one perpetrator behind this attack; only one man who would benefit from Isobel's death: Bentley. He stood to gain from her demise. But it didn't make sense. Only an expert shot could have hoped to hit his target from that distance, and Bentley was no rifleman. God's teeth! His wits were wandering. Bentley was in London, which made it even more unlikely he was involved.

This needed further thought. He wouldn't draw a hasty conclusion; he needed to be certain before he confronted his erstwhile heir. If his conjectures were correct, the man wouldn't survive the meeting.

★　★　★

'Alexander, I can't believe Bentley's behind these attacks. Remember, you plucked him from his miserable existence and gave him an allowance, a fine wardrobe and a home. He might be irritating, but surely he's not a villain?'

'Perhaps you're right, sweetheart.' He rubbed his eyes. 'But Bentley's the only one who stands to gain from your . . . who stands to gain.' He straightened and his eyes blazed. 'I have it! Of course. It has to be something to do with those ruffians who accosted Bentley. If I find their master, I'll find the perpetrator.'

'If that's true, then poor Bentley must be in the thrall of this monster. You must go to London and discover the truth. I fear that young man might also be in danger.'

'I shall, my love, as soon as I'm certain Newcomb is safe.'

She smiled. 'Will you stay in town for long?'

'No longer than I have to. If you recall, I decided my place is here, taking care of you.'

She waved away his arm as she pushed herself upright. 'Then I'll not delay you. Take care, Alexander.'

Isobel suffered Mary and Ellie's fussing in silence and was relieved when they left her to read in front of the fire with a tray of freshly baked cakes and a large pot of coffee. The fright from the unpleasant incident had faded and she reviewed the event more objectively.

She prayed Alexander was wrong and that no one was trying to kill her. The very idea was like something out of that silly novel, *The Mysteries of Udolfo*. Admittedly the man had aimed the gun in her direction, but her dogs were running towards her so he might well have been hoping to hit one of them.

A poacher with a rifle must be unusual. They were more likely to creep about with snares and cudgels than with such sophisticated weaponry. What other possible reason could there be for a man with a valuable gun to be in Home Wood?

Concentrating was difficult whilst the infant inside her was apparently dancing a jig. Smiling, she placed her hands across her belly and could feel the movement through her garments. Mary had told her she was likely to become twice the size but that beggared belief. Already she'd lost sight of her toes and bending down to retrieve a dropped object was impossible.

Bill appeared at the open door. 'Could you spare me a moment, your grace? There's something I need to tell you and I reckoned you'd like to hear immediately.'

'Please come in. I've been puzzling over this morning's events and have come to no satisfactory conclusion. Have you got an answer for me?'

The young man grinned. 'I reckon I might have. It's like this, your grace. Jed went down to the village this morning on an errand. They were talking about a group of renegades who've been stealing and demanding money with menaces in neighbouring villages.'

'Thank God! That explains it; no doubt the villain intended to burgle the house but my dogs chased him up a tree. The militia must be sent for. His grace will know how to go about that. Do you know how many people have suffered at their hands?'

'A fair few, your grace. There's been a couple of coaches held up and several farms attacked, but none of them on this estate so far. I reckon your dogs disturbed them and they took to their heels, apart from the one who ended up the tree.'

'Well, I can't think why something hasn't already been done about it. I wonder why we didn't hear of this before today?'

Bill bowed. 'Shall I tell this to his grace when he returns?'

'Yes, the duke will wish to send word to the appropriate authorities. I intend to forget it ever happened.'

The men involved must be desperate to attack villages. Maybe if the government had been more generous with the soldiers dismissed from the army after Waterloo — had provided them with a decent pension or found them employment — then these unfortunate men wouldn't now be terrorizing the countryside.

This didn't excuse them but it did explain their motivation. Had she not been driven to violence herself when confronted by Sir John Farnham's licentious behaviour? She shuddered as she remembered. Desperation and anger made people behave badly; whoever these footpads were they would eventually be hanged.

She blinked back tears. She was a veritable watering pot nowadays and the slightest thing seemed to set her off. When Alexander returned she'd make her peace. Her unexpected brush with mortality had given her the push she needed. She doubted she'd ever forget what he'd done, but was ready to give him a chance to demonstrate his metamorphosis was genuine.

What a strange day it had been. First there had been Sally's funeral service, and then an encounter with an armed man. She prayed life would be less eventful in the ensuing months, for her constitution was no longer so robust. She feared that many more shocks of this sort might bring on a miscarriage. She now loved and wanted the baby and wished the infant to be born at full term and not prematurely.

Good grief! Alexander wasn't the only one who had changed. She wasn't going to abandon her baby to go and live on an unknown estate in Essex. Her life was here at Newcomb bringing up this child.

Dusk had fallen when he eventually joined her. He looked less grim than he had when he'd set out. She greeted him with a smile. 'You have spoken to Bill? It's a great shame

Jed didn't return before you all left for the funeral and I took my walk.'

'Indeed it is, sweetheart.' Wearily he dropped into the armchair opposite the daybed she was relaxing on. 'He was correct. We found evidence of others having been in the wood. The trail led to the back lane but there we lost it. I've spent the remainder of the day riding around the farms warning my tenants to be vigilant, and to ensure they've bolted the doors before they retire.'

'Couldn't Hill have done this for you?'

'Of course, but I wished to let my people know I have their safety at heart.'

'Will the militia be here tomorrow to search for them?'

'I've written a letter to Squire Rollins telling him what happened. I can do no more. I must insist you take no more solitary walks until these men have been apprehended.'

She bristled. 'You insist?' His shout of laughter sent her teacup flying and it smashed in the hearth. 'Now look what you made me do.'

'Don't ruffle your pretty feathers, my love; I'm certain one broken cup won't be noticed. I'll rephrase my sentence.' His wicked smile played havoc with her equilibrium. 'My dear, might I request you reconsider your daily promenades? I should be most distressed if you were shot by an itinerant veteran.'

'You're being ridiculous, sir. However, I'll bow to your position as head of the household and follow your instructions. In future I'll expect you to be downstairs at seven o'clock each morning to accompany me on my walk.'

'A hit direct, my love. I'll be delighted to come with you. I'm also certain the two outside men who must check the grounds before we go out will be equally thrilled you wish to walk so early.' He grinned. 'I'm relieved I don't have to thunder off to London today. My thigh is deucedly painful.'

'I'd quite forgotten about that. Indeed, you've been racing about without the slightest sign of a limp.'

He clutched his chest and fell back in his chair. 'I'm in need of your loving care, sweetheart. See — I'm swooning.'

'Don't be ridiculous, Alexander. You're perfectly well.' Her smile slipped — he did look a trifle pale. 'My dear, shall I fetch Bill to take care of you?'

'Absolutely not! I'm funning; my leg's sore but will be perfectly fine by tomorrow.'

There was little point in changing to dine so she spent a further delightful hour discussing the high price of corn, the woeful provision for ex-servicemen and whether it was now safe to tour the continent. When Bill came in to announce dinner was served she couldn't remember having spent such a relaxed afternoon with Alexander.

After dinner she smiled at him as he lounged at the table. 'Do you wish to remain on your own to drink port? I warn you I'll be retiring soon so won't be in the drawing room when you come through.' Isobel had been persuaded to drink a glass of champagne in honour of the passing of her abigail. The unaccustomed alcohol had quite gone to her head, making her feel skittish as a schoolgirl.

'I've had sufficient to drink, thank you, my dear. I've finished off the bottle — far more than I normally have.'

She snorted inelegantly. 'Your *normal* intake, if I remember rightly, would include three bottles of claret, port *and* a decanter of brandy. Heavens! I'd consider what you have imbibed this evening as a mere bagatelle.'

Not remaining to hear his reply, she almost skipped through the communicating door into the drawing room. She wasn't unduly surprised to hear his chair crash back and to see him right behind her.

'I've changed, sweetheart. I no longer drink to excess, nor do I gamble. I'm a reformed man.'

'I've come to a decision, Alexander. The

more I think about it the less I want Bentley to have anything to do with Newcomb. Neither can I in all conscience abandon this baby. You were quite right to point out children need both parents in order to prosper.'

His eyes widened, and he looked shocked. Didn't he want her to remain? Then he was beside her and before she could tell him to desist she was in his arms. She meant to push him away but her hands crept around his neck and buried themselves in his hair.

He drew back before matters progressed to their inevitable conclusion. 'Darling, we can't make love here. We must retire to your bedchamber.'

Her lips glowed from his kisses and every inch of her tingled from his touch. There was nothing she would like more than to experience the ecstasy they'd shared at the beginning of their marriage, but common sense returned. She wasn't certain such activities wouldn't be harmful to the baby.

'No, Alexander, we mustn't. I don't feel my pregnancy is secure enough to risk such vigorous activity, especially after the double shocks I've suffered today.'

At her words the hectic colour along his cheekbones faded and his eyes returned to their normal blue-grey. 'I've no wish to jeopardize the health of the child. I hadn't realized something so pleasurable could be harmful.' He smiled ruefully. 'It's just I find you irresistible. I'll have to find other outlets for my energy.'

She couldn't allow him to believe things were fully restored between them. She still wasn't quite sure. 'There's something else I wish to tell you. If this baby is a boy, then at the moment my role as your true wife will be ended. I'll live here in the east wing, but not depart from Newcomb entirely.'

'And if it's a girl?'

She couldn't look away. She was pinned like a butterfly on a board beneath his gaze. 'If a female then I'll remain as your wife until you have your heir.'

★ ★ ★

Alexander tried to school his features and not show his elation, for she might misinterpret his reaction and think it triumph not joy. He knelt down beside her and took her hands within his own. They were all but lost beneath his. 'Then, my darling, I'll pray every night it's a girl.'

'And I'll pray for the opposite. I might never be able to produce another child

— remember, we thought I was barren. I thought securing your title was everything to you?'

Gently he raised her fingers to his mouth and kissed each one in turn. 'No, Isobel, you're everything to me. I'll count myself a lucky man if we produce a dozen daughters if it means you remain as my loving wife.'

Giggling, she snatched back her hands. Good grief! She was a trifle bosky. Would she have committed herself if she had been entirely sober? He must pray she didn't recant in the morning. 'Come along, darling. I'll carry you to bed. It isn't *I* that have consumed too much alcohol tonight, but you.'

He left her in the capable hands of her new maid and returned to the drawing room to wait for the coffee. There were still aspects of today's events he wasn't happy with. It seemed odd these renegades should choose to burgle Newcomb in broad daylight.

The men had known the house would be empty. Jed would have mentioned the girl's funeral whilst he was in the village and told all and sundry his master was allowing the entire staff to attend. The vagabonds must have seen this as the perfect opportunity. If Othello hadn't found them, God knew what might have happened.

He stretched his legs on the daybed; Isobel's scent lingered on the upholstery and he sniffed appreciatively. She was almost convinced he'd become a man she could love again, but he wanted to do something else, something tangible, to prove his credentials as a loving and caring husband.

When he eventually retired he was sure he had the perfect solution. What he planned to do for her would not only surprise her; it would make her life at Newcomb more enjoyable.

★ ★ ★

Something woke Isobel. Had Alexander changed his mind and ignored her strictures to remain out of her bed? A familiar heat spread from her toes to her fingertips. Despite her protestations she knew she couldn't refuse him.

'I shouldn't be here, darling; I promise I haven't come to importune you. I've come to tell you what I plan to do next door.'

'Could it not wait until tomorrow? I can't think of anything worth waking me up in the middle of the night.'

By this time he was lighting candles and she'd no option but to listen to his proposal. Her irritation was mainly because she was disappointed he hadn't come to make love to her.

'There, my dear. Tomorrow I'm going to move the kitchen at Newcomb so in future you'll have your meals served to you hot.'

Whatever she'd expected him to say it hadn't been this. What an extraordinary conversation to be having at midnight. 'Move a kitchen? It can't be done. What about the chimney, the scullery and everything else? The kitchen was put there for a reason . . . '

'That was to make sure we had unpalatable and unpleasant food and all our staff ate better than us.'

His playfulness was infectious. 'So why don't we move into the servants' quarters and move them into Newcomb?'

'A sound idea, my love, but I've a better one. I still have the drawings the architect made and have been perusing them for hours. We've more rooms on the ground floor than any sensible family could ever use. I doubt I've been into half of them and I've lived here all my life.'

She yawned and was too late to disguise it. 'Tell me tomorrow, Alexander. Go away now and let me sleep.'

In answer he strolled across and sat on the edge of the bed. 'There's something else I wish to tell you, darling girl. I'm irrevocably in love with you. No, don't protest. I don't expect you to reciprocate my feelings, but I wanted you to know.' He leaned down, placing his hands on either side of her, and his kiss was sweet and loving. The ice around her heart finally melted.

17

'What kind of day is it today, Ellie? Do you think it will be hot?'

The girl flung back the shutters letting the sunlight into the bedchamber. 'It's a beautiful day, your grace. I reckon as his grace was right to delay your move back into the main building until them April showers had gone.'

'Have you seen the improvements, Ellie? I've not been allowed to peep. Do you know I've not felt so excited since I was a small child waiting for my name day?'

Her brow creased. Today was in fact her anniversary and she would be one and twenty. Alexander had never acknowledged her birthday. Indeed, she'd no notion when *his* birthday was, but he must be well into his thirties. What a ridiculous situation! How could she have been married to a man without actually knowing how old he was?

'I've not been in; no one has apart from the workers. That lot who came back from London know what's been done.' The girl carefully placed the tray on the bedside table. 'Shall I put out the pale green dimity, your grace? The one with the pretty daisies sewn around the neck and hem?'

Isobel stretched and the baby protested by punching and kicking as if desperate to get out. The eminent medical man who'd come down from town last month had assured her she was in perfect health and that her hips were wide enough to produce the infant she was carrying. Her delivery couldn't come soon enough. She felt like a brood mare about to drop a foal. Maintaining any sort of normal activity was becoming increasingly difficult. Alexander still insisted on accompanying her on her early-morning promenade even though the small band of renegades had long since been arrested, but even this gentle stroll must soon stop.

Only a few more weeks and she'd be holding her baby. What must take place in order to produce this miracle she didn't dwell upon. Mary had told her what to expect as she'd produced three stillborn infants in the early days of her marriage.

Alexander had been remarkably elusive, spending all his days either overseeing next door or on the estate. Regular reports were sent from Grosvenor Square by Bentley, who was almost betrothed to the pretty daughter of a minor aristocrat. The young man was to visit with the family when the season was over and wouldn't be returning to take up residence in the east wing until the renovations and repairs were completed.

She no longer bothered to wear a multitude of petticoats or stockings, she didn't go about in public, and Alexander scarcely seemed aware of her nowadays. No, that wasn't true. Every evening they dined in perfect harmony. He was witty and charming but treated her as if she was a sibling rather than his wife.

'I'll get dressed immediately, Ellie. I intend to demand to see next door.' She smiled at her maid. 'Tell Cook I'll eat nothing further until I'm established in Newcomb.'

She stood tapping her foot in her sitting room. Why was he tardy? Every morning he came to escort her downstairs as if she were a decrepit octogenarian, not a healthy young woman with nothing wrong with her. Pregnancy was making her unbalanced, as if she might tip forward from the weight in front of her.

Eventually the door opened. 'My love, forgive me. You must have wondered where I was. Come, shall we go down?' He drew her arm through his, his eyes tender. 'Being with child has made you even more beautiful, sweetheart; every day I thank God you came back to me.'

Isobel returned his smile. 'And every day I begin to believe I made the right decision.'

Downstairs the hall was empty, the usual footmen absent and no sound of the parlour maids. Good gracious! Even her dogs were missing. Where was everybody this morning? He led her straight outside, not pausing to ask if she wished to eat before her morning walk.

A thrill of excitement rippled through her. 'Alexander, are we finally going next door? Why have you chosen today?'

'Why do you think, darling?'

She pursed her lips and glanced up at him. 'It's May Day? The first day of summer?'

His free hand came round and cupped her face, turning it towards him. 'No, you pea-goose, it's your name day. I thought this the perfect time to surprise you.'

Her feet stuck to the ground and her eyes filled. 'I didn't think you knew. I can't tell you how much this means to me, Alexander. I'll never forget today.'

His eyes flashed and he dipped his head. His lips covered hers in a kiss so sweet she wished it could go on forever. He raised his head and smoothed away her tears. 'I love you, Isobel; I hope one day you'll be able to reciprocate. Now, I want to show you the changes I've made.'

He guided her around the corner of the building. A huge cheer from the assembled staff startled her. They were freshly garbed and waiting to greet her. To her astonishment Mary, magnificent in bombazine, stepped forward and curtsied formally.

'Welcome, your grace. I'm housekeeper here. Watkins at your service.'

Then Bill, resplendent in a black tail coat, was beside her bowing deeply. 'Welcome, your grace. I'm Brown, butler here, at your service. Allow me to present your staff.'

Isobel could scarcely believe her eyes. Alexander had appointed *her* staff to run his enormous establishment. 'Thank you; having my people in charge is the best birthday gift you could have given me.' She could hardly ask what he intended to do with Maynard and Foster, but as long as they weren't here she didn't care. They were both well past retirement age, so hopefully he'd pensioned them off.

'My love, you haven't had your birthday gift yet; I've more to show you. However, I'm delighted you approve. I want you to be happy here and I know you weren't, under the old regime.'

Bill, keeping a commendably straight face, introduced each of the footmen from senior to junior, and there were a prodigious amount of these. Mary did the same with the females. As each one heard their name they bowed or curtsied appropriately and she nodded regally. By the time she reached the front door she was biting her lips trying not to laugh.

He must have felt her vibrating because he raised his eyebrows in a comical manner which was almost her undoing. It would be unkind to laugh when the staff were taking the matter so seriously, but the whole business was risible. She was relieved to be escorted inside, leaving the servants to disperse.

She breathed deeply, trying to control her amusement. The sweet scent of hothouse flowers filled her nostrils. Everywhere she looked there were vases overflowing with beautiful blooms; this lessened the austerity of the vast, rectangular entrance hall, making it more welcoming.

Forgetting they had an interested audience of several dozen, she flung her arms around his neck and kissed him. The old Alexander would have pushed her away with a look of distaste on his face because she'd made a public display, but the new one laughed out loud and swung her around like a child.

'Darling girl, you haven't seen everything. I want this to be the happiest day of your life, I want you to remember the day you came of age as a turning point for both of us.' He gently set her down but kept his arm around her waist in case she was disorientated by his flamboyant gesture.

'I'll keep flowers in the hallway always; it makes such a difference. Perhaps you could commission some studies of the grounds to hang in place of the gloomy portraits.'

'I'll have you know, my girl, you're casting aspersions on my ancestors and the ancestors of our children.' He grinned and dropped a feather-light kiss on the end of her nose. 'But I agree, they shall be banished to the east wing for Bentley to appreciate.'

'I'm sharp set, Alexander. May I have my breakfast?' He looked quite dejected at her suggestion; he obviously had further surprises awaiting her attention. 'However, I'll wait until you've shown me everything, as long as you promise to sit down with me when we've finished.'

Like a boy, his expression lightened and he almost whisked her off her feet as he took her down an unfamiliar passageway. 'Where are you taking me this time?'

'To see the new kitchens and other offices on this floor. The downstairs rooms have been given over to the staff. There's a separate hall for the senior servants, a bathing room and an apartment for the butler.' He grinned. 'I've also refurbished a neat house in the grounds for Mr and Mrs Watkins.'

'How kind of you to think of them. They've always had to make do, apart from the year they spent in the cottage. I don't believe I've the energy to go down and inspect all that; show me the new kitchens today and I'll see the rest tomorrow.'

The rooms were ideal for the purpose, having access to the cobbled backyard where the barnyard creatures were kept. No expense had been spared — a massive closed range had replaced the open fireplace and would reduce the temperature and smoke.

She was surprised to find Mrs Boothroyd, her own cook, in charge. She prayed Alexander's faith in her inexperienced staff wouldn't be misplaced.

'I'm most impressed with the changes. In future I'll eagerly anticipate my meals instead of dreading them.' She gazed imploringly at him as her stomach gurgled loudly. 'Can I have my breakfast now, please, Alexander? I'll faint if I don't eat soon.'

'Not quite yet. You might have noticed they were getting it ready. I believe we've a quarter of an hour at our disposal.' His arm once more encircled her and she found herself back in the entrance hall. Without a by-your-leave he slid his second arm under her knees and carried her upstairs. Even he couldn't have lovemaking on his mind, not at eight o'clock in the morning and her the size of a heifer.

'I can walk from here, thank you, my dear. Have you redecorated my apartment again — is that why we're here?'

'Yes and no, my love. Contain your impatience for a few moments longer.'

His arm was once more around her and when she tried to turn into her apartment she was whisked past and he didn't stop until they were at the rear of the house. This part of Newcomb abutted the east wing. Why had he brought her here? As far as she could recall these were dreary and unwanted chambers, rooms used for accommodating governesses or companions.

'Here we are, sweetheart. This is your name day gift from me.' He flung open the door he stopped beside and stepped away.

Her mouth opened. Instead of an unloved guest chamber she saw a perfect lady's boudoir. Two rooms had been made into one, an arch the only indication there had once been anything else but this beautiful sitting room.

The furniture was exquisite; she recognized the pieces as Chippendale, but until this moment she'd only seen drawings of such items in *Ackerman's Repository*. The walls were freshly papered — she loved the pale green and gold stripes and the similarly patterned carpet.

'I love it. How did you achieve this without speaking to me? Green and gold are my favourite colours. I don't remember telling you that.' She was too overwhelmed to continue. Shaking her head in disbelief, she walked from item to item, running her hands along everything in delight.

Ellie appeared from the door that led into the bedroom. The girl was bouncing with excitement. 'Oh, your grace, you'll never guess what you have through here.'

Isobel wandered in a happy daze to see what other wonders he'd provided. The bedroom was as superb as the sitting room, the dressing room and closets everything they should be, but the room that had caused her abigail so much excitement was a genuine bathing room.

He was glowing with happiness. 'See, darling, if you stand here you may take a shower bath. The water escapes through the drain hole and goes down pipes attached to the outside wall. I think perhaps it might be wise not to use the bath until you're delivered.'

She viewed the enormous bath; this was long enough for him to stretch out. She would be obliged to swim if the water were filled to the brim. 'You're quite right, Alexander. Not only might I drown in there, but I'd be unable to get out without assistance.'

'I hope you'll give me permission to use this bathing room sometimes, sweetheart. I don't have one installed at my end of the house.'

Her eyes widened. It hadn't occurred to her she'd been moved on her own. He couldn't have made it plainer. He was giving her the freedom to choose. Her throat closed. She held out her hand and he took it. He was quite right: today was the start of a new life for both of them.

'There's just one more thing to show you, darling, and then we'll go downstairs and eat.'

What else could there be? Hadn't she got everything she could possibly want in this apartment? Keeping hold of her hand, he led her back into the corridor and across the passageway.

'I remembered what you said about your baby being taken away and brought up in the nursery by a regiment of nannies and nursemaids. It's what's customary but I intend to set a precedent. I hope you approve.' This time he opened the door and stepped in with her.

He had converted this suite of rooms into a nursery wing. Here there was everything a baby could possibly require. There was even a bathing room for the use of the nursery staff as well as the baby when he or she was old enough. The rooms were freshly plastered, each with a substantial grate, but there was no furniture or curtains.

'I thought you would like to choose for yourself how this will be decorated. The nanny's room, the nursemaids' room and the kitchen for making nursery teas are finished; the furniture and fittings are the same as everywhere else in the staff quarters. But the rest I'll leave to you.'

'Are you saying the baby can be down here? Can I choose who will have charge of the infant?'

He frowned. 'Didn't I just say exactly that?'

'You did, but a while ago you said it would be your prerogative to select the nursery staff.'

'Damn it, Isobel, must you keep throwing my idiocies back to me? I thought this was to be a new beginning — the past put behind us? How can we move on if you're constantly reminding me of my failings?'

Flustered by his irritation, she stepped back, treading on the hem of her skirt. She lost her balance and even his lightning reactions weren't quick enough to save her from a fall. The air was knocked from her lungs and she gasped for breath like a fish landed on the riverbank.

'My God, let me get you upright.' He snapped his fingers and Ellie appeared, her eyes round with horror. 'Downstairs. Go at once and have Watkins send for the physician.'

Slowly the band of pain around her chest eased, her breath rasped and then she was breathing normally. 'That was stupid of me. I've almost fallen several times doing the same thing.' Experimentally, she sat up. 'I believe with your assistance I can regain my feet. This tumble wasn't your fault, Alexander. I've been increasing long enough to remember I can't move with the alacrity I used to.'

'Here, slip your arm around my neck and I'll carry you. I think you should rest until the doctor can examine you. You fell heavily; it doesn't do to take chances, not at this stage.'

He carried her across the passage and into her splendid apartment. Her eyes prickled. She'd ruined everything by her clumsiness. She wouldn't argue; her back ached unpleasantly and she feared there was something seriously amiss. However, she'd no intention of worrying him until the physician arrived.

18

Doctor Jamieson stepped back, courteously turning away in order to allow Ellie to pull down the bedsheet. Isobel shuffled upright before attracting the venerable gentleman's attention. 'Doctor, is there any danger of my delivering prematurely?'

He smiled, his startlingly blue eyes twinkling. 'If you're asking me if the baby's going to arrive early because of your fall then the answer is a categorical no. However, I must warn you, your grace, that you won't go full term. I suggest you have everything in place for the middle of June, not the first week in July.'

This was good news indeed; the sooner she was delivered the happier she'd be. 'But the backache? I understood this could be a sign of labour.'

'That's sometimes the case, but not for you. The fall has put additional stress on your back muscles; you can feel that. If you rest here for the next week the pain will go.'

'A week? I'll go mad from inactivity. I like to walk every day and I've yet to see all the improvements made here.'

He shook his head. 'I must insist. No doubt you've noticed your baby isn't moving much at the moment. The accident will have put a strain on it. I'm sure you don't wish any harm to come to your child through your inattention?'

'Of course I don't. I'll do as you suggest. Must I remain in bed the whole week, or can I walk about in this part of the house?'

'Remain where you are for twenty-four hours. When I see you tomorrow I'll give my decision. If the baby's active again, and your back no longer painful, then walking around these rooms will be beneficial. Remember, your grace, absolutely no stairs until I give you leave.'

Her lips twitched. Perhaps now wasn't a good time to tell him Alexander carried her from floor to floor. 'Please could you ask my husband to come through on your way out, Doctor Jamieson?'

He bowed, collected his bag and moved briskly into her parlour. He would be interrogated so there would be no need to repeat what she'd been told.

* * *

The physician gave her permission to get dressed when he called the following day and

251

she did so forthwith. The infant was pummelling her stomach and from the strength of the kicks and punches she was convinced the baby would be a boy.

'Alexander, place your hand here. Did you feel that?'

'Good grief! You've a pugilist in there, my love. If I put my ear against your bump could I hear the heartbeat?'

The idea of having his face resting so close sent a frisson of excitement along her spine. How ridiculous! She was an unnatural woman thinking of making love when she was so vastly pregnant. 'The doctor listened through a cow horn. Why don't you try the same thing with a glass?'

Should she offer to pull back her skirts? Instead she pulled the muslin tight and laid back whilst he placed the open end of the glass against her belly. He was on his knees beside her, his jacket casually discarded and his cravat untied; when he spent time with her nowadays there was no tension between them. The momentary irritation which had caused her to step back unwarily was forgotten. After all, she couldn't expect him to be in perpetual perfect humour.

His hair was longer than previously and flopped endearingly over his collar. She barely resisted the urge to sink her fingers into it, the last thing either of them needed was excitement of *that* sort. A wave of bitter disappointment engulfed her. He'd told her he wouldn't be unfaithful, but he might not consider visiting a bawdy house as infidelity.

She pressed herself into the back of the chaise longue and attempted to quell her dismay. He'd given her his word he wouldn't renew his liaison with his mistress. She could hardly demand to know if he slaked his physical needs with a lady of the night. She no longer wished to touch him and wanted him to leave her in peace.

He sat back, a rueful grin making him dangerously attractive. 'All I got for my effort was a bruised cheek. Do you think this baby of ours is a boy?'

Something prompted her to say the opposite of what she intended. 'I sincerely hope so. I've no wish to be obliged to produce more children in order to protect your title.'

Her words were like a slap. He was back on his feet, his expression closed — a formidable man replacing the approachable friend. There was no point in apologising; the damage was done. She'd all but destroyed the fragile affection that had been growing.

'I'd thought your antipathy towards me was gone, Isobel. I can do no more. If you won't accept I've changed, and meet me halfway in order to make this marriage work, then it will be best for both of us if I no longer spend time with you.'

Helplessly she gazed at him, willing him to understand that sometimes she spoke without thought and didn't mean what she said. Pregnancy was making a veritable shrew of her. 'I enjoy your company. I'd be sad if you returned to Grosvenor Square.'

'I've no intention of returning to London. This barracks of a place is big enough for us to avoid contact. I must attend to estate business. Reynolds has been clamouring for an interview since yesterday.' He nodded and strode away. The bedchamber seemed empty without him.

Life confined to her apartment was going to be tedious without him. These past weeks she'd come to eagerly anticipate the evenings, but now her sharp tongue had driven him away. Her life would be so much simpler if she could learn to trust him again.

*   *   *

'What do you think, Mary? Is lemon yellow a suitable colour for the curtains and upholstery in the nursery?' Isobel viewed the samples spread out on the table in her sitting room. 'I must make a decision today, as it could be as little as four weeks before I'm delivered.'

'It's an unusual choice, your grace, but will suit either a boy or girl. I know you've selected two girls from here, but what about the nanny? Does his grace have someone in mind for that position?'

'No, he's leaving it to me. When he went to town last week he set enquiries in motion. There's always a family who can recommend someone suitable.' She heaved herself to her feet. Her mobility was sadly restricted lately as her girth had dramatically increased. Alexander had laughingly told her this morning if she didn't give birth soon she would pop. She hadn't found the comment particularly amusing.

Fortunately since her outburst a few weeks ago their relationship had drifted back to amicable. Unlike her, *he* didn't bear a grudge. 'Mary, do you think he has changed? That he's no longer the violent and arrogant gentleman who abused me?'

This was a highly unsuitable topic of conversation between a member of staff and herself, but Mary was first and foremost her friend. Even Alexander appeared to accept the closeness of their relationship and no longer stared down his nose when he came in and found them together. Mary was a far better housekeeper than ever Maynard had been, which would improve his opinion of her.

'At first I thought it an act in order to win you over, but as the months have passed I truly believe he loves you and has made himself a better person because of it.'

'I've always loved him deep in my heart but was too scared to admit it. I must find him at once and tell him. He'll be so happy.'

* * *

Alexander rubbed his eyes and yawned. He was finding it damned difficult to sleep. Having his chambers so far from hers meant he was constantly on the alert in case she needed him. He'd got up three times last night to check on her.

The list of possible candidates for the position of nanny wasn't over-long and the first two seemed possible. He would take the information to Isobel immediately. He had been told that most households had everything in place three months before the due date and did not leave it so late. A decision must be made today; Jamieson had told him the baby was readying itself for delivery.

He jumped to his feet as the familiar

footsteps of his beloved approached the study. This was no longer a place where she wasn't welcome, and she often joined him in the afternoon and sat reading with her feet up whilst he worked on his papers. He stepped into the spacious corridor to greet her.

She smiled at him, her face illuminated by such love his chest squeezed, making breathing impossible. He couldn't speak; his heart was full, and tears filled his eyes. He opened his arms and she fell into them.

'Alexander, I had to come right away. I've just discovered I still love you — indeed that I love you more today than I ever did.'

She was obliged to stand sideways as even *his* arms were not long enough to embrace her nowadays. 'My darling, you've made me the happiest of men. Come in. You know you shouldn't have come here but sent for me instead.'

'I'd no wish to wait another second to tell you.' Her eyes shone. He wanted to sweep her up and make love to her despite her advanced pregnancy. 'I've finally chosen the fabric for the nursery and sent Sam to the warehouse. Fortunately Mary has a team of seamstresses assembled and the covers for the furniture, the curtains and everything else will be completed by the end of the week.'

'I've a list of possible candidates to take

charge of the nursery. There are two that I think we should interview but I'll leave the decision to you.'

He knelt at her side and tenderly lifted her feet before fetching the various letters of recommendation. He watched her peruse the contents; he loved the way her nose crinkled when she was concentrating. He slid in behind her legs and dropped them back into his lap. As usual she was wearing no stockings and had kicked off her slippers as soon as she'd sat down.

Whilst she read he massaged her feet and ankles, worried they were more swollen than they had been yesterday. Jamieson had warned him swelling of this sort was a sign that she needed to do less. He would insist she stayed in bed until noon and then rest on her daybed.

'I like the sound of Nanny Cooper. Which one did you prefer?'

'She was top of my list; the woman from the Everton household was the second. Would you like me to write and offer the position to Nanny Cooper?'

'Please. It might be better to send it express. Mary thinks I should be resting more and leaving the organisation of the nursery to a nanny.'

'Exactly so. I'm going to insist, sweetheart,

that until the baby's born you spend most of the time with your feet up. Jamieson told me swollen ankles aren't a good sign.' He braced himself for the argument but she nodded.

'I'll do so on one condition, my love: that you move into my apartment with me.' Her eyes danced as she continued. 'I'm quite certain from the size of the bed you never intended I sleep alone.'

★ ★ ★

His shout of laughter sent the papers flying. 'Thank the good Lord for that. I've been prowling the corridors these past nights checking on you. If I'm at your side I'll have a decent night's sleep.'

'Then you'd better get your man to bring your belongings down. There are, I couldn't help but notice, my dear, two quite distinct dressing rooms and enough closet space for an army to place their garments.' He tickled her feet in a bid to avoid answering but she was having none of it. 'You always intended to be with me, didn't you?'

His mischievous smile answered her question. 'I hoped to one day, but I never dreamt you'd welcome me so soon.'

'We've been through so much these past months, but I truly believe I can finally move forward and look to the future with happiness. There's something I wished to ask you and now seems as good a time as any.' She needed to have his guidance on a matter she knew nothing about and couldn't in all conscience discuss with Mary. The only person she could talk to was her husband. Until today she hadn't believed the matter of any urgency.

His eyebrow quirked. 'Go on, sweetheart. What do you wish to know?'

'I haven't enjoyed being pregnant. It doesn't suit me as it does other women. If our baby is a boy . . . ' His eyes dimmed as if a candle had been blown out inside him. Surely he didn't believe she meant they were not to make love in future? 'My darling, don't look so conscious. It's because I wish to . . . to share myself with you as frequently as possible that I've broached this delicate subject.'

The relief on his face was comical. 'Are you asking me if I know of any ways to avoid a yearly pregnancy?'

'I am. There must be other couples who wish to be intimate but don't want an overcrowded nursery. How do *they* manage this situation?'

He frowned. 'I've no idea, darling girl, but I promise you I'll find out from someone who knows about these things. We've a few weeks before that particular problem presents itself.'

Satisfied with his answer, she settled back to doze, leaving him to return to his desk and write the necessary letter. His pen scratching across the paper and his frequent curses and muttering made her smile. He would always be irascible — this was part of his nature — but he would never mistreat her again.

Having him sleeping peacefully beside her every night improved her own slumbers. Even when they'd been first married he'd never remained all night. Ellie's shock when she came in that first morning still made them laugh. Indeed it had been more of an adjustment for Duncan and her abigail than it had been for them.

Alexander's valet was unused to sharing bedchamber duties, having worked alone these past years. For a day or two he feared Duncan might hand in his notice. As there were two distinct dressing rooms, and separate chambers where mending and such things were done, there was no need for the two servants to meet.

The only place there could have been difficulty was over the bathing room. Mary solved this by appointing a chambermaid whose sole duty was to keep it in pristine condition and to carry up the necessary hot water.

Alexander had been happily ensconced for a week when Nanny Cooper arrived to take up her position. Isobel liked her on sight; the woman could be no more than one and thirty and had a calm, practical air about her.

'Nanny, you'll find things are done differently at Newcomb. The nursery suite is opposite the rooms the duke and I occupy. It's my intention to feed the baby myself, but I expect it might be wise to have a wet nurse available as well.'

Instead of pursing her lips the woman smiled. 'Your baby will do better being nursed by you, your grace. My previous employer always did so.'

'I knew as soon as I saw your letter, Nanny, that we'd get on splendidly. The midwife's arriving tomorrow and I'll put her in your charge. If there's anything you require just speak to the housekeeper, Mrs Watkins, and it will be arranged.'

Nanny Cooper curtsied. 'Thank you, your grace. I'm sure I'll be content here. For all its size Newcomb is a happy house.'

When Alexander climbed in beside her that night she was eager to tell him how delighted she was with the new appointment. However no sooner had she settled into his arms than she felt a flood of liquid pour from her. Horrified she'd disgraced herself, she cried out in distress, but he hushed her with a kiss.

'That was not your bladder emptying, my love. It was your waters breaking. Let me help you out of bed and we can send for assistance.'

'Good heavens, how do you know such a thing?'

'You forget, sweetheart, I've been through this process twice before.' He found the tinderbox and lit several candles before returning to her side. 'Although I'll admit, my dear, that on neither occasion was I drenched when it happened.'

That light-hearted comment did much to dispel her fear, but there was no midwife in residence. It was four weeks to her due date and the baby was coming.

19

'Alexander, come back — you can't fetch Nanny Cooper like that.'

He glanced down at his nakedness and laughed. 'Very well. Where the devil's my bedrobe?'

She directed him to the heap of navy silk he'd tossed carelessly to one side when he'd joined her ten minutes ago. 'Hurry up; someone must ride for Jamieson and things must be prepared downstairs.' Isobel tried to control her panic but her voice wobbled.

In two strides he was back beside her. 'Darling, the baby won't arrive for several hours. There's no need to worry. Everything will be ready in time.'

'That's all very well for you; you're not sitting in a growing puddle feeling as though your insides are falling out.' With hindsight perhaps she should have mentioned the nagging backache she'd had all day.

His expression changed to one of alarm. 'Isobel, have you had contractions or pain before this?'

'Only a backache. No contractions at all.'

'Stay where you are. I'll rouse the house.

There won't be time to fetch a doctor. We must deliver the baby ourselves.'

She was about to protest when a band of pain gripped her stomach and took her breath away. A further gush of water added to her discomfort. She prayed Nanny and Mary had enough experience between them to deliver this baby. He was right — the infant was on his way.

Not wishing to sit in a soaked chair or to wear her ruined nightgown, she struggled to her feet and walked unsteadily to her closet. She needed something dry. As she was reaching up a second contraction almost floored her. Gasping, unable to keep back the moan of pain, she hung on to the edge of the shelves waiting for it to pass.

'Your grace, whatever are you doing? Here, let me get you into a clean night rail. Nanny's preparing what's necessary whilst the girls strip the bed.'

Thankfully, she leant back into Mary's arms. 'Even Alexander thought my travail would be long — how can the baby be almost here after only two contractions?'

The soiled nightgown was removed and a clean one dropped over her head. 'Sometimes it can be like this. You're one of the lucky ones, your grace.'

Alexander appeared in the doorway, his

hair standing on end where he'd raked his hands through. 'Isobel, I told you to stay put. Now isn't the time to be wandering about.'

'Go away, Alexander. This isn't the place for a man — you'll be called in due course.'

His grin was a trifle lopsided but he nodded. 'First, my love, I'll help you into bed, and then I'll wait next door.'

Halfway across the carpet she was convulsed again; having his arms around her was a comfort. Her eyes blurred with pain and her body was no longer under her control. The band of agony passed and she breathed again. Next moment he picked her up and carried her to the prepared bed.

'I can stay here with you, if it's easier.' The chorus of dissent made him step back, shaking his head apologetically. 'Very well, but I'm ready if you change your mind, my dear.'

★　★　★

Reluctantly he released his hold, but not before cupping her face and kissing her gently. He hated to see her suffering. He recalled the agony involved when his two daughters had been born. He prayed fervently Isobel wouldn't suffer as badly.

Watkins had ridden to fetch Jamieson but it

266

was unlikely the doctor would arrive in time. The baby was almost four weeks premature. Did this mean it would be sickly? Was this because of the fall she'd had last month?

He paced the room, wincing every time she cried out. This was happening too fast. It couldn't be safe for baby or mother when things were rushed like this. Where was the damned doctor? He stared at the tall-case clock. It had only been three quarters of an hour since he'd been ejected from the bedchamber. It seemed far longer.

An ear-splitting yell halted him and he rushed to the door. Nobody was going to keep him away from her, not when she was in such distress. He burst in and he was stunned by what he saw: a wriggling red-smeared object still attached to Isobel was resting on her stomach. Ignoring the shocked exclamations of the nanny and housekeeper, he surged forward.

'Alexander, you shouldn't be here, but I'm glad you are. See, we have a daughter. Isn't she beautiful?'

He took Isobel's sweaty hand and kissed the palm. 'Not as beautiful as her mother. How are you? I heard you scream. I thought things had gone wrong.'

'Your grace, it isn't seemly for you to be here. I must insist you leave and allow us to complete the delivery.'

'Please, my love, come back later when everything's clean and tidy.'

He was bundled from the room. As the door closed behind him he realized he hadn't looked at his daughter, and had been more concerned for Isobel than the baby. Would his omission have been noticed?

★   ★   ★

Isobel watched him leave with a heavy heart. He'd wanted a son and was obviously bitterly disappointed they'd a daughter, for he'd scarcely glanced at her, giving her no more attention than a newborn kitten.

'Lucinda Rose, that's your name, little one. I think you're a beautiful little girl but maybe I'm a trifle biased.'

'Shall I take Lady Lucinda and give her a nice bath, your grace?' Nanny Cooper beamed down at both of them. She could see how lovely the new arrival was even if her papa could not.

'Is she a good size, Nanny? She's almost four weeks early you know.' The baby was gently removed from her arms and wrapped in a warm towel. Mary was still hovering at the end of the bed, her work not quite done.

'Lady Lucinda's a perfect baby, no smaller than many at full term. I should think she'll weigh about six pounds.'

Isobel flopped on the pillows whilst Mary dealt with the arrival of the afterbirth. Thankfully this was less painful than producing Lucinda. 'I should dearly like a warm bath. Is that allowed so soon after giving birth?'

Mary smiled. 'You must do as you please, your grace. I should think a lovely soak would do you good. I'll arrange for water to be brought up, then the girls can tidy up in here.'

No one referred to the fact that Alexander had burst in or that he hadn't admired his new daughter. 'Nanny, when do I get to feed my daughter?'

'As soon as you're both clean and tidy I'll return with your baby, your grace.'

'Mary, I think I had better remove myself to the bathroom before Jamieson arrives. He's a mite old-fashioned and will probably expect me to remain in bed for three weeks. Apart from being a little sore and fatigued, I'm remarkably well. The experience wasn't half as bad as I'd expected.'

'That's because it was over in a flash. Next time you mightn't be so lucky.'

'I wonder why Lucinda arrived three and a

half weeks early when she isn't a particularly large baby.'

'You were so big because you carried extra water. With your next pregnancy everything might be different.'

This was the second time Mary had referred to another child. Although she must produce a son, at the moment the thought of another nine months of increasing filled her with horror. She was eager to get back to riding every morning. Until Alexander could assure her his attentions wouldn't result in a baby, she was going to make him remain in his old chambers.

They'd already agreed that during her lying-in they would sleep apart. One thing was certain; as soon as they were sharing a bed he'd want to make love. She'd no wish to carry another child for at least a year, but would be unable to refuse him.

Doctor Jamieson arrived when she was in her bed with Lucinda suckling contentedly. Alexander hadn't reappeared even though word had been sent that they were ready to be visited. Where was he? Why didn't he come?

'Your grace, I don't believe there's any need to examine either you or the baby. I can see you're both in excellent health. However, if you'll forgive me, it's better to be sure and

I'll just give you a cursory examination.'

After enduring the indignities of childbirth this was nothing. He declared she was a perfect mother and should be able to produce any amount of children without difficulty. She was getting tired of being told to reproduce. When he left, dawn had broken and the birds were singing as if to celebrate the new arrival.

Nanny had taken Lucinda, insisting a new mother must sleep. She'd promised to return when the baby needed her next feed. Still *he* didn't come. Isobel's joy was dimmed by his absence. Eventually she asked Ellie to discover where he was. It would be impossible to sleep until she knew.

Fifteen minutes trickled past before her abigail returned. 'Your grace, we've searched the house and can't discover him anywhere. Should we make enquiries in the stable yard?'

'No, Ellie, you get to your bed — no doubt everything will be clear tomorrow.'

Instead of falling into a satisfied slumber Isobel curled up and buried her face in the pillows, fighting back her tears. This should have been a wonderful time, a shared experience. Why had he abandoned them now?

★ ★ ★

271

Alexander stared at the closed door tempted to knock, to insist he be allowed in to hold his baby, but this would be unpopular. Men weren't wanted when babies were born. He must find something to occupy his time until his two darlings were ready to receive him.

Taking a candlestick, he wandered downstairs and into his study. It would be dawn soon. He'd open the shutters and the French doors and stretch out on the daybed and listen to the birds. When the sun came up he'd rouse Duncan, get himself shaved and return.

He should have found himself some clothes before he left. He couldn't be discovered downstairs in his bedrobe. All his garments were now installed in the closets at the rear of the house and he couldn't go back there for the moment. However, there were some items in the guest rooms he'd occupied in the east wing.

Exiting via the doors that led onto the terrace, he headed for the east side of the house. By the time he found a window to prise up, his feet were sore and he was more than a little irritated. All the rooms were under covers whilst the workmen improved the kitchens, installed bathing rooms, and repaired the roof.

Several times he trod on something sharp

and his cursing echoed through the empty building. He lit several candles before searching the closet and was delighted to discover all the necessary undergarments, a pair of decent breeches and a shirt. However, the only footwear was evening slippers which looked odd but were better than bare feet.

There was still an hour before full light; he'd catch up on his missed sleep. As he relaxed, his eyes misted. He was the luckiest man in England. Six months ago he'd been in despair; now he had a wife and daughter and a life to look forward to.

The sound of banging and hammering woke him. He jolted awake. Dammit to hell! He'd overslept — Isobel must wonder what had become of him. As he raced back through the house workmen scattered, buckets were dropped and ladders toppled over, but he ignored the chaos. Would his feeble explanation be enough to make up for his disastrous lack of attention to his new daughter and wife?

$\star$ $\star$ $\star$

'There you are, little one. I don't think you could take another mouthful even if you tried.' Isobel rested the baby on her shoulder and rubbed her back as Nanny Cooper had shown her. It would seem infants needed to bring up their wind before they could settle.

The tall clock in the sitting room struck for the third time since she'd awoken. The time was seven o'clock. Alexander had been absent for five hours. Had he ridden off to hide his disappointment at her failure to provide him with a son? For all his protestations that he'd prefer a dozen daughters, his absence demonstrated his disappointment.

'Let me take Lady Lucinda for you, your grace. Ellie has brought you a delicious breakfast. A nursing mother needs to keep up her strength if she's going to produce sufficient milk for her baby.'

Nanny made her feel like a complete ninny, but when it came to motherhood Isobel was remarkably ignorant. 'I'm sharp set. The tea and toast I had in the middle of the night seem a very long time ago.'

She was halfway through her repast when the sound of running feet alerted her to the imminent arrival of her missing spouse. 'Ellie, please fetch another tray. His grace will wish to eat with me.'

The chamber door almost flew off its hinges. Her mouth dropped open. Never in her life had she expected to see her immaculate husband appear so dishevelled. 'Alexander, where have you been? Why are you dressed like a scarecrow?'

He skidded to a halt beside her, looking round like a man demented. 'Sweetheart, I went next door to find something to wear and fell asleep. How can I apologise? Where's my daughter? I owe her an apology for not greeting her when she was born.'

Whatever explanation she'd expected, this had not been it. What he said was quite ridiculous and perfectly understandable. 'My love, you're forgiven. We searched the house last night but didn't think to look next door.' She smiled. 'I'd also quite forgotten your state of undress and that your garments were unavailable. Lucinda Rose is next door in the nursery; go and see her there.'

She expected him to refuse, to say he'd wait until Nanny brought her in again, but he didn't. He blew her a kiss and rushed from the room. She'd been worrying needlessly. Everything was explained away. She must learn to trust him, but this was difficult when his behaviour was so unpredictable.

She'd almost finished her breakfast when Ellie hurried in with a laden tray at exactly the same time Alexander returned with their daughter cradled in his arms. 'I couldn't put her down, my darling, so Nanny said I could bring her back to you.' He sniffed appreciatively. 'Is that food for me? You're an angel to think of me after I abandoned you last night.'

The baby was tenderly returned to the crib, which was to remain in the bedchamber for the moment. There was a second identical one in the nursery for when she was with Nanny.

'There, little Lucy, you're as beautiful as your mother and I already love you almost as much as I do her.'

'She is tiny but perfectly healthy, so the doctor told me. He also informed me I would have no difficulty producing a dozen children.'

He pulled up a chair and examined what was under the cloth. 'I think one baby alternate years for the rest of your productive life will be sufficient, my dear.' He then picked up his cutlery and set to with gusto, ignoring her dagger looks.

'Gracious! Do you realize by my reckoning that could mean, let me see, fifteen further children? I can promise you when we reach four or five you'll be banished to the far side of the house.'

Pausing between mouthfuls he grinned at her, his eyes sparkling with humour. 'It shan't come to that, sweetheart. Didn't I promise you I'd make enquiries before I return to your bed?'

She nodded. 'I can't resume *physical*

relations, as Jamieson put it, until Lucinda is six weeks at least. However, Nanny let slip that by nursing myself it could prevent a pregnancy. I think she was warning me against breastfeeding rather than encouraging me. Everyone appears to think we're desperate to produce another baby.'

'I'd be perfectly satisfied with just Lucinda Rose. By the by, I don't remember agreeing to that name.' He raised his eyebrows and she giggled.

'You may choose the names for boys, my love, but I'll select for girls.'

He nodded solemnly. 'In which case, my darling, our first son will be Horatio Peregrine Everard, and then the second, Peregrine Everard Horatio . . . '

Spluttering through her mirth, she finished his sentence for him. 'And the third no doubt will be Everard Peregrine Horatio.' Their laughter woke the baby and brought Nanny clucking into the room.

Isobel sent him away to write letters announcing the arrival of their daughter to Aunt Lucy, Uncle Ben and her parents. He also had instructions to send word to London so Bentley was aware he was still in line for the title for the next year or two at least.

20

Isobel was finding nursing exhausting; Lucinda refused to wait the expected four hours between feeds and was constantly at her breast. Not that she minded. Unlike her pregnancy, she loved every minute of being a mama. She was sitting with her feet up on the chaise longue four weeks after the baby's birth when Alexander strolled in, several letters in his hand.

'That daughter of yours is insatiable. Small wonder she's gaining weight and you're losing it.' He stroked the baby's downy head and kissed Isobel on the brow. Since her delivery he'd been less inclined to kiss her lips; in fact his eyes no longer darkened when he looked at her.

'I've almost done. Another few minutes and Nanny will collect her.' She nodded towards his hand. 'Is there something from my family? Can they come to the baptism in July?'

'Shall I read them to you?' He sprawled on the window seat. He looked relaxed, happy — so why didn't he kiss her anymore?

'Just tell me what they said; there's no need

to read the whole.'

His smile faded at her terseness but he made no comment. Being tired was making her snippy, but she shouldn't be uncivil to him. 'I'm sorry, Alexander, I shouldn't have snapped. It's not your fault I'm getting little sleep.'

'Then stop feeding Lucinda. The young woman you've employed as wet nurse looks perfectly wholesome. Let her take over.'

He didn't understand that the bond between a baby and mother was forged in the first weeks. However tired she was, she would persist for another week. 'Not yet, my love. Nanny says if I continue until she's six weeks old it will be good for both of us.'

'I'm heartily sick of hearing that woman's name a hundred times a day. Dammit, Isobel, can't you make these decisions yourself?'

Why did they end up cross with each other nowadays? *He* had no excuse; he was able to sleep undisturbed and to roam around the estate enjoying the beautiful weather whilst *she* was trapped upstairs on doctor's orders. How was she going to get fit with no exercise?

He tossed the letters aside and sat beside her. 'I shouldn't criticise the nanny; she's doing the job we employed her for. But, darling, I'm getting as little sleep as you. I can't rest without you at my side. When may I return?'

'As soon as I'm allowed to resume my normal life, which hopefully will be tomorrow. The doctor makes his weekly visit then. He said I've recovered quickly. But are you sure you wish to be woken up when Lucinda comes to be fed?'

He yawned and shook his head. 'Perhaps I should wait until you've stopped nursing. I'm going to see my lawyers next week. I'll be gone several days.'

This time there was no mistaking the desire in his eyes and she responded. His smile widened and ignoring the entrance of one of the nursery maids to collect the baby, he stretched out and placed his hands on either side of her face. Her insides somersaulted and she leaned forward to meet his embrace.

Lucinda, who had fallen asleep, woke and wailed her protest at being sandwiched between her parents. He sat back and picked up the baby, kissing her puckered face. 'Little madam, already wishing to be the centre of attention.'

Miraculously, the crying stopped and the baby snuggled into his shoulder. Isobel blinked back tears. He was such a good father, as confident as she in handling the infant. He gave her to the waiting nursemaid and returned to collect the letters, allowing Isobel time to rearrange her clothing. Of course he was competent; she kept forgetting he'd been a father before.

'Here, darling, read the contents. I've Reynolds coming to discuss estate business so I'll visit later this afternoon.'

Excellent news — her entire family was coming from Norfolk. The last time she'd seen her parents had been her wedding day, and she'd not seen her siblings since before she went to London. Her aunt and uncle were also coming, and her cousin Petunia was to bring her future husband. He sounded pleasant and not much older than Pet, with no title but a considerable fortune. He must be prodigiously handsome to have captured her cousin's heart.

She recalled her cousin saying she wouldn't marry until she'd had at least three seasons. The unfortunate young man must believe Petunia would never be his wife, as the engagement was now of more than a year and a half's duration.

Mary was due to make her morning visit to discuss the menus. If there was to be a house party next month plans would need to be made well in advance. The nursery upstairs must be opened to accommodate her four brothers and three sisters, who would be accompanying her parents.

'There will be a governess and tutor as well as the nanny and nursemaids, plus several other members of staff, Mary.'

'I'll prepare several guest suites as well as rooms for the junior staff. Don't worry, your grace, we could accommodate a hundred extra folk and still not be quite full.'

'I can't like this house. I've really tried, but it's far too large. I don't understand why anyone should choose to build such a monstrosity.'

'Lawks! The Duke of Rochester must have a grand establishment as his main seat, your grace. It goes with the title, never mind how uncomfortable for the family.'

'I shouldn't cavil; since the installation of the new kitchens the food's excellent. I don't know what's wrong with me, but since I was delivered I'm no longer a watering pot. Instead I've turned into a shrew.'

'What you need, your grace, if you'll forgive me for speaking out of turn, is to get outside and enjoy the sunshine. I know what the physician told you, but he doesn't know you. Shall I call Ellie to help you change into a promenade dress?'

'Yes, I shan't delay until tomorrow. Also, my dogs will be thinking I've abandoned them. I haven't seen them for weeks.'

The brisk walk she took with her pets frolicking around her ankles, Ellie at her side, restored her equanimity and blew away the cobwebs. On her return she met Alexander in the entrance hall.

'Isobel? I'm delighted you're down. I've the most amazing news — Reynolds is to be married.'

The estate manager was a relatively young man. Why was this news so astounding? Was he a misogynist, only just discovering women were to his taste? 'I'm pleased for him, but why are you so excited?'

He grinned ruefully. 'I've known this man since he was a boy. He grew up on the estate and followed his father into the position of factor. Like me he was married young, but his wife ran off with a soldier. He has been moping about unable to declare his love to a local girl. He had word yesterday that he's a widower.'

'How long is it since the first Mrs Reynolds ran away?'

'It must be more than ten years; I can scarcely remember the girl. The banns are to be read this week and the marriage to take place at the end of the month. He's asked me to stand up for him and I've agreed.'

'Lucinda is to be baptised then. I should

like the church flower-filled for our celebration; if it's done a day in advance Reynolds and his new wife can share them with us.'

His eyes dropped to her milk-engorged breasts. 'I think our baby must be crying for her lunch, my darling, so I shan't detain you longer.'

She ran lightly up the staircase, revelling in the fact she was free to go anywhere. She could feel the milk but hadn't known this was apparent to anyone else. She glanced down at her bosom. Good gracious! She was leaking and her lovely muslin gown had two damp patches.

Much as she loved feeding her child, she could hardly appear in public as she was. If she was obliged to remain in her apartments until the baby was weaned she would be fit for Bedlam. Today would be the last day. She would ask Jamieson what to do to discourage milk from flowing so copiously.

Over dinner Alexander told her he was going to London the next day to see his lawyers. 'I suppose Bentley will wish to come back with you. He must be delighted our baby is a girl.'

'Exactly so; I'll discourage him from returning until his accommodation is complete. Sam Watkins is proving extremely useful; he's been overseeing the improvements and is making a splendid job of it.'

'I no longer need a man of business and was wondering how to best employ him.'

'I've already spoken to him and offered him the position of under-estate manager. Reynolds can now visit all my other properties knowing there's someone capable taking care of things in his absence.'

'I can't believe how happy I am, my love. Have you noticed how staff are smiling too?'

He reached out and stroked her hand. 'Happiness is infectious, darling, but Maynard and Foster's absence has a lot to do with the good humour of the staff.'

Despite being held captive in her apartments during the day, she always came down to dinner. They'd taken to sitting on the terrace after their meal. He joined her on the padded bench and slipped his arm around her shoulders, encouraging her to lean against him.

'I shan't be away more than a few days. I can send for my lawyers to attend me here if you'd prefer I didn't go.'

She hadn't told him of her decision to stop feeding and decided to surprise him when he returned. Whatever the physician told her, she was eager to welcome him back in her bed. 'Alexander, have you written to your friend to ask how he and his wife avoid yearly pregnancies?'

'No, I'll do so whilst in town.' His smile sent waves of desire racing around her body.

'Then I'm happy for you to go. Remember, I'm used to being here on my own and things are very different now.'

They parted outside his bedchamber. As usual he kissed her lightly on the lips and bid her good night. She was disappointed he hadn't shown more passion. She was worrying about nothing — the smile he'd given her earlier was sign enough he still desired her.

★ ★ ★

Sultan, the gelding she'd purchased whilst living in Norfolk, might well have forgotten her by now. Although she'd visited him in the stables she hadn't ridden since they'd returned to Newcomb. Leaving Lucinda entirely in the care of Nanny was going to be difficult, but if she was to stop nursing, this was the only way.

Dressed in a smart royal-blue habit, she hurried to the stables. Both dogs were as keen as she to go out. Her mount was saddled and waiting. The groom holding his head was Jethro, who'd come back with the staff from

Grosvenor Square.

'I don't wish to go too far this morning, Jethro. It's been many months since I've ridden.'

'A brisk canter around the park will suit Sultan, your grace. He's not as fit as he could be. He's been a mite crabby with the stable lads.'

She rammed her foot into the single stirrup iron and gathered the reins. The gelding's muscles bunching beneath her, his neck arched and he mouthed the bit impatiently. Perhaps she ought to ride the grey mare instead. Before she could decide, Ebony saw a stable cat and chased it across the yard, scattering the fowl pecking for stray morsels of corn. Sultan reared, snatched the bit between his teeth and took off at a gallop. It took all her skill to remain in the saddle. There was no way she could stop such a powerful animal. She must sit tight and pray he exhausted himself before they came to grief.

★ ★ ★

The business with his lawyers was completed within a morning and left Alexander ample time to visit Lady Fulbright. She was of childbearing age and yet didn't get pregnant.

287

Therefore, unless she was barren, she must have a method of avoiding unwanted conception.

He sent a footman to her townhouse in Albemarle Street, asking if he might visit her as he had a favour to ask. He hoped she'd forgiven him for his rebuff all those months ago. Whilst he waited for her reply he gathered up the morning's mail and took it into the study to read.

Of Bentley there was no sign; according to Foster the young man had been out until the small hours at some social function or other and wouldn't rise until midday. He detected a stiffness in his ancient butler. There was generally an unwelcome atmosphere amongst the staff. They were not any less attentive, but no one met his eyes or smiled when he approached as they once did.

No doubt this was because they'd been obliged to remain in London looking after Bentley. The groom who delivered the post every day would have taken back the information that Brown was butler at Newcomb and Watkins was the housekeeper. He must reassure them they weren't to be turned off. This was one reason he'd seen his legal people. His elderly retainers could retire with a good annuity and live in comfort for their remaining days.

He flicked through the pile of invitations, pleased he was back in favour with hostesses who had dropped him. Perhaps he'd attend one or two events; he'd like people to know he was a father again and that he and Isobel were happy.

The reply from Gloria arrived later that afternoon. She suggested they meet at Vauxhall Gardens as there was to be a firework display to mark some anniversary or other. It would probably be wise to meet in public and not visit her house, as this might be misconstrued. He wrote a quick reply agreeing to meet her at nine o'clock.

Bentley drifted into the drawing room as he was preparing to leave. 'Your grace, I beg your pardon for not having written to you to congratulate you on the birth of Lady Lucinda. I hope that both mother and baby are doing well?'

'They are, thank you, Bentley. I hope you'll come down for the baptism. Your accommodation will be finished and you can spend the summer with us.'

The young man nodded and smoothed his blue-and-gold striped waistcoat lovingly. 'I'd intended to return with you, your grace, but will now postpone my visit until the house party. I see you're about to depart. Are you going to Lady Simmons's soirée?'

'No, I'm meeting friends at Vauxhall Gardens. There's to be a firework display that shouldn't be missed.'

'I might well see you there; if not then we'll meet tomorrow. I bid you good evening, your grace.'

Alexander left the house seething. God's teeth, one would think *he* was the hanger-on and Bentley the duke. It hadn't been such a good idea to leave the young man in sole residence in Grosvenor Square. He'd got ideas above his station. Tomorrow he'd put the young man straight, but tonight he must speak to Gloria. The thought of being able to make love to his darling girl without fear of a second pregnancy was reason enough to renew his acquaintance with his former mistress.

21

Alexander sent a letter saying he was delayed and wouldn't be returning until the following week. Isobel was disappointed as she was almost free from unwanted milk. If she avoided Lucinda's feed times she could safely spend several hours with her baby daughter.

'Ellie, can you start altering my gowns? Now I've regained my original form I don't need them so full in the chest.'

Her maid looked up from her task. 'I thought you might like to leave them as they are, your grace. You've a closet full of beautiful gowns.'

'You're quite correct. Why don't you put the ones I wore during my pregnancy at the back of my closet?' Everyone thought she'd be increasing again by the end of the year. Her pulse raced just thinking about the possibility. An image of Alexander naked in her bed sent a wave of heat from head to toe. Ellie was looking, her eyes wide with concern.

'Are you feeling unwell, your grace? Have you got a fever?'

Isobel forced her thoughts away from bed sport. 'I feel a little overheated. I'll take a walk in the garden to cool down.'

She enjoyed her stroll and was ready to continue with perusing more lists with Mary. A footman held out a silver salver with a letter.

She paused in the window to read it. The missive was brief but said everything it should.

My darling wife,
I am desolated I have further business to attend to before I can be with you. I am returning next week. I have the information we both wanted. I can't wait to try out the efficacy of this with you.
Your devoted husband

In the post script he'd scribbled the names and number of some extra guests. The staff must know the names so she'd better speak to Mary immediately.

The next week dragged. She rode for an hour or two every morning, spent time with Lucinda, and oversaw the arrangements for the house party, but still his arrival seemed no nearer. A second missive arrived unexpectedly from her aunt and uncle. It appeared they'd be in the vicinity a week earlier than planned and would now be arriving the day before her husband.

She sighed. She longed to see her relatives and couldn't ask them to languish in a hostelry whilst she and Alexander . . . she could hardly bear to think of what they might be doing. It sent her dizzy with excitement. Newcomb was vast; surely they could be private somewhere?

The house was looking as welcoming as it could. She'd filled the chambers with flowers and the furniture and glass sparkled. The extra indoor staff necessary for a grand house party were coming from Grosvenor Square. She wondered how they'd adjust to the new regime. Bill (she could still not think of him as Brown) limped towards her. She scarcely noticed his infirmity nowadays. She was confident everything would run smoothly.

'Your grace, Mrs Watkins and I've trained three footmen and three maids to act as valets or abigails for guests without servants. I hope this will be satisfactory.'

'Yes, of course. I believe I can see a carriage on the drive. Did Sir John and Lady Illingworth's luggage cart arrive earlier this morning?'

'It did, your grace, and the trunks are unpacked and their apartments ready.' He hesitated. 'I've put all single gentlemen on one side of the house and the young ladies on the other.'

Her lips twitched. Good grief! Did he believe this was the kind of house party where gentlemen prowled the corridors looking for their lovers?

Smiling to herself, she returned to the drawing room. She was wearing a new leaf-green muslin, perfect for a hot summer's day.

Eventually Bill stepped in to announce her aunt and uncle, Cousin Petunia, Cousin James and a stranger. This young gentleman was obviously Petunia's intended.

'My dear girl, you look wonderful. One wouldn't know that you're now the proud mother of an infant daughter.' Aunt Lucy embraced her fondly. 'Is Rochester not here?'

'No, he'll be here tomorrow. He's been delayed in London.' She hugged her uncle, kissed Petunia and nodded to the gentlemen. 'I'm so pleased you've come earlier. It's been an age since we saw each other. I must show you the improvements Alexander has made for me after you've settled in.'

There was no time for a private conversation with Petunia until late afternoon. Lucinda was much admired and the newfangled bathroom declared a wonder. Eventually the young gentlemen retired to the billiard room and her aunt and uncle to their apartment for an afternoon rest.

Petunia was obviously bursting with a delicious piece of gossip that couldn't be shared in public. 'Pet, shall we take a stroll around the garden? It's far cooler under the trees than in here.'

'I should like that above anything. I've something most particular to tell you.' When they were alone her cousin turned to her. 'Isobel, I must tell you, I've heard the most malicious rumour. Fortunately it hasn't reached the ears of my parents, but it's been talked about everywhere. I can't allow you to remain in ignorance of what your guests will assuredly know.'

Isobel's heart sunk to her slippers. 'What is it? It is to do with Alexander, isn't it?'

'Oh, my dear, the duke was seen in Vauxhall Gardens in a private booth with Lady Fulbright.'

'My husband doesn't need my approval to visit his friends. If that's all, then I can't see why anyone should be interested. Don't *all* gentlemen have a *chère amie* in town?' She was amazed her voice sounded unperturbed when inside she was falling apart.

'I haven't told you the rest of it. He was seen leaving Lady Fulbright's house in Albemarle Street the next morning. I'm so sorry to be the one to tell you that this.'

'What Alexander does in London is no

concern of mine and certainly no business of yours, Petunia. I can't think why you'd believe telling me was beneficial to either of us.'

Her cousin shook her head in dismay. 'I'm sorry; I shouldn't have mentioned it. Please forgive me. You're quite correct. I can't think why anyone should consider such a thing worth gossiping about.'

'Do you see the marquee they are erecting for the garden party? Reynolds tells me there will be several hundred villagers and tenants attending. We are to have fire-eaters, stilt-walkers and conjurors to entertain.' She rattled on about the ale that had been ordered and the food that was to be prepared until she was certain her cousin was convinced the news was of no interest.

'I can see your young man approaching. I'll leave you to continue your walk with him. We dine at seven as Alexander doesn't keep country hours.' Somehow she made her way back to her apartment without betraying her dismay. Once safe from prying eyes she gave way to tears. Eventually her head cleared and she came to a decision.

When he came back she'd make it clear she knew that he'd broken his promise and everything had changed. George must remove his belongings and set him up again in the master suite. He was no longer welcome. Leaving him wasn't an option she considered. She would remain at his side and fulfil her duties as his duchess but there would be no more children. Bentley could remain his next in line.

On impulse she decided to hold a celebration ball and invite all the prestigious families of the neighbourhood. She would establish herself in the area; after all, she'd been married for more than two years and had yet to hold a grand event. Although she didn't have his permission, the ball would go ahead whatever his views on the matter.

★ ★ ★

At her morning meeting with Mary she broached the subject. 'We're already having a garden party and I wish to hold a ball on the following evening. This gives you two weeks' notice. Will that be sufficient?'

'Yes, indeed, your grace. It's high time you established yourself as the Duchess of Rochester. I've a list of the suitable families.'

Her unhappiness lifted a little. Perhaps if she made new friends and was no longer so isolated, living here would be bearable. She sincerely hoped *he* would return to London, or remove himself to some other part of the country.

Her stomach revolted. Her hand flew to her mouth and she swallowed furiously. How could she deny him access to her bed when it had been agreed they must produce an heir? She closed her eyes. Being estranged from Alexander was going to be harder this time because her love had blossomed. To lose him a second time was more than she could bear. Should she pretend she didn't know?

She was tempted to discuss her heartbreak with Mary, but this was too personal to share even with her. 'How many local guests will there be, Mary?'

'Well, your grace, I can't say exactly without referring to the list, but around fifty or more. Pray excuse me; I'll fetch it directly. Do you wish me to begin planning before the cards are sent?'

'Do that, Mary. We have more than thirty staying here. I'm quite sure they'll appreciate a dance even if no one else accepts my invitation. Do you know, I've been in the ballroom only three times?'

'I'll have it cleaned immediately. There's ample time to send to the warehouses for provisions. Bill will speak to you about the champagne and wine; he'll know exactly what's in the cellar.'

By the end of the day cards had gone to fifteen families within an hour's drive of Newcomb. If everyone attended there would be in excess of thirty couples — more than enough to make the enormous room full.

Having the dance to look forward to, as well as the other two events, alleviated her misery somewhat. However, she wasn't looking forward to Alexander's reaction when he discovered there was to be a ball and every guest would know he'd been visiting his mistress.

She shuddered as her mind went back to the night of Lucinda's conception. Would his reaction be the same? No; although he'd broken his promise to remain faithful, she believed he was a different person now. He no longer drank to excess, and didn't gamble or associate with ne'er-do-wells.

He wouldn't mistreat her however angry he was. No doubt he considered his behaviour acceptable. The difference in this case was that somehow it had become gossip amongst the *ton*. If he hadn't given her his word, the knowledge wouldn't hurt as much.

Despite her unhappiness her lips twitched. She recalled families with whom she'd mixed in her younger days. Some of them had three or four children, others too many to remember all their names. Goodness! The very thought of her own parents still indulging in bedroom sport was shocking. Her youngest sibling had been in leading strings when she'd left home, so her parents had a loving relationship.

Did a lack of children in the other families mean the couples didn't share a bed? Had she been too hasty in her condemnation? No, his letter had intimated he'd discovered a way of preventing conception; therefore he'd no excuse for indulging himself with his mistress.

Her door burst open and Petunia ran in. 'Is it true, Isobel, that you're to hold a ball?'

'Indeed we are. I decided on a whim that Lucinda's baptism should be celebrated by my neighbours as well. I hope you've something suitable to wear?'

'I have. Mama insisted I bring a formal gown. I'm glad you're not too dispirited about the news.'

'Pet, this is the way things are. Alexander and I are very happy together. He knows I've no wish to be increasing every year. I'm sure he believes he's doing me a favour by finding an outlet for his passion.'

Her friend turned an unbecoming scarlet. Isobel's sudden laughter did nothing to improve the situation. 'I apologise for mentioning something so indelicate, but you'll be married soon and would do well to understand these matters.' She offered her arm. 'Let's continue our stroll and talk of other things.'

★　★　★

'Duncan, I've just received a missive from Newcomb informing me we're having a ball. Does that mean that I must become involved? I'm glad I invited some friends to come down; it's far too long since Newcomb held a big event.'

His valet smiled. 'I should leave such matters to her grace. I'm sure she has everything in hand. A few extra guests will barely be noticed.'

'I must inform Bentley. He'll need to purchase something more suitable than the dandified costume he prances about in.'

'A wise notion, your grace. It wouldn't do to startle your guests.'

'Mind you, the thought of him appearing in his high-heels and hideous waistcoat is entertaining.'

Why had Isobel decided to invite the entire neighbourhood to Newcomb without consulting him? Was this his punishment for delaying so long? Grinning, he reviewed the business that had kept him at Grosvenor Square. Leasing a luxury yacht hadn't been straightforward and he'd been obliged to interview the captain and the purser before the deal was done.

Isobel and his infant daughter were to accompany him on a cruise after the celebrations. He'd also pensioned off the old retainers, and the remainder were on their way to Newcomb to help with the preparations.

His meeting with Gloria had been informative. He had in his possession a letter explaining how to use vinegar and a sponge in the most efficacious way. His parting with his former mistress had been amicable. She'd found herself another benefactor, someone less demanding and almost as rich as himself.

His lawyers wanted him to return to sign the papers. Once the dratted house party and ball were over he'd slip away for a day whilst Newcomb was put under holland covers and the staff given leave of absence. The custom was to put servants on half-pay when the family was absent, but as he was feeling benevolent, he'd not do so. He was happy and he wished to share his joy with all those within his domain.

This summer was a fresh start. He was a loving husband and father again. He blinked; he didn't deserve to be happy after the way he'd behaved. Isobel had forgiven him and he'd never let her down.

Alexander's garments were gone and the preparations for the garden party and the summer ball all but complete. There was nothing more to be done. His carriage was approaching at a spanking trot. She was dreading this meeting; had veered from rage to almost understanding his reasons for betraying her. Her relatives appeared to have accepted her explanation and saw no reason for disquiet.

She hurried through the house and into his study. Bill would make sure his master knew where to find her. They wouldn't be disturbed in here. Whatever took place between them would remain private. Twenty minutes later footsteps approached and the door was thrown open.

He stood there, eyes blazing, and she quailed. He'd been upstairs, seen the changes, and had come to demand an explanation.

22

'Sweetheart, what's wrong? Why are you looking at me like that?'

Isobel had mistaken his expression. He looked bewildered, his eyes wide with hurt. Suddenly his infidelity no longer mattered. He loved her and she loved him — that was enough for her.

'Alexander, it's nothing . . . I thought . . . they said . . . it doesn't matter. I love you.' She flung herself at him, wanting his arms around her.

'You're making no sense. Has someone upset you? Tell me, darling. We mustn't have secrets.' She pressed her face into his jacket, shaking her head and refusing to look at him. 'Isobel, you're worrying me. I intend to know even if we remain in here all day.'

Her words were somewhat muffled in his shirt. 'It's nothing. I've missed you and my aunt and uncle and cousins are here.'

He stiffened. 'Come, we'll sit calmly whilst you tell me what's so discomforted you.'

There was only one thing she could think of that would stop his interrogation. She slid her hands up his chest until they were buried in the hair at the base of his neck, then relaxed and tilted her face expectantly.

'Baggage! You shan't distract me so easily.' He dropped a swift, hard kiss on her parted lips and then swung her into the air to stride across the room and drop her none too gently on the sofa. 'Now, young lady, tell me everything.' He gathered her hands into his own. His strength reassured her. This wasn't the drunken, callous man she'd run away from, but her own dear Alexander, the father of her child.

With lowered eyes she told him. He didn't answer and she risked a glance upwards. He was smiling slightly. 'I don't know whether to be offended you didn't trust me or delighted you forgave me.'

'You've come back to me. You love me and our daughter and that's all that matters.'

Leaning forward, he stared earnestly into her eyes. 'I did meet Lady Fulbright and go to her house. It's *she* that has supplied the information we require.'

'My goodness! That's not an explanation that readily came to mind. I thought you'd ask a friend.'

He chuckled. 'Would you have preferred I discuss our personal business with someone you might meet socially?'

'No, and I wish people wouldn't jump to

conclusions and be so ready to pass them on.'

'That puzzles me also. I was most discreet, and I don't think my visit would arouse the slightest interest in most drawing rooms. I wonder how your cousin came to hear of it.'

'I'll ask her, and make sure she knows the information was erroneous.' She fluttered her eyelids, hoping she looked irresistible. 'I've something else to tell you. You've another opportunity to decide whether you're offended or if you'll forgive *me*.'

'Mmmm . . . let me see if I can guess. Could it be that in your high dudgeon you've banished me to the master suite?'

A bubble of laughter rose inside her. He was irresistible when he was teasing her. 'And, sir, let me remind you, there are locks on the inside of all my doors.'

His eyes darkened and he trapped her face between his hands. 'It would take more than a few keys to keep me out of your bed tonight, my darling.'

She swayed closer and his mouth hovered tantalisingly. Why didn't he kiss her? Then she was crushed against him. His lips burned hers and she was lost to the world, to sense and decorum. She no longer cared if she conceived. She wanted to make love with him.

With a groan he pushed her away. 'Darling,

not here. When we make love I want it to be without fear of interruption or embarrassment. I'm as eager as you, but one of us must be strong.'

'Shall we go and see our daughter? She's adjusted well to being fed by the nurse and is thriving. You won't believe how much she's changed whilst you've been gone.'

Hand in hand they strolled through the house. 'Isobel, I intended to suggest I move from your apartment whilst our guests are here. Such unusual sleeping arrangements would have given rise to further gossip.'

She giggled. 'But at least everyone would know the rumours are untrue. The butler has put all the single gentlemen as far away as possible from the young ladies. I wonder if you'll meet any of them when you're creeping down the corridor tonight.'

Petunia was suitably contrite over her misinformation. To explain the true circumstances wasn't possible; such revelations would be unsuitable, as her cousin was unmarried.

'When do your parents arrive, Isobel?'

'Tomorrow, as do four other families Alexander invited. Finally I'm to meet his oldest friends. After this house party I doubt I'll be lonely or lack company again.'

'From the way the duke follows you with

his eyes I doubt you'll need anyone else.'

She blushed. 'We've resolved all our differences. I didn't know such happiness existed. Nothing can come between us now.'

Petunia observed Bentley's arrival. 'Isobel, one of the duke's carriages is here and the most extraordinary young gentleman has stepped out.'

'I'd hoped Bentley might have adopted a more conventional mode of dressing for this visit.'

Her cousin stepped away from the window in case she was seen. 'I've seen one or two gentlemen dressed as he is, but have never been introduced.'

'I have to warn you, Pet, he's as silly as he looks. We pray we eventually produce a boy; I shudder to think what harm he'd do to the Rochester estates if he took control.'

Petunia pulled a face. 'Don't say such things. Your husband's a young man. To talk of his demise is depressing, and today of all days.'

Alexander dashed into the room and laughed. 'He's here; I thought I'd seek your company. I must speak to him, but I can't bear to do so alone.'

Bill solemnly announced their visitor. The butler's lips were trembling. Bentley bowed extravagantly and Isobel was sure she heard the creak of corsets. She studied him closely. The young man had gained weight; in fact he was decidedly stout.

'Your grace, I'm delighted to be here to celebrate the arrival of Lady Lucinda. Might I enquire if my accommodation's ready for occupation?'

'Unfortunately the workmen have been involved with other things these past few days, which has delayed matters. However, you'll be installed next door within a week.' Alexander didn't bow, merely nodded. Isobel followed his lead and did the same; however, Petunia curtsied.

'Allow me to introduce Miss Petunia Illingworth, my cousin. Miss Illingworth, might I introduce you to Mr Richard Bentley, a distant cousin.'

A deal of simpering and banalities followed, as if her cousin found Bentley amusing. Alexander took her hand and they tiptoed out, leaving them together.

'I can't understand why Petunia should wish to make his acquaintance; perhaps she's taken pity on him.'

'I think it more likely, my darling, that she's allowing us to escape. Your parents arrive this afternoon. It will be a pleasure to have Newcomb filled with children's laughter. I'm anticipating the garden party tomorrow. The weather's set fair; it should be a memorable occasion.'

She shook her head in mock severity. 'Aren't you forgetting something, my love? Tomorrow morning our daughter will be baptised. I rather think *that's* the event you should be looking forward to.'

In answer he swept her up in his arms and twirled her around, causing two footmen carrying a trunk to stumble. 'Put me down, Alexander.'

He let her slide down his body, holding her still when her breasts were touching his waistcoat. A wave of heat enveloped her; she forgot where she was and tilted her face.

Someone cleared their throat and her cheeks coloured, this time from embarrassment not passion. 'Alexander, this is disgraceful. You must behave yourself whilst we have visitors.'

'I daren't let you go,' he whispered. 'My desire's all too evident.'

She had no idea who was waiting to speak to them. If it was Aunt Lucy or Uncle Ben she'd never be able to look them in the face again without discomfort.

'Turn me round; if I remain in front of you and you keep your arms in place I believe we shan't cause an upset.'

He did as she suggested. She found herself face to face not with her uncle or aunt, but with her parents. Alexander recovered his composure first.

'Welcome, my lord, my lady. You must forgive us; I've been in town and, as you observed, we're delighted to be reunited.'

Her father frowned; he was obviously not impressed. For a second she was worried about offending him, and then remembered *she* was a duchess, this was *her* home, and here she could do as she pleased.

'Papa, Mama, we didn't expect you until later. Are the children not with you?' If they thought it a breach of etiquette for her to remain within her husband's embrace they would be even more scandalized if she moved away.

'Nanny's following in the old coach; we travelled in our new carriage, which is why we're here early.'

They couldn't remain as they were for much longer. She must greet her parents. Alexander gently pushed her forward. Thank God; the situation was becoming ridiculous. Isobel curtsied. 'You must come and see your grandchild. She's the most beautiful baby in England.'

Alexander spoke from behind her. 'I've estate business to attend to so I'll leave you with my wife. I look forward to renewing our acquaintance at dinner.'

She glanced over her shoulder and he winked. He was still holding his coat-tails across his front. Stifling a giggle, she turned to escort her parents to the nursery, where Lucinda was much admired. She then led them to their apartments and left them exclaiming happily over the luxurious appointments, the basket of fruit and the spectacular arrangements of flowers in their private sitting room.

Not long after she'd returned to her own chamber, her cousin came in to speak to her. 'It's as I thought, Isobel. Bentley spread the rumour about you and your husband. As soon as I saw him I knew he was the gentleman who'd been described to me.'

'So that's why you were talking to him. We wondered at your sudden interest in such a nincompoop.'

'You know why he spread the rumour, don't you?'

'It could only have been because he wished us to become estranged and not produce another child and disinherit him.' She could hardly credit the silly young man could be so devious.

'Do you know, Isobel, I had the distinct feeling Bentley was ashamed of what he'd done. He might be a popinjay, but I can't believe he's malicious. I think it might be the company he's keeping. That vile creature, Farnham, is one of his cronies.'

'Good grief! I must tell Alexander. Bentley must be removed from the influence of that man. Pray excuse me, Pet. This information cannot wait.'

She discovered her husband in his study, his feet on the desk and a tray with coffee beside him. He was reading the paper and quite obviously hiding. He jumped to his feet.

'Alexander, I know how the rumours spread.'

'Sit down, darling, and catch your breath.' He took her hand and led her to the armchair. He waited until she was settled before swinging a straight-backed chair around and straddling it. 'Now, tell me what you know.'

'Bentley was the perpetrator, but Sir John Farnham's behind it. Your cousin has become embroiled with that horrible man.'

'God's teeth! Farnham could have been the instigator of the attacks on Bentley. I paid his gambling debts but I fear, if Farnham's involved, that he owes far more.'

'What is it? Alexander, what aren't you telling me?'

'I blame myself for having Farnham here. I should have known of the man's reputation and steered well clear of him.'

'You are scaring me now, Alexander.'

He stretched forward and clasped her hands. 'Nothing has been proved, but blackmail and extortion are the least of the crimes I've heard him accused of.'

'Thank goodness your cousin will be here for the rest of the summer.' She returned the pressure of his fingers. 'Do you intend to speak to Bentley?'

'Of course. Believe me, sweetheart, by the time I've finished with him he'll regret his gossip-mongering.'

'Don't be too hard on him, my love. He's vain and foolish, but not a truly bad person.'

★   ★   ★

The next few days she was busy with guests and parties, and at night had more pleasurable things to occupy her mind, so she quite forgot to be cross with Bentley. He was so subdued after his dressing-down that she almost felt sorry for him. Several days after the ball their last visitors departed, and Bentley moved to the east wing.

'Sweetheart, I must go to town to sign the agreement for the yacht. Is there anything you wish me to purchase for you?'

'Nothing. I've everything I need as long as

you're here. Don't delay too long, for I'll be lonely without you.'

His eyes darkened and his lips covered hers in a hard, demanding kiss. 'You're insatiable, my darling. I pray this strange system we've adopted proves adequate. I can't keep away from you regardless of the consequences.'

She stroked his face, loving the feel of bristles beneath her fingertips. 'I'm now resigned to having a big family.'

'I've instructed Bentley to remain next door and not bother you. I trust he does as he's bid.' Alexander wasn't so ready to forgive as she was.

★ ★ ★

Alexander discovered the papers wouldn't be ready for another day. He was obliged to kick his heels in Grosvenor Square when he would rather be at Newcomb. He decided to visit his club and walked to the stable yard. Nowadays he preferred to do things for himself and not be waited on.

On entering White's a close friend, Sir Richard Taylor, beckoned him over. 'Rochester, good to see you. Must say I enjoyed your hospitality. Your wife's quite delightful.'

'Thank you.' Alexander glanced round the room. Was he imagining the covert looks?

'Am I missing something, Taylor? What's going on?'

'No idea. Why don't you ask them?'

He strode across and glared at the nearest gentleman. 'Well? Out with it.'

The man blanched and he stepped away. 'Your grace, Smithson was just telling us some news about Farnham that concerns your family.'

'What? For God's sake, man, tell me.'

'Farnham was bragging last night that he'd got Bentley in his pocket. That when Bentley comes into the title half your fortune will go to him.'

His fist unclenched. This was news to him. He nodded at the men. 'Both Bentley and Farnham will be disappointed. I can assure you, I'll have a son of my own before too long.'

The circle of men relaxed. 'Glad to hear you say so, Rochester. Still, if I were you I'd have a stern word with Farnham. Can't have this sort of rumour bandied about the place.'

'Thank you, Smithson. I've every intention of doing so.'

He left the club and headed for one of the less salubrious haunts he'd once drunk in. Someone here would know the whereabouts of his quarry. He shouldered his way through the press of inebriated riff-raff. One could hardly refer to these as gentlemen.

He spotted a friend of Farnham's and barged across. 'Where's Farnham?'

The man stared, glassy-eyed, not recognising his questioner. 'Gone to Newcomb. Got a bit of unfinished business down there.' The man half-slid from his stool. 'He's meeting someone who owes him.' Perspiration beaded Alexander's brow. His heart raced and his hands were clammy. Somehow he groped through the crowd of stinking drinkers and emerged, shaking, onto the cobbles.

Everything fell into place. He swallowed hard as bile rose in his throat. The grease on the stairs that had killed poor Sally had been meant for Isobel. The soldiers shooting had not been a random event but a deliberate attempt to kill his wife. My God! He'd left her with no protection and a madman intent on murder heading for the house and his accomplice living next door.

He ran back to Grosvenor Square, ignoring the shocked faces of those he elbowed aside. He erupted into the yard and yelled for a groom.

'Saddle my horse. I leave for Newcomb immediately.' He couldn't arrange for grooms to accompany him — every minute counted.

Moments later he thundered through the arch onto the cobbled street, scattering an unwary flock of pigeons from his pathway. Several heads turned to gape as he guided his mount through the diligences, carriages and hackneys with scant regard for his, or anyone else's, safety. Eventually he was in open country. He crouched forward, urging Rufus ever faster, praying he would be in time to save the woman who was his life.

23

'Ellie, I don't think I'll have sufficient closet space to take those gowns. From what the duke has told me, living on a yacht's rather cramped.'

'Your grace, we'll need morning, promenade and afternoon gowns as well as evening gowns. We're going to be away for six weeks; with the few garments you've selected you'll be seen several times in the same ensemble.'

Isobel smiled at the horrified expression on Ellie's face. 'As there will only be ourselves aboard, I can't see it matters. When we go ashore it will be at different ports, so even then there's no problem.'

Her maid nodded. 'I hadn't thought of that, your grace. What about laundering? Will there be fresh water available?'

'I should think so. I'm going to oversee Lady Lucinda's packing; Nanny must be warned not to take too much.'

Alexander's belongings were packed by Duncan. Although the yacht was well appointed the cabins would be small and storage space restricted. They would be taking Duncan, Ellie, Nanny and the wet nurse, but the remainder of the staff were to have two weeks' holiday in order to visit family wherever they might be.

Bill and Mary were arranging for them to leave in rotation. The others were to begin redecorating and cleaning the building from top to toe. Late for a spring clean, but much of the building hadn't been touched for years.

This was the last night before their holiday. Alexander was returning first thing and they would set out directly he arrived. The yacht was moored at Dover, in Kent, so they would have to stop overnight.

She was so excited she couldn't sleep. Tonight was a perfect evening, the oppressive heat replaced by a gentle, cooling breeze. Her clock struck midnight.

Ellie had been instructed to call her early. Alexander had advised her to wash her hair and take a bath, as the facilities aboard were basic. The shutters and windows were open, she strolled across and leant on the windowsill to hear the owls calling.

She was just drifting off to sleep when something woke her. The dogs were barking. This was unusual — something had disturbed them. The hair on the back of her neck rose. The last time they'd barked had been the night before Sally's death. Perhaps one of the yard cats had ventured through an open window and they were expressing their disgust at this intrusion.

The racket continued. Was she the only one to hear the noise? The open window meant the sound carried from downstairs. Othello and Ebony slept directly below her in a little-used withdrawing room. She scrambled out of bed and pulled on her robe.

She found the tinderbox and lit a candle. At the chamber door she paused. Something wasn't right. She sniffed. What could she smell? She opened the door and reeled back. Smoke drifted along the passageway, filling the air. The house was on fire.

★　★　★

Alexander's stallion sailed over another five-barred gate. This would save him a precious mile or two. The bullocks in the field eyed him with disfavour. His horse was tiring; when he reached the lane he would slow his pace and let the poor beast recover, but first he must gallop across this final meadow.

The horse lurched and he was somersaulting through the air to land on his back, the breath knocked from him. He was too winded to move, then slowly he pushed himself up onto his elbows. His throat closed. Poor

Rufus was standing with his right foreleg raised.

He knew with a sickening certainty his mount had broken his leg. The animal must have put his hoof into a rabbit hole. Dammit to hell! Why hadn't he slowed down? This was his fault and his horse must be put out of its misery.

Reaching into his inside pocket, he removed his pistol. This was already loaded and primed; he only had to cock and fire. He walked across, keeping the gun behind him, all the time talking soothingly to the dejected beast. 'All right, old fellow. Stand firm; the pain will soon be gone.'

He raised his gun and fired point-blank; Rufus buckled at the knees and toppled over. A shuffling behind him made him glance over his shoulder. The bullocks had come to investigate. Angrily he rubbed his eyes. There were still fifteen miles to Newcomb and he'd have to walk the rest.

He pulled out his watch and flicked it open. The hands pointed to seven o'clock. It would be dark by nine, so he must complete his journey before then. He shoved his discharged weapon into his pocket. He would make sure to reload before he reached home.

As he strode across the field towards the gate he cursed his impetuosity. Why hadn't he brought men? The death of his horse would then be tragic and inconvenient, but not an unmitigated disaster.

Too late to repine; he must concentrate on covering the ground. He could no longer cross the fields; for the remainder of his journey he'd be obliged to stick to lanes. This would take longer than travelling as the crow flies.

There was bound to be a farm or dwelling, maybe a roadside inn, where he'd hire a nag to continue the journey. As he jogged he checked his pockets; he'd several flimsies in his wallet and a purse full of coins. Hopefully this was enough.

A further hour passed before he saw a substantial manor house in the distance. He could barely see his way by the time he approached the front door. He was frantically thinking of a reasonable explanation for his urgent need to return home. He would have to invent an emergency, without actually mentioning that Farnham and Bentley might be intending to murder his wife.

★ ★ ★

Isobel coughed; the smoke wasn't dense enough to prove a serious hazard. She thanked God the nursery was close. If Lucinda had been in the attics there mightn't have been the time to reach her. The sound of crackling, of flames taking hold on the other side of the wall, was terrifying. Her courage almost failed. The house had thick panelled walls; with luck this would give the fire something to burn before it reached them.

The air was hotter. Delaying for a second might prove fatal. Bursting into Lucinda's room, she snatched her from the crib. With the baby in one arm, the candlestick in the other, she ran to the first chamber and shouted, 'Quickly, the house is on fire! Get up, there's little time!'

The three nursery staff appeared in various states of disarray but fortunately all had put on clogs and cloaks.

'Nanny, take Lucinda downstairs. Jenny, go with her to unbolt the door and carry the candlestick. If you have time, bang the dinner gong. Anna, come with me to make sure everyone's awake.'

Nanny hastened across and took baby; Jenny and Anna picked up candlesticks and were ready to leave. Was there time to put on something more substantial? No, every second counted. Leading the way to the corridor, she opened the door. Already the air was more polluted; she prayed there'd be time to escape without harm.

'Don't touch the walls; they're hot. The fire must have started in the kitchens and will be burning up the back stairwells and corridors. I'm hoping the main part of the house won't be aflame.'

'I reckon them panels will take a while to burn, your grace, so there'll be plenty of time to get out.' Anna hesitated in the passageway.

'We must use the main staircase; with luck it'll be possible to reach the bedrooms that way.' Now wasn't the time to remind the girl the servants' quarters might already be cut off. She had to try. Her staff mustn't perish.

At least Mary and Sam were safe. The sudden clang of the dinner gong meant Nanny was safely downstairs. The air was cleaner at the top of the house and she breathed deeply, clearing the smoke from her lungs.

'Through this way, Anna. I'll knock on the doors this side. Go through and ensure the men are awake.' Anna was courting one of the footmen so would be eager to see that he was safe.

When she reached the women's quarters there was pandemonium: girls screaming, coughing, and general panic. 'Enough of this. Be silent and listen if you wish to survive.' Her authoritative tone was sufficient to halt the hubbub. 'As you can see, the house is well alight. Put on your clogs and cloaks and follow me; the only way out will be through the original nursery wing and down the main staircase.'

Two of the girls — it was hard to see who they were in the smoke-filled darkness — ran from door to door to check everyone was out. She heard a call: 'All the rooms are empty, your grace. We can go now.'

Anna had disappeared with her candlestick to the far side of the attics, where she hammered on the wall and screamed a warning. There were no communicating doors but the racket should be sufficient to rouse everyone.

A man shouted that everyone was awake. Isobel prayed the second staircase wasn't burning as fiercely as the one to the women's quarters. Anna returned.

'They must use the schoolroom stairs, your grace, as their own are well alight.'

She turned to the terrified group of forty women waiting for instructions. 'Quickly, cover your faces with your cloaks; the smoke will be thicker as we descend.'

The two flights of stairs converged in a lower passageway and she was relieved to see men emerging as her party arrived. The atmosphere was thick, the heat stifling, and all were coughing, their eyes streaming, but none complained or cried. They stood waiting to be told what to do. In minutes the stairs behind them would be too hot. She had to lead them through the choking smoke or else they'd all die, trapped inside the house.

Holding her hand over her nose, she plunged forward, terrified she'd pitch head-first down the stairs before she found the banister. She gripped the smooth wood and began to descend. The candles were useless and the feeble flicker of the flames not enough to see by.

★ ★ ★

The door was flung open as Alexander leapt up the steps.

'My dear Rochester, what mishap has brought you here on foot?' Sir Frederick Campion greeted him. 'I spied you from the terrace where my dear wife and I were taking supper.'

'Campion, good God! I'd no idea this was your house. I was riding across country and my mount broke its leg.' Sir Frederick looked even more bewildered, if that were possible.

'Come in, come in, sir. I'll find you refreshments. Do you wish to stay overnight, or borrow a fresh mount?'

He followed him in, trying to think of a

reasonable explanation for his arrival. 'Thank you, sir. I'm travelling alone. I received disturbing news from home. You might recall that many years ago I failed to arrive in time.'

This was a masterstroke. Immediately the man's face changed; the whole neighbourhood remembered the tragedy.

'I'll send word to the stables for them to saddle up my best horse. I'll not delay you longer than it takes for you to take eat.'

Ten minutes later he was mounted on a magnificent bay gelding. It would be foolhardy to go across country in the dark; he must stick to the lanes and hope the moon was enough. He'd heard the tall clock in the entrance hall strike ten; it would be midnight before he arrived.

He was several miles away when his eyes were drawn to an orange glow. He almost fell from the saddle. It could be only one thing: Newcomb was ablaze. Those snivelling bastards had set light to his home. He dug in his heels and galloped headlong towards the conflagration.

★ ★ ★

As Isobel reached the halfway point there was a horrible groan, like a giant in pain, then the ceiling in front of her collapsed, spewing flames and searing heat. 'Back, back, into the master suite — we'll be burnt to a cinder if we continue!'

Everyone turned and fled, leaving her to stumble along behind them. Then Ellie was beside her and took her arm, dragging her through the press of people on the stairs. They parted willingly, urging her ahead of them, more concerned for her safety than their own.

George and Duncan had taken the men into Alexander's apartment. This was now uncomfortably overcrowded. Men and women were mingling together, some spilling into the bedchamber, others obliged to hide in the dressing room itself.

Duncan seemed to know what to do and she left the decision-making to him. He'd organised men to soak bedcovers and press them along the bottom of the doors. This would prevent smoke from entering for a while. Should she open the windows and let in some fresh air?

She was walking towards them when George called out, 'No, your grace, leave them be.'

Surprised she paused. 'Why's that? I thought with so many people inside . . . '

'When I were a little'un I remember a fire in a neighbouring cottage. The family, trapped in their house, opened a window and were consumed by the flames what came into the room.'

'How dreadful! I'll leave it closed.'

The room was oppressive, for blocking the smoke also prevented fresh air from entering. There were more than ninety people huddled in these rooms. They wouldn't suffocate, but one or two of the older women were already suffering from the foetid atmosphere.

They couldn't remain incarcerated indefinitely. If the outside staff didn't arrive they were doomed to die a horrible death. Alexander's sitting room had a substantial balcony overlooking the garden. Surely they could manufacture some sort of rope from the remaining bedlinen?

'Duncan, how long will the doors hold if we open the windows?'

'Long enough for you and the women to escape, but I doubt we'd all get out in time. But we've no choice. I'll start making a rope.' They'd been conversing quietly; no one had overheard.

'I doubt all the women could climb down the thirty feet to the terrace.'

'I thought of that, your grace. If we attach something around them as well I think we'll be successful.'

She walked through the group, reassuring

and comforting. She told them what was planned and asked Ellie to explain to those she couldn't reach. The older women would go first, then the youngest, and after that by seniority. She was determined to remain until the end.

Soon two ropes of knotted linen were ready. Somehow the staff had been grouped appropriately, but she'd resisted every suggestion she go first. 'If you think we're ready, Duncan, then George must open the windows.'

'Right, your grace, but you must go. Nobody's leaving until you're safe outside. Ain't that right?'

A chorus of assent rippled round the room. She'd no choice. If her staying meant more people would perish, then she must go. She remembered the hideous collapse of the ceiling; she'd sent Nanny that way. If anything had happened to her baby . . . She mustn't think of it. The Almighty couldn't be so unkind as to take away something so precious.

24

Alexander thundered up the drive expecting to see staff organising a bucket chain to douse the flames. The place was deserted but there was shouting and banging coming from the lofts. Swearing volubly, he vaulted from the saddle and raced to release them. 'Raise the alarm — someone ring the stable bell — bring ladders and as many horse blankets as you can find!'

Not waiting, he raced to the front of the house where the seat of the fire appeared to be. As he arrived the front door opened and three women stumbled out coughing and spluttering, one carrying his daughter.

Thank the good Lord. Lucinda was safe; now he must pray he could save Isobel. Two black shapes hurtled round the corner. He paused to scratch their heads, glad the dogs had survived.

'Nanny, is Lady Lucinda unharmed?'

The woman wiped her streaming eyes with one hand. 'She is, your grace. We escaped in the nick of time. I fear opening the front door increased the flames. Her grace was intending to lead the servants down but she'll have been driven back.'

'Let me see my daughter.' She handed him the sleeping bundle. He pulled back the damp shawl and lightly kissed her face. 'Sleep on, little one; I must fetch your mama.' He handed her back with a smile. 'Do you know where Mr and Mrs Watkins live?'

Nanny was about to answer when they ran up to him. 'Your grace, we've only just seen the flames or we should have been here sooner. Is her grace out?'

'No, Watkins, these are the only three. Mrs Watkins, take my daughter to your cottage and take care of her. I'll bring my wife when I rescue her.'

'I'll be waiting, your grace. Come along, Nanny. It's a mild night, but you've had a nasty shock and would be better for a hot drink.' Mrs Watkins stopped. 'Peggy Simpson, the wet nurse, didn't she come with you?'

'She prefers to sleep in the attic with the other women. Since her man and her own baby died she doesn't like to be alone.'

Damnation! If the baby woke there'd be no food. He must make sure the Simpson woman was the second one to come out. 'Please don't worry, Mrs Watkins. I'll have her grace and the wet nurse with you shortly.'

The flames had taken a good hold and the windows on the first floor were as bright as if a thousand candles glowed inside. Where could a hundred souls hide safely with such a furnace burning? With two dozen men behind him he raced round to the south side. Thank God! Here the windows were black; the fire had not reached these chambers.

'Up there. Do you see, Watkins? There's light in my apartment. Get ladders up against one set of windows; the rest of you divide yourselves into groups and take hold of the edges of a blanket. The only way we're going to get everybody out is if the ladies jump.'

'I can organise that, your grace. Two blankets at a time, the others waiting to replace them when they're full.'

'Good man. I'm going up to get things started. I'm hoping the men can come down these, leaving the blankets for the women. The wind's getting up. We don't have a moment to lose before the place is engulfed.'

A small forest of lanterns on poles lit his way. A sudden gust of wind almost knocked him off the ladder, and an ominous roar from the front of the house made him climb speedily. There couldn't be more than a quarter of an hour before everyone perished.

He tipped headlong over the stone balustrade, landing inelegantly on his face. As he sprang to his feet the French windows flew open and Isobel fell into his arms.

'Alexander? What are *you* doing here? Lucinda, have you seen her?'

He crushed her in his arms for a second and then picked her up and placed her on the ladder. 'Our daughter's fine. No time to talk; get down the ladder now. Leave things to me. I'll send Simpson next. Go to Mrs Watkins' cottage and wait there.'

'Take care, my darling. I couldn't bear to lose you.'

Descending the wooden ladder in slippers and a nightgown was difficult, but when your life was at stake you managed somehow. No sooner was she off the bottom than someone else followed. To her astonishment two more windows were flung open and the next thing she saw were women jumping from the other balcony to land in stretched-out blankets.

Peggy arrived at her side, breathless and red-faced but smiling. 'What a lark! I've never seen the like. I hope me milk don't dry up because of it.'

'Go to Mrs Watkins right away; she's expecting you. Do you know the way?'

'I do that. It ain't far and there's a fine big moon to show me.'

By now there were a dozen men and women milling about on the terrace getting in everybody's way. 'Inside staff, listen to me,' said Isobel. 'Go to the coach house. It's warm and dry there. Get a fire going and put water on to boil. I'm sure the stablehands have the makings for tea. You must share cups, as there won't be enough for everyone.'

Two of the outside men offered to guide those rescued. She should go with them, but she wanted to be sure everyone got out safely. Soon there was a constant stream of the rescued heading for the coach house. She greeted each one in turn, congratulating them on their bravery and promising they wouldn't be dismissed because of this.

Heaven knew how they were going to accommodate so many when Newcomb was likely to be razed to the ground. Too soon to fret; as long as all were safe, that was all that mattered. Smoke was billowing from the bedchamber and sitting room above. How many more had to come down?

'Sam, I've not seen Bill. Is he up there?'

'Your grace, you shouldn't be here. Let me take you to Mary's, where you'll be safe and warm.'

Alexander appeared on the balcony and shouted to the men below, 'Just a dozen more to come and everyone's out.'

Four more men scrambled down the ladders, while others were jumping into the blankets. Her nails bit into her palms. Why didn't *he* come? She counted frantically as the sound of crackling and burning grew. There couldn't be more than three inside including Bill, Alexander, and one other.

There was a scream and a figure fell from the far window, his garments on fire. He landed in a blanket and those who'd caught him rolled him over to douse the flames. Bill and Alexander emerged, pursued by the fire. They would be too late. They would be swallowed by the blaze behind them. Her beloved locked his arms and legs around the wooden ladder and slid down. By the time he hit the ground the top of the ladder was burning fiercely.

Bill could only use his arms; his injury prevented him from moving swiftly. His ladder was on fire before he'd descended more than a few rungs. Frantically a group of men ran towards him with a blanket. Too late. He had no choice. He must drop to the flagstones or be incinerated. He plummeted to the ground and Isobel expected him to die before her eyes.

A collective gasp rippled round the group as, instead of falling flat, somehow he managed to roll himself into a neat ball and land on his shoulders. Because he was curled up, the impact sent him tumbling head over heels onto the grass. He was sitting up rubbing his elbows by the time the first man reached him.

She was transfixed. Everyone had got out unscathed. This was a miracle. Then Alexander was beside her, hugging her fiercely, mumbling incoherently into her hair.

'My darling, you could have been killed. I thought I'd be too late; that for the second time I'd be bereft.'

'How did you come to be here in the middle of the night? I thought you weren't to come until tomorrow.'

'I'll explain later. You shouldn't be here, sweetheart, but I'm glad you are. I still have things to attend to. Can I trust you to join our daughter at the cottage?'

There was no point in arguing. He was lord of the manor; of course he had to ensure his dependents were accounted for and were as comfortable as they could be in the circumstances. A sudden crash of thunder jolted them apart; from nowhere a summer storm had drifted in and the heavens opened.

'Take care, my love. I'll do as you bid. I've no wish to stand out here in the pouring rain. Will this put out the flames? Shall anything be saved?'

'God knows! The Almighty has done a wonderful job tonight so I'll leave this in his capable hands. Hurry; you'll be drenched if you stay here any longer.'

She stretched out and pulled his head down to kiss him. His lips tasted of smoke. 'I love you, Alexander. Come to me soon. I think I see Hill and Reynolds heading this way. Can't you leave everything to them?'

In answer he pushed her gently in the direction of Mary's house. 'Go, and take your dogs for company.' He beckoned to a lad holding two lanterns. 'Here, boy. Go with her grace, then come back and tell me all is well.'

Fortunately it was a short distance to her destination and much of it under a canopy of leaves. 'I'm safely arrived, young man. See, Mrs Watkins is waiting for me in the doorway. You can return to your duties in the stables. The horses will be unsettled by the smoke and the smell of the fire.'

He grinned and bowed awkwardly, the lanterns bobbing furiously on the end of their poles. She hurried down the path, eager to see her baby. She reached the cottage and realized Mary wasn't smiling. As she stepped into the cottage, the door slammed behind her. Her dogs were snarling and barking, flinging themselves at the wood in a frantic effort to get in.

★ ★ ★

'Hill, Reynolds, Watkins, with me,' said Alexander. 'There's unfinished business to attend to. Bentley's behind this fire and was also responsible for that girl's death and the incident with the rifleman in the woods.' The three men nodded, unsurprised by his revelation. 'On both occasions my wife was the intended victim. He's embroiled with that bastard Farnham — without his manipulation I doubt any of this would have happened.'

'I had my doubts about Bentley from the start; there was something behind his eyes that made me think he wasn't the simpleton he wished us to believe,' said Sam.

'Farnham has convinced himself he can blackmail my fortune from Bentley when he inherits. God knows what maggot has got into his brain.'

Reynolds chimed in, 'You're right, your grace. When little Sally slipped I thought it a rum do, but kept my opinions to myself.'

Alexander glared at Reynolds. 'Why the hell didn't you speak up? A bit too late to be telling me now, don't you think?' He swallowed his ire. They'd all been fooled; now wasn't the time for wringing hands. 'Have any of you got a pistol?' They shook their heads. 'I've two. I'll keep one. Any of you a marksman?'

Watkins held out his hand. 'I am, sir. Do

you have sufficient powder and shot for both of us?'

When both guns were loaded and primed he explained his plan. 'I doubt Farnham has hung about to see the results of his machinations. Bentley will be cowering in the east wing waiting to see if his latest attempt has succeeded.' He stared hard at each one in turn before continuing. 'I don't intend him to survive this encounter.' Again all three responded in unison; this time they nodded. 'If Farnham's with him, I'll kill him too.'

He was turning towards the east wing when he heard dogs barking in the distance. He froze. Once again he'd been outsmarted; his quarry was in the cottage, and he'd just sent Isobel there. 'He's in your cottage, Watkins. We're too slow!'

His heart was pounding as he raced across the park. He prayed Bentley hadn't completely lost his senses, and would realize murdering Isobel in cold blood would gain him nothing.

★   ★   ★

'Come in, your grace. As you can see, I'm expecting you.'

Isobel's eyes widened. The monster was standing beside Lucinda, one hand resting

341

close to her mouth. 'Mr Bentley, if you give me my baby and leave immediately, I promise no further action shall be taken against you for tonight's fire.'

His laugh was shrill and the hair on the back of her neck prickled. She was dealing with a madman. 'And shall my dear *Cousin* Alexander feel the same? I've already murdered once. My life's forfeit whatever your avowals. When your husband arrives he won't be so merciful.'

'I beg you, don't harm my child. Kill me if you must, but let Lucinda go.'

The dogs continued to hurl themselves at the front door. Would Alexander hear them? Then she saw the madman held a pistol in his other hand. The world stood still. It wasn't her baby or herself he intended to kill, but Alexander. With him dead this lunatic would be the Duke of Rochester and there'd be nothing anyone could do about it.

If justice took its course and Bentley was hanged then the title would be in abeyance, the good name of the family forever tainted. She wouldn't let that happen. When Alexander burst in she would throw herself in the path of the shot; she'd willingly die to save the man she loved and keep his heritage intact.

'Where are Nanny Cooper, Peggy and the maids?'

Mary answered, 'He's locked them in the bedroom, your grace.'

'Be silent, unless you wish me to finish off this brat right now.'

★ ★ ★

Alexander wanted the two dogs to continue to bark. If they stopped it would warn Bentley he was close. 'Watkins, we must approach from the rear. You know those animals. What can you do to make them continue to attack the front door and distract that bastard?'

'They've a fine hatred of felines, sir. If we put a yard cat on the roof that'll keep them going.'

'Do that. Hill, you assist Reynolds with this; Watkins, come with me. Is it possible to get in through the kitchen without being heard?'

'I reckon if I go in by the coal cellar and you through the scullery window, one of us will get him before he can harm anyone.'

They approached stealthily. The cat secreted under Reynolds's jacket seemed unperturbed by this unusual mode of transport. Alexander watched his estate manager scramble up a convenient wall and push the unfortunate animal onto the roof. The yowl it made attracted the

343

dogs. Suddenly they were howling and barking in their frustration. Excellent — anyone inside would believe he was approaching from the front.

He gestured to Hill and Reynolds to go to the front door, knock and demand entry. With luck that would concentrate Bentley's attention whilst he approached from behind. The scullery window was a tight fit but somehow he wriggled through and slid to the tiles. Thank God there'd been nothing beneath his feet to clatter and warn of his arrival.

He pulled off his boots then crept forward, listening for a clue that might tell him where Bentley was standing. He would get one shot and he must be certain he didn't miss; the lives of his family might depend on it.

He heard Bentley talking. He almost surged forward, forgetting to be cautious when he heard what was spoken.

'Firstly I'll kill your husband and then I'll smother your baby. I'll do both things before your eyes. After that I care not what happens to me. I'll be the Duke of Rochester until they hang me.'

★ ★ ★

The dogs were at the back of the property, but someone was running up the path. Isobel must warn Alexander. She saw Bentley's hand move to cover Lucinda's face, and closed her mouth. She was in agony. She couldn't save her baby *and* her husband. How could she make such a dreadful choice?

Bentley raised his pistol and she gathered herself to make the ultimate sacrifice. How long would it be before Alexander realized the door was unlocked and burst in? A slight movement behind the monster drew her gaze. There was the hideous sound of a pistol shot and Bentley pitched forward, shot through the head. It was over. They were safe.

Ignoring the body on the floor, she flung herself at Alexander. 'He was going to kill you and Lucinda! I thought . . . oh, my love, I can't believe we've all survived this night.'

He tossed his spent weapon aside and embraced her. 'Isobel, my darling, I never want to go through that again. If I lost you or Lucinda I couldn't go on living.'

The infant, terrified by the retort, was screaming. Isobel turned to scoop her up. 'Hush, little one. Your mama and papa are here to take care of you.' Lucinda snuggled in between them and was comforted by their closeness.

Isobel scarcely noticed the body being removed or Mary picking up the soiled mat; she was safe in the arms of the man she loved.

'What are we going to do, Alexander? Where are we going to live? What about the staff?'

He smoothed back her hair and kissed her tenderly. 'I've a dozen other properties. Tomorrow you must decide where you wish to live. Then half the staff can remove there and prepare it for us and the rest can go to Grosvenor Square. They might as well be idle in London as anywhere else.'

Leaning back in his arms, she stared at him. Could this be the arrogant, autocratic Duke of Rochester speaking so casually about the destruction of his family seat? 'Newcomb has been destroyed. Doesn't that bother you?'

His arms tightened. 'Why should it? I've everything I want right here.'